BETTY SERVES THE MASTER

- by -

MADELEINE TANNER

CHIMERA

Betty Serves the Master first published in 1999 by
Chimera Publishing Ltd
PO Box 152
Waterlooville
Hants
PO8 9FS

Printed and bound in Great Britain by
Caledonian International Book Manufacturing Ltd
Glasgow

All Characters in this publication are fictitious. Any resemblance to real persons, living or dead, is purely coincidental.

Copyright Madeleine Tanner

The right of Madeleine Tanner to be identified as author of this book has been asserted in accordance with section 77 and 78 of the Copyrights Designs and Patents Act 1988

BETTY SERVES THE MASTER

Madeleine Tanner

This novel is fiction – in real life practice safe sex

Chapter One

Betty Meets her Master

Winter 1783 – Kismet – Liza likes a licking – Divining the future – A clouded crystal ball – A demand for virgin blood – A face revealed – Fellatio – Kiss of the whip

'I see Betty in the glass, beautiful, innocent Betty Ellis bowing humbly afore the Master, an' a-kissing his feet. Who'd ha' thought it, eh?' Liza nudged her companion, heaved her heavy petticoats and nestled one hand comfortably over the head of the little maid lapping assiduously at her fat cunny. 'Naked, too, an' showing everythin' she's got! Huh! She ain't changed much.' She pressed the girl's skull, forcing her to lick harder. 'Get on wi' it yer bugger! I ain't got all day. If you don't learn ways o' pleasing fancy ladies, you won' make no money in the cunny warren!'

'Master,' she whispered huskily. Betty's eyelids fluttered open, the delicate trembling of a butterfly clinging to a leaf, but frightened to meet the Master's dazzling eyes she lowered her head in submission.

'Just as the oracle predicted!' The Master grasped Betty's tiny hands, drawing her to her feet. She stood awkwardly, ashamed of her nakedness before the powerful stranger whose law was absolute in his own domain. 'You are mine at last, Betty, my property, my slave. Many suns have passed...'

'I changed these last few years. There's girls more lovely'n me in the harem.'

'You are a treasured possession of great pulchritude, a

matchless beauty, a peerless prize.'

'But I ain't as comely as I were, Master.' Betty tossed her golden hair. It had grown a little darker and her face a little leaner but her black eyes shone as bright and clear as ever.

'The Master, eh?' Zillah interrupted impatiently. 'Give us the crystal. You've no right to it.'

'As much as you, you old crone!' Liza relinquished the ball and temporarily satisfied with the action of the maid's tongue, folded her arms under her drooping bosom. 'An arter all she's been through, the chit's as wilful as ever. She won't never make no lady! Why, the jumped-up trollop deserves a sound thrashing!' To emphasise the point, Liza gave the poor maid a resounding slap on the rump. 'I'd like to smack Betty's slit good an' proper, an' force 'er little tongue right up me. 'Stead I got to make do wi' this piece o' pigeon's pizzle!'

'So, the almighty Master returns to claim her!' Zillah spat the words through her teeth as she watched the picture changing. 'I smell incense.' Her nose wrinkled as her fingers beckoned the invisible powers. 'I feel the cold draught of mountain air. I see a horseman, a black head-dress, robes parting and a thrusting, throbbing manhood. What use is that to me? I must see his face!' Furiously, she rubbed the crystal ball with her sleeve, but the fantastical image dimmed.

'Talking o' faces, this sprat'll get a smack on 'ers if she don't do better with 'er friggin' tongue!' Liza pushed the maid's head down firmly. 'Do it faster, or else!' She leaned over the ball, thus obscuring Zillah's view. 'Why, there's Betty lying on them cushions, all fancy-like. I can see 'er cunny curls plain as day – lick harder you trollop – but Master do look much thinner than afore. An' darker. They reckon 'ard labour in them forin countries shapes a man's flesh. Mind you, 'is portion bulges big as ever! I reckon 'is ballocks is bigger'n ever...'

'God's lid, never mind his ballocks! What of his face? I must see the Master's face!'

But Liza was concentrating on her carnal pleasures. 'He's parting 'er legs wider, rough hands are a-roving all over her cunny, fat fingers is splitting them pink lips apart. Mind you, I don't like the look on 'is hands, see. Ooh, I'd like to smack that cheeky look off 'er face, so I would, the hussy! I'd make 'er suck 'is cock an' lick me bum... Ah, the trollop! She's a-makin' me come afore me time.' Liza jerked her hips against the maid's face then pulled her up roughly. 'An' as fer you, puke-stocking, wipe yer dirty mouth an' get back up to the house.'

'Shush!' Zillah put a bony finger over her skinny lips. 'I hear summat.'

The ugly hags cocked their ears towards the crystal ball and listened intently.

'You are infinitely more beautiful than I could have dreamed.' Gently, he ran a calloused hand over the faint silver streaks on her white rump. 'Such loveliness,' he murmured, 'can only be enhanced by motherhood, by the bearing of many sons!'

The Master held her closely to his broad chest. 'Will you serve me as a woman should?'

Betty sank to her knees. 'What is your will, Master?'

'I demand that which is priceless, your virgin blood!'

Zillah grimaced as the sound faded. 'Ungracious wretch, she still retains her beauty!' The old hag growled, then muttered some unintelligible oaths. 'But will she lose her virgin prize? Come, come. Show me! Show me!' But the crystal clouded as the powers she'd conjured refused to oblige. 'Ah, they speak again but I cannot hear!'

Betty breathed heavily and sighed in resignation. 'I shall submit, sir, submit to your authority because I must.'

'Submission is not enough! You must swear your love for me, Betty, your true Master! That is my command!'

'Sir, how can you command love?' Betty's eyes filled with tears. 'I have but one love.'

'Then you must take the consequences of your refusal.' The Master unwound the black head-dress, his dark eyes probing the depths of her soul.

Zillah began to rock back and forth, chanting to herself. 'Past is past, present calls, hereafter beckons! Surely the scurvy whoreson will take her now? And after he has had his way, throw her from the precipice to the depths of the gorge!'

Suddenly the clouded image before her cleared and the picture reformed. 'No! No! It is he! It is he! What have I conjured? May hell gnaw his bones!' With an ugly grimace Zillah seized the crystal ball and dashed it to the stone floor where it shattered into a thousand pieces.

Unperturbed by the outburst, Liza picked up one of the larger fragments of glass and crept out of the cottage.

The Master reached out for his riding crop. His lip curled with intense pleasure. Shivering with desire and anticipation, Betty parted his robes, released his pulsating member, and sucked deeply as the whip struck her perfect marble shoulders.

Exhausted, Zillah lay slumped over the mean oak table muttering to herself, 'No, Black Prince, no!' She reached out to stroke the black cat beside her. With a nonchalant glance it merely lifted its tail, sniffed, then curled up against her withered face and slept.

Chapter Two

Destined for Madame Farquar's

Autumn 1778 – Dreams of a naked virgin – Zillah's potion – Harold's patience – Edward's vicious passions – A thumb in a tight cunny – Betty eavesdrops – Evil lies – A plan for revenge

'Why, I ain't got no clothes on!' Betty's startled but unseeing eyes opened wide. 'I'm near enough stark naked!'

The velvet cloak had been shrugged from Betty's shoulders by the joltings of the coach-and-four. Now she wore nothing but a ragged veil, a blue pocket containing her lucky stone, and a gold chain running from her waist to the piercing in her cleft. Strands of seaweed laced her sandy skin, creating a mermaid-like effect.

'But I ain't a trollop.' Almost as quickly as her eyes had opened they closed, and gathering the cloak around her, she drooped into the padded upholstery, apparently fast asleep. She was not to know that Zillah, the old gypsy, had conjured her picture and was gazing at the scene with relish.

'Good, good, so the twins have captured the hussy.' She rubbed her hands eagerly. *'Let them mount her while they may! Pierce her virgin flesh to the bone and dash her hopes! Meanwhile let her dream...'*

Betty lay quietly for some minutes. Then her eyes began to move rapidly, her breath coming in short gasps as, thus prompted by the evil woman, she relived the strange drama of her wedding day.

'William, William, where are you?' In her agitation Betty threw the cloak aside, thus exposing her cunny. 'I love you, Master.' Her hands sought the soft cleft and her little fingers ran over the delicate pink labia. 'Forget the fortune! Take me! Take me...!' Betty arched her back as if to receive her Master deep in the womb.

Edward licked his lips lustfully. 'See, the trollop is asking for it!' He nudged Harold gleefully. 'See how her hips rise, how she pulls her licunny-nny lips apart!'

'But the girl is delirious and we are nothing if not gentlemen. You must stem your rising passion!'

'Ah, t'would be a crime against nature to stop the flow of unctuous juices! See how she yearns to be plugged to the hilt. We should breech her right away! You take her mouth and I shall distend her little cunny!'

Harold's passions had begun to rise too, and his tight breeches strained manfully, but he wanted the virgin to himself. 'She has no idea where she is and, besides, she may not wish it.'

'Bah! You heard her begging for it. "Take me" she said, as clear as daylight!'

'Quiet! She may hear you!' Harold put a finger to his lips and shook his head.

'Surely she won't wake now!'

Much to the frustration of both Edward and Zillah, Betty's dream moved on. 'Ah! The dogs! So much juice!' Betty emitted a piercing scream, which to her observers sounded more like a muffled grunt. 'The hounds are biting. Ah! William... Where are you?' Betty suddenly sat up, her vision blurred.

'Why, sir, who are you?' With glazed, uncomprehending eyes she tried to focus on Lord Edward Clancy and his twin, Harold, but they merged into one figure, one face. Without waiting for an answer she collapsed into a stupor.

'I must possess the virgin.' Edward gripped his brother's arm until his knuckles whitened. 'I have spunk a-plenty to dispose of and she is ripe for rumping. I have not savoured the flesh of a pure maid for a long while.'

'And do not merit such pleasures! You have no patience. This pink rosebud deserves more than your unbridled lust. As a bloom in nature she must be given time to blossom, time to blow, time for those exquisite petals to open slowly and tremble with anticipation.' Harold shivered and sighed like a parent sorely irritated by his child. 'Save your energies for later.'

'I do not see why it is always you who must decide,' Edward grunted, then seeing Harold's angry face, spoke to himself: 'I should be the one in charge. I am far more important!'

For some while there was silence inside the coach as it rumbled inexorably towards London, taking its occupants to Madame Farquar's, a high-class brothel specialising in every variety of corporal punishment.

'Harold, what was all that nonsense the girl was muttering?'

'Later, Edward, later.' Harold had begun to nod off. 'Take a nap and leave well alone. Let Zillah's potion do its work.'

'And you do your work, dear brothers. Do your worst to sully the chit. Ah, if only I had the power to force your actions.' Zillah *grasped the crystal with both hands, and summoning her thoughts, concentrated on the scene. 'Dream, dream, fair coxcomb, and may most evil thoughts suggest themselves! Thoughts to set the lowest scurvy fellow a-blushing!'*

Hunched under the cloak, Betty slept fitfully, dreaming of her extraordinary ordeal. Eventually the brothers slept too, but their dreams were of a very different nature. Edward imagined sating his vicious sexual passions upon the helpless body of Betty, his victim. Harold dreamt of setting Betty up as his mistress. In exchange for a life of luxury she would surely be willing to satisfy his greedy appetite for incessant sexual congress.

Edward licked his lips. He'd been watching Harold through slitted eyes and decided he was definitely fast asleep.

'The trollop is a perfect beauty,' he muttered through his teeth as he brushed sand from Betty's neck. His eyes gleamed lasciviously. 'What luck, eh?' Edward gently lifted aside the tattered remnants of the wedding veil and kissed Betty's delicate nape, afterwards wiping his gritty mouth on a handkerchief. 'She tastes of salt and weed.' He slid the cloak aside and kissed her shoulders.

As Betty stirred under the velvet, the coach jolted violently over a rut, rousing both her and Harold from slumber. She rolled over and the cloak fell away, revealing her naked charms. She'd been sleeping for some while and would have remained so if it hadn't been for the changed motion of the coach, the sound of Edward's voice, and his soft wet lips dripping on her ivory shoulders.

'How tender her skin is!' Edward withdrew reluctantly, torn between his intense desire for Betty and his fear of Harold. He clenched his fists with repressed passion and his heart pounded fit to burst.

Betty squinted through her eyelids, but could see little in the gloomy interior. She'd no idea where she was or with whom, though she guessed by the jerking that she was travelling by horse-drawn coach. Its movements now rolled her over so that her face was deep in shadow, her body hidden by the velvet cloak. She listened intently. Perhaps she'd recognise the voices.

'Zounds, you fool, control yourself!' Another male voice, deeper, more masculine than the first. Betty stiffened.

'But we have the girl to ourselves, Harold. We can do just as we like.' Edward rubbed his hands gleefully. 'What a delight to kiss her ruby lips, to squeeze her little bubbies, to...'

Betty shrunk from Edward's searching hands. She curled

up, one thumb in her mouth, the other wedged between the tight lips of her cunny.

'Do not attempt to rouse her!'

'Why not?' Edward whined, sulking now, and then muttering under his breath. 'I shall see you dead, brother!'

'Because, dear Edward, if she wakes before Zillah's medicine takes full hold it will have the reverse effect. Instead of being fast asleep, she'll be fully conscious and therefore might object to your unwonted lascivious attentions.' He laughed quietly but mockingly. 'And indeed, who would not, oh King of codpieces!'

The voices seemed familiar to the half-sleepy Betty, but their subject somewhat alarming. At the mansion she'd taken Zillah's potent medicines and knew she must force herself awake. Betty carefully shifted position and clenched her fists, digging the nails into her palms. She must keep her wits about her, follow the conversation and feign sleep if necessary.

'Do not call me that again!'

Harold knew how far he could go. 'Then do not deserve it!' He patted Edward's knee patronisingly. 'You know I have your best interest at heart. Am I not constantly right in these matters of the heart?'

'Mm.' Edward hated to admit that Harold's judgements were invariable correct. 'Why did you not give her a larger dose, Harold?'

'Do you want to kill the girl?'

Edward shrugged. 'Why should I care one way or another?'

'Because I promised her to Madame Farquar, you dolt, and that means much needed money!' Harold smiled smugly at his brother. 'A beauty such as Betty is a rare and valuable commodity in a cunny-warren. Neither pox nor plague has touched her. She commands a good price!'

'What luck!' The nasty Edward laughed cheerfully, ignoring the insult. 'I had no idea that was part of your plan. It will suit perfectly.'

'Yes, the girl believes she is to take tea in high society with your bosom friend, a gentle lady, whereas...'

'She is to be held prisoner in the steamiest bordello in London, and frequented by the most depraved of the aristocracy.' Edward curled up with laughter and his waxen white ears glowed bright pink. 'How I shall love to see her face when she discovers that! The foolish girl was so immensely pleased to be rescued by a Lord!'

Betty's cheeks coloured. She was reminded of her escape from the mansion. She'd been swept out to sea, but the tide had turned and she'd been tossed onto the beach to be found by Lord Clancy. He'd carried her up to the cliff-top in his strong arms, promising to take her to Aunt Rowena's after visiting his friend Madame Farquar. She'd not realised it was a bawdy house, nor made the connection that it was the very establishment patronised by her husband William. Instead of removing her to safety, the Clancy twins were abducting her! Betty's heart beat harder.

'Madame requires a wench with flawless skin, not the usual pock-marked tail. And for extra spice, I have arranged for Candace to join her... What a contrast! The one pure white, the other as black as ebony!'

Betty drew a sharp breath. Her friend must've escaped the mansion only to be captured too.

'Ah, brother, it's as if you read my very mind. The beautiful Candace will submit to anything. Squire William has trained her well in the art of pleasing men.' A lusty expression distorted Edward's features as he considered the humiliations Candace suffered at the mansion. 'And there is extra delight in knowing she comes from a long line of powerful queens!'

'Madame has some very special customers in mind, the noblest of aristocrats and various esteemed members of the clergy, one of them being the Bishop of London. Then there is the Mistress Emma, who would pay dearly to...'

'Hm!' Edward folded his arms grumpily. 'Why should Emma have the advantage? If Betty is to be sold into prostitution and given to whoever Madame sees fit, we may as well make use of her first. Why should the hussy refuse us? She is hardly innocent, so it would be no mortal sin. And she has been saved from drowning.'

Harold had been watching Betty for any signs of consciousness. It was obvious to him, though not to Edward, that she was now awake and probably listening. It would not do to frighten her. 'Let the girl sleep.' He nodded meaningfully towards Betty and touched his ear. *'If she awakes...'* he emphasised, lifting his brows... 'She is a lively creature...' Harold raised his voice. 'The beauty needs good care. She is no ordinary village girl.'

Edward, not known for his brightness of intellect but a wily enough creature, took the meaning: Betty was listening. He nodded. Now he had the opportunity to make an impression for himself.

'I do not think the girl would object to the attentions of a Lord and his brother,' he drawled pompously, craftily thinking what he should say to poison Betty against her husband. 'Her beloved William has deserted her! She is penniless and entirely at the mercy of fate.'

At the mention of William's name Betty's heart pounded wildly. She vaguely remembered the marriage ceremony, but was it real or part of her wild dreams? William had mounted her on the altar of the chapel. His erection had been enormous. There was spunk everywhere and she'd rubbed it into her flesh, but had he actually entered her? She didn't remember, but she was sure he hadn't and her cunny still felt very tight, her hymen unbroken. But where was her husband now?

'Beautiful as she is, the Squire is unlikely to claim this prize for himself.' Harold knew that Squire William was incarcerated in his own dungeon below the mansion, but he was not about to impart that piece of information to Betty.

Betty peeped through her fingers. How different the twins were; both handsome, both muscular, but Edward was fair, slim and effeminate, whereas Harold was swarthy, stocky and strong-looking.

'So we have in our possession William's lovely wife, totally helpless. A prize indeed! Harold,' Edward gripped his brother's hand and whispered quietly. 'I must have my way with her before we deliver her to Madame! I beg you, consider my weak constitution!'

Betty stifled a nervous laugh. Having endured the cruelties of William's sadistic servants, she'd escaped Father Loughran and the evil Mistress Emma. She'd survived the hounds' attack and a drowning. If she still retained her virginity she was not about to sacrifice it to the brothers. She'd pretend to be asleep, escape, and join her husband wherever he might be. She would have the virgin birth required by the will, inherit the fortune and live happily ever after, surrounded by her children. William could not have deserted her. It could not be true. Could it?

In her counterfeit sleep, Betty gave a tender sigh which somehow touched the more sensitive brother, Harold. True, he was a selfish man, and like most gentlemen of the time, used to having his way. However, even though he was capable of cruelty, he would not have thought of himself as either callous or heartless. Seeing her beauty, his heart opened tenderly to her. 'Be patient. The girl loves William. She must not be forced!'

Good, thought Betty. Harold, the stronger of the two, could be depended on to defend her.

'Ha! She loves a man who consorts freely with the lowest harlots at Madame's disposal? No, the trollop is after his money!'

That ain't fair! Betty wanted to shout.

'And at the least chance he'd be in the arms of another harlot,' Edward continued. 'The Squire has spent thousands lining the pockets of the greasiest whores to satisfy his scandalous tastes. Such a man is incapable of love. The nuptial vows were a mere convenience, a mockery! In any case, if Father Loughran's connection with Rome is discovered, who knows what would happen to those who harbour him?'

Betty tried to recall the details of the marriage service, and the more she thought of it the more bizarre it seemed. She remembered standing at the altar, naked except for a white veil and a daisy crown. The ceremony had been rushed, she'd lost the daisy ring, and there had been no banns. Did that nullify the marriage?

'You cannot know what is in another's mind. The Squire in particular.'

'No, but after he'd had his way with Betty he was seen riding away from the chapel on his stallion, escaping to the filthy comfort of a scheming whore.'

'Hm.' Harold was thoughtful. 'I had not heard that item of intelligence. As far as I knew...'

'Even his serving maids benefit from his depravity. Both Grace and Liza have left for London to set up a whorehouse for themselves.'

At the mention of the vile, bullying servants Betty's anger grew. Had William given them money? If so, why?

Edward continued with his venom. 'Then, of course, there is the matter of William's betrothal to Lady Marmaduke. I hear she is making early preparations for the wedding breakfast and a honeymoon in Italy. Apparently she wishes to make acquaintance with the ancient treasures of Rome.'

Harold glanced at the captive young woman, and could not resist adding to Edward's poison. 'So, he does not care for Betty? Poor child, to be abused so! And all without the compensations and satisfactions of love.'

Stifling a jealous sob, Betty buried her face deep in the velvet cushioning. She'd been a fool to imagine the powerful Squire William could hold in his esteem anyone other than a true-bred lady. She should have taken notice of Giles. He'd rightly warned her not to dream, not to have ideas above her station. Betty bit her knuckles to stop the screams.

'Poor Betty. The child is infatuated with the monster. He has charmed Lady Marmaduke too, but I doubt the innocent bride knows of his base proclivities.'

'Hardly! A lady of her high reputation and rank is too well-bred to even imagine the existence of such debauchery.'

Edward lifted an eyebrow and tightened his fists. 'I hear, dear Harold, that he ties the hussies, beats them black and blue, whips them until the blood runs, then forces them to...'

'Yes, dear Eddie, what exactly does he make them do?'

Edward had a sudden inspiration. 'Ah! He has the filthiest strumpet whip him to ribbons and is not content until his flesh is as crimson as raw meat!'

Hearing this, Betty gasped, disguising the sound by turning onto her back. She moaned as if dreaming, rested one arm across her face, and peeped through her eyelids. How could the man she loved, the man for whom she'd suffered countless indignities, scourge her without mercy yet pay for the unloving lash of a harlot? Jealousy swelled the anger in her breast. To desert her for a real born lady was understandable. To leave her for a whip-wielding whore was unforgivable!

'He is probably in some filthy stew this very moment!'

'Yet I hear she loves him to distraction.'

'His cruelty only draws her closer to him, but she cannot know his evil plans for her.'

'Which are?'

'In the Squire's own words: "When I've used her to the utmost, filled the strumpet with my spunk, impregnated her with my seed,"' Edward lied, '"I shall stitch the foolish virgin and send her back to the pigsty where she belongs. There she may give birth to her bastard offspring in the mire. Once the child is born – and it need live no longer than a few hours – the entire fortune is mine!" He then swore to throw Betty and her mewling infant to the hounds.'

'So the hunting rumours are true? I'd thought it malicious gossip!'

'Yes, he dresses the unfortunate hussy in a red corset and

a fox's tail, setting the dogs loose shortly afterwards. It is an unpleasant business.' Edward had unwittingly touched upon Betty's fear of the pack and the vision that had always haunted her since her childhood: a bloodied infant pursued and trapped by hounds.

Betty could bear her silence no longer, and a stifled sob gurgled from her strangled throat as she sought to control the sudden hatred surging in her breast. She thought the unthinkable. Her husband had contemplated the murder of his own unconceived child – her child! Almost paralysed by the enormity of such a crime, Betty trembled with rage. She wanted to hurt William, hurt him badly. To kill him. How? How? She would find a knife and stab him to death in his sleep! Cut deep into his flesh, and hurt him as he liked to hurt others. No, she would set the hounds on him, giving him the violent end he deserved. No, she would... Think! Think what would hurt him most! Yes! Yes! The sacrifice of her precious virginity to another man, thus ensuring his disinheritance! But, no! That was her most valuable asset. She must stay intact until she'd won the money for herself. William could be damned to hell!

The carriage made its way through the countryside, and despite her seething thoughts, Betty managed to keep up her pretence. Harold lay back contented. Having said very little to influence Betty, his conscience was as clear as it would ever be. He'd been watching her closely and guessed that seeds of doubt had been sown in her mind. He hoped those seeds would grow into strong weeds, strangling her love for William. Edward cared nothing that he'd lied. He imagined what he'd do with Betty when he found himself alone with her.

Betty forged a plan.

She'd befriend The Clancy brothers on their journey to Madame Farquar's. There, no doubt, she would find out what had happened to William. She'd obtain the twins' assistance in revenging herself against him. Meanwhile, she'd use every artifice she could to drain them of their vital juices, rendering them powerless to assault her and take her virginity. They were obviously hot-blooded, but Betty knew how to please a man. She'd tantalise the brothers and satisfy their carnal instincts using her mouth, tongue and fingers. Eventually she'd take her full revenge upon her unfaithful husband, afterwards leaving him to the whores he apparently loved. Now she'd formed her plan, Betty relaxed into a half-sleep and the soporific effect of the laudanum took hold.

Chapter Three

Lusting after Betty

Delicate bubbies – An uncut gem – A born trollop – Diamonds – Tonguing a cunny – The Devil's offspring – Betty chooses a lover – Dressed for exposure – A convenient slit – A spending cunt – Double frigging – The Sisters of Nommerci

Edward had been waiting for both Harold and Betty to fall asleep again. He plucked at the cloak. An entrancing vision lay before him: Betty's golden curls, intermingled with strands of seaweed, were tossed wildly about her. She held one thumb in her mouth, the other split the darker curls of her cunny. Edward moved nearer, sighing as he stroked her white rump. 'Such magnificent rounded hips and flawless skin! They would mark so well.'

Betty sighed too, pursed her lips, and brushed a hand to her neck as if to swat an irritating fly. The young lord flinched, controlling the desire to embed his teeth into Betty's vulnerable flesh. He ran his fingers over her torso, between the hillocks of her youthful breasts and along the chain around her waist.

Betty shivered, and a sleepy moan escaped her as she drifted in and out of consciousness. The feather-like touches felt pleasantly soothing. Gently she coiled her arms around Edward's body.

'How I should like to nip this soft, pink shell.' Edward held her ear in his teeth and disentangled himself from her limbs, wincing slightly. Unless it were to his express order, he did not like a woman's touch, nor indeed any sign of human affection. He slithered his tongue over her girlish breast meanwhile, muttering to himself: 'Such delicate bubbies. Ah! Her rosebuds pouting so innocently. How I should like to leave my mark upon them...'

'One false move, dear brother, and *you* shall be marked permanently.' Alerted, Harold's eyes flashed threateningly and his hand slid to the dagger tucked in his waistband. 'I thought you were cured of your malicious illness.'

Edward drew away without biting, swallowed, and spoke sullenly. 'I thought you were asleep, Harold. In any case, she is only a peasant. They come ten a penny. What does it matter in God's scheme if the girl should suffer?' Edward caught the look in Harold's eye and shrugged. 'You needn't concern yourself. I can wait.' He hummed a soft melody as his hand played the gold links running from Betty's waist, over her belly and betwixt her thighs. 'She suits gold.' He cocked his head to one side.

'But not that filthy rag. Untie the string, brother.'

Edward picked at the twine holding the pocket at Betty's waist. Eventually he untied the knot and brought out a red stone of irregular shape. 'What do we have here?'

Betty's heart thumped as Harold examined the stone.

'An uncut gem, a garnet no doubt.' He held it to the light. 'Hardly worth ten or twelve guineas,' he lied, knowing full well it was a ruby.

Betty gasped inwardly and bit her lip. Granma Wylmotte's lucky stone was worth a fortune!

'I have acquaintance with a gentleman who buys property, however hot. He'll give a good price. Otherwise we might have it set in silver. Betty must look the part for her gentlemen clients.'

'You may as well sell the stone. The ready cash would be most useful since mother keeps us short. Still, I warrant the girl will look pretty enough with my jewels.'

Betty had intentionally slumped to one side, but Edward pushed her upright. He supported her by two large bolsters, then pulled out a choker, which he affixed around her neck. 'What a prize, indeed. She'd satisfy the lustiest Turk.'

Betty looked the image of innocence. Her golden curls were flung in disarray about her marble bust, and one hand joggled limply with the rhythm of the horses whilst the other pressed to her lips.

'What a picture, eh Hal?'

A small, deliberate sigh of pleasure from Betty's voluptuous lips. It was exciting to be admired, and she gradually arranged herself in the most fetching pose.

'If I promise to take care...' Quivering with lust, Edward placed both hands on Betty's milk-white breasts.

'Mm. Mm.'

Now the pressure of Edward's palms on her nipples.

Harold leaned over Betty and lifted an eyelid. 'She has gone off for certain, now.'

'The girl's a born trollop! Even in sleep the girl is not averse to my touch! Her bosom is deliciously stiff!' Edward massaged his swelling groin. 'How long will the sleeping draught last, brother?'

'Long enough for you to play about with her bubbies, if you must. Though the Devil knows why a Lord should want to romp with a filthy peasant.'

With mock disdain, Harold observed Betty's perfectly formed body. He ground his teeth jealously, but he couldn't admit to himself that he'd fallen in love for the first time. He'd fallen in love with Betty. Harold, who prided himself on his numerous conquests, had never chased a woman nor had his heart suffered pangs other than those of lust, but this pale beauty had reached his heart. Putting thoughts of romantic love aside he decided he'd allow his brother to touch the girl a little, but the main prize, her virginity, he must reserve for himself.

'I should like to chafe and knead these pretty playthings.' Edward brushed his hands across Betty's pert breasts. He'd have been surprised to know of his brother's feelings, but was too insensitive to interpret the jealous look in Harold's eye. Besides, the finer sensations of passionate love would never enter his callous heart, which would remain thus unloved to his grave.

Betty continued to feign sleep as Edward grasped her neck. She'd believed she could only love William, yet Edward's mastery drew her to him. Why the thrill of desire for a man who cared only for his own gratification? Gita's words came to mind: '...voluptuousness... humiliation... pain... sexual appetite...'

'Don't worry, I shan't cause her to make a noise.' To Betty's disappointment, Edward removed his hand. 'You know I can't bear to hear a woman's screams.'

Then I should scream on purpose to drive you mad! Betty thought, her nerves tingling, her cunny growing wet.

'And yet you would like to be the cause of her agony!' Harold sneered, despising the cowardly cruelty of his sadistic brother. 'Just as you enjoy whipping the servants.'

'It is the born right of a gentleman to chastise his servants when necessary. How else would the social order be maintained?'

Betty imagined herself at the mercy of Edward. Adrenalin flowed as she imagined him tying her, teasing her with the whip, and then satisfying his lust in her mouth.

'But the birching of innocent women...?'

'There is no such creature as an innocent woman.' Edward pressed his fingertips into a roof shape. 'I cannot help my inclinations. It is natural in a full-blooded man. And the flagellation of whores is hardly a crime. Why, in Church doctrine...'

'Ha! One with such *unnatural* preferences should become an Inquisitor for the Roman Church!'

'If only, if only I had the means to go to Europe... perhaps sometime I shall. How long before she wakes?'

'Are you so mean-spirited that the hussy must know who graced her neck with diamonds?' Harold could read his brother well. 'Cover her. She'll take cold in her condition. We must keep her warm until we reach the inn.'

Betty pretended to stir in her sleep, changing position so that her face was in the dark corner. She felt the necklace. Diamonds? Once she got away from the brothers she could sell the jewels and set herself up as a lady, perhaps a foreign lady running from a wicked father. Of course, she'd have to wear a mask and a wig when in company. Suddenly Betty's small world opened to a whole range of possibilities, limited only by her vivid imagination.

Edward surveyed Betty's neck and shoulders. 'I should like her to be aware that a true lord, one that is legally deserving of that title, favours her with his attentions,' he whined. 'A girl from lowly beginnings will be nothing but grateful to her benefactor.' Edward's hands moulded the beautiful white orbs and with difficulty he refrained from squeezing hard. 'She will be only too willing to please me in the way I like! She is sure to offer herself to me enthusiastically. But I shan't care if she does not. I will gag her if she protests.'

Betty's first instinct was to throw herself at the mercy of the brothers. She was normally an impulsive creature, and in the past had abandoned herself to her strong submissive urges, risking the direst of consequences. But now she was beginning to develop a certain cunning combined with a degree of patience. No, Betty would not reveal herself yet. She'd take her time and choose the moment. Meanwhile, she'd abandon herself to her brilliant imagination.

'Your squawking tone belies your words, my Lord!' Swarthy Harold made a gesture of mock-obeisance and then stared moodily out of the window. 'The truth is, you wish to hurt the girl and at the same time make a favourable impression. Yet you cannot bear to part with anything better than paste! Those imitation diamonds look a trifle dull against her ivory skin. Wouldn't you agree? I would have given her the originals.'

'I could hardly remove the jewels from mother's safekeeping. The girl must make do with the copies! I doubt she'll know the difference.'

Betty was heartily disappointed at the latest turn of the conversation. Still, perhaps the gems would pass as diamonds.

Harold smirked to himself, since the necklets had been swapped and Betty was, in fact, wearing the real thing. For years Edward had been in the habit of 'borrowing' his mother's paste – he did not dare take the real jewels – and giving away the trinkets as gifts. Harold had informed Lady Clancy of his brother's thieving and they had devised a scheme which would give them both an income. She would replace the paste in her jewellery box with the original articles, which Edward would be subtly encouraged to steal. With Harold's collusion, and the compliance of each girl in question, the jewels could be sold at a considerable sum, perhaps less than market value, but sufficient to satisfy Lady Clancy's growing need to import large quantities of Claret from the best vineyards in Bordeaux. However, the good lady was unaware that on each occasion Harold had pawned the jewels and after redemption was keeping them at a secret location in London.

'Your arse is tighter than a wild duck's. Mother wouldn't miss them. She's too blind to tell the difference.'

Edward moved to the edge of the seat and his voice grew shrill with annoyance. 'The girl is ignorant. What if she should lose them? What if they should be stolen and my inheritance squandered as a result?'

'So you're worried she might run away with mother's precious jewels and when she drops dead there'll be nothing left for you! Ha! There are plenty more to be had in the world – jewels and girls! She looks exhausted. She must have been in the water quite a while. And water is known to chill the blood.' Harold adjusted the cloak around Betty.

'But Hal, I would touch her now!' Edward rummaged in

his breeches and played about with his cock. 'What could be more delightful for us, and more humiliating for the wench, for her to be told, on awakening, that she has been frigged in her sleep? Such shameful blushes! I shall not last the whole journey, indeed I shall not! I must have a little satisfaction, else God knows what I shall do to quench my thirst!'

'Draw the cloak aside. I shall watch your play. But take good care. Do nothing that will shock or hurt the girl. We cannot afford to arrive with damaged or soiled goods.'

Edward frigged himself rapidly whilst he slid his other hand gently over Betty's limbs. 'See, the laudanum has warmed her. She's hot in more ways than one.' He started to hum discordantly. 'Why don't *you* have a feel of her flesh?'

'Perhaps I shall.' Harold affected disinterest. 'Meanwhile, take care what you do.' Harold was irritated with his brother, but more so with himself for succumbing to Betty's charms. The resultant jealousy, lurking toad-like in his breast, was an uncomfortable emotion. 'Must you hum that silly tune? I am heartily sick of it!'

'Betty doesn't seem to mind, and she likes my attentions.' Edward rubbed the wetness at the closed aperture of her cunny, then tried to insert a finger. Betty was enjoying the light touches, but she tensed her muscles at this attempted intrusion. 'Her cleft is strangely tight.' He rubbed then sniffed the digit as if to determine whether he'd risk a taste for himself, simultaneously increasing the friction on his cock. 'Oh, oh, I shall spend if I don't take care!'

Harold laughed: 'Lick her cunt if you dare!' He knew his brother's preferences, how he'd rather inflict pain than give pleasure, how he balked at activities which came to himself quite naturally.

'Lick and eat the fruit, but do not bite!'

'Mm, she smells better than any other hussy I have met, a strangely delightful scent for a village girl! Most unusual for such a low-bred wench.'

'Mingled with the "coarse stink of peasantry", I hear you say! And thus a reason to leave the girl alone!'

'Far from it.' Edward was genuinely surprised at his own reactions. In the past his sole reason for performing cunnilingus was because he imagined it would humiliate the girl in question. Thus he would overcome his aversion to the task. Betty's scent, however, had made him unusually excited. 'She smells of roses and the sea. I should like to bury my tongue in her treasure house...'

'Bury, bury! Your ardour surprises me. Such eagerness to pleasure a woman. I hope you are not weakening in resolve, or falling in love!'

'Hardly! But you know how greasy these village chits are as a rule. They are useful in as much as they might perform a service, fellation or analingus perhaps, but that is all. I rarely touch one with my tongue!'

'Well, if you must gamahuche the girl, get on with it! Your fingers don't seem to be having much effect.'

'But they are. Her cunt is awash with juices.' Edward bent over again, and with his fingertips he tentatively parted Betty's cunny-lips and gently licked them. But all Betty did in response was to draw the cloak tighter around her. She was enjoying herself immensely, and would draw out the game for as long as possible.

'Huh! I'd have thought she'd be a deal more fiery.' Edward was disappointed at the lack of reaction, but he nuzzled in a little closer.

'Your thin white fingers are too soft for a girl whose grown used to the rough hands of farm labourers. Likewise she is used to the action of stronger, more practised tongues upon her nether lips!' Unlike Edward, Harold instinctively knew the ways of women, their desires, their pleasures. Edward had only ever thought of himself. 'And as for your failing tongue, I'd say it's had little practice in the past! Perhaps you have never learned how to pleasure a woman!'

Edward, feeling slighted, diverted his annoyance. 'Hal, I

would prefer it if you did not address me as "Eddie". It is a title hardly befitting of a Lord.'

'Lord or no, you are still a man! And like any man, must spunk, as I see you soon will!' Harold had noticed how Edward had increased the frigging motion and seemed about to spend. His face had reddened and his nostrils curled, but Harold knew his liver was white!

Edward's eyes brightened: 'Spunk inside her cunny? What luck!'

'So, the odour of Betty's fragrant cunny has truly fired you!' He handed his brother a linen handkerchief. 'Spunk here, you lack-brain. And then we will attend to the lady.'

'But brother,' Edward whinged as he spurted into the cloth, 'you should have let me enter...'

'Enough for now. There is plenty of time and we must attend to Betty. See, she is restless!' From a bag Harold fetched a small pot containing a potion of bear's grease and belladonna. 'This should calm her nerves, Eddie, rest the spleen, and gently but slowly arouse her deepest passions. Zillah makes a fair concoction.'

'But I am a Lord,' Edward continued weakly, throwing himself back into the upholstery. 'You should have let me... and I am not a lack-brain! Indeed I am not!'

Harold laughed coarsely and his eyes twinkled with mischief. 'You may have secured a title, dear Eddie, however dubiously,' he paused, a mocking smile on his lips as Edward winced, 'but Nature has given the powerful figure and the demeanour to me rather than you! In short, whilst you are a Lord in name, I am a Lord amongst men. And that, of course, puts in question your ideas of what constitutes a true Lord!'

'Confound you and your rhetoric.' Edward's intelligence was no match for Harold's superior brainpower. His orgasm had drained him, and in any case, he was too cowardly to oppose his sturdy brother.

'Another thing you should remember,' Harold sneered, 'you are beholden to the Old Girl until you come of age.'

'Come of age! Ha! At five and seventy! God's teeth!' Suddenly angry, Edward began to shake as he controlled his desire to give pain. Spunking into a lace kerchief was no substitute for the infliction of pain and humiliation upon an unwilling victim. Edward would have liked to take out his anger and frustration on a servant, as was his custom, but there was only Betty and he could not mark her yet. 'Confound our poxy Father's will! What difference does it make that Father thought fit to leave everything to me? I shan't live to see that bountiful anniversary! Mother is barely a generation older than us and apart from her failing sight is as robust in physique as he was weak. She is bound to outlive both of us, the demented, old hag!'

'She is far removed from that state, I assure you.'

'Well, I have seen no signs of her intelligence.'

'Her premature senility is for outward show only. She is not as far gone as she pretends! At least when she is not a drunken sot.'

'Drunk! Your coarseness is insulting, Harold. Mother does not drink.'

'You're more of a fool than I thought, dear Eddie. There is no one else in the household to empty the wine cellar! Ye gods, without me you would not be clever enough to pizzle, let alone worm money out of the old girl!' Harold studied his brother's face and laughed.

'Why mother should prefer you to me I have no idea. And yet Father's affections were the very opposite!'

'Edward, you deceive yourself if you think that is the case.'

'I have always been more in his favour.'

'Nothing is further from the truth. Father despised your weak, effeminate ways, your cruel nature. However, as a man of absolute rectitude he must favour the first-born son.'

'But I thought it was you that were first-born.' Edward pouted childishly. 'And that Father wrote you out of his will because he preferred me. Why is it that I am the last person to find out anything important?'

'Because, Edward, you do not see what is obvious. As a child you were the bane of your teachers. The simplest facts would not sink in, the easiest mathematical computations were a mystery to you, Literature and Poetry you could not understand, and as for the Natural Sciences...'

'Never mind all that. Tell me, pray. Tell me the truth!'

'I was the first-born – you are right about that – but not the first to breathe. I was the first-born but considered to be the spawn of an interloper. I struggled from the womb encased in a heavy caul, and the fool of a midwife declared me dead. Whilst my tiny limbs fought to release themselves from their shroud, mother expelled you, the second babe. The midwife uncoiled the cord from around your neck and you apparently let out a robust yell. Father rushed into the room as mother ripped the caul from me and kissed life into my failing body. He naturally assumed my birth to be the second.'

'But surely mother put him right.'

'Mother fell into a faint and the servants attempted to tell him otherwise, but you know how Father would not stand opposition. When he saw my squashed and dark features, which seemed to him to resemble those of a close gentleman friend, he accused mother of cuckolding him and swore that I was no son of his but the Devil's offspring. Nothing would alter him from that persuasion and he swore over the Holy Bible that he would leave his fortune to you.'

'So, you are a cuckoo in the nest with your dark feathers sorely crumpled.'

'Not proven, dear Ed. But rather be the bastard spawn of an alley cat than have the brains of a wren. Father always said the midwife should not have cut the cord strangling you at birth.'

'If he so despised and hated me why did he not change the will in your favour?'

'Because, dear Eddie, unlike his sons, he was a man of honour, a quality which neither of us has either inherited or learned! He was also a stubborn, tyrannical, old fool.'

'But mother cannot take away my title or my future riches, and neither can you!' Like a petulant child Edward shook his head triumphantly as if to say "so there".

'Hm,' Harold snorted, thinking it would be an easy business to get rid of his brother and take the inheritance for himself if he had the need. 'You are as dependent upon me as I on you. Quiet, the girl is moving.'

'Let me touch her again.'

'Why not? Since you are the Lord!' Harold had obtained a perverse enjoyment in his brother's sexual frustration.

Betty had stirred into an awkward sideways position. Edward's hands now roved over her back, and then between the cleft of her arse. He muttered to himself weakly: 'What a beauty. As white and cold as marble. Her skin as sheer as silk, her blood showing blue through each tiny vein, her plump hips so voluptuous.' Edward clenched his skinny fingers into tight fists. *Ah, to split that tender virgin arse with my piston, to plunge it to the ballocks, spunk into that narrow hole and drain myself of vital juices!*

Betty knew she must appear to wake soon, but she was enjoying Edward's frustrated touches.

'Later Edward. Curb your sickly passions.' Harold had guessed his brother's thoughts. 'I don't want the girl hurt, not yet anyway, and you have so little control over the base instincts!'

'Let me shaft her now, Harold.' Edward's pale complexion had reddened with his rising libido, his eyes had reduced to points, and he grimaced asymmetrically as one of his hands went to his groin again.

'You have spunked enough!'

But Edward was of a different opinion. 'She'll put out her tongue and after she has poked it in my ear, I'll bid her poke it up my...'

Harold fingered his dagger again and glared angrily. Whilst his brother was cowardly, his manic streak would occasionally erupt and he'd be difficult to handle. 'You've had a good look and feel of the girl, you have released quantities of sperm which should satisfy you for a while. You may taste her full and intimate charms another time. We mustn't allow her to chill. Madame Farquar is expecting a perfectly healthy, unmarked specimen, and she will be perfect for her new role. It would not do for her to start work with a cold or a fever. Move over. You begin with her feet.'

Harold rolled up his sleeves and gently lay Betty along the length of the seat. He brushed off the dry sand and began to massage her white flesh until it became a delicate rosy colour. Meanwhile Edward kissed and rubbed Betty's pretty feet as he surreptitiously attended to the growing bulge in his nether regions.

The maddening caresses had heightened Betty's senses until she was near driven to distraction. Peeping under her lids, she watched the men's expressions. Harold's dark complexion had entirely reddened, his lips seemed to have swollen and his eyes stared with sexual passion. Edward's face had turned a ghostly white, apart from spots of bright red on his cheekbones and the tips of his ears. His nostrils flared as if he were controlling an impulse. Betty stretched out one leg, placing her foot deliberately on Edward's groin. Immediately he jumped up and began furiously kissing and gnawing her feet.

Betty curled into a ball, retreating into the cushions as far as possible.

'That'll do, Eddie. Take your lips from her feet. I wouldn't want you to get carried away with your fangs. You might soil your breeches!' Harold glanced at his brother's groin and laughed loudly.

Edward covered the wet patch with his hand and giggled, shamefaced as Harold laughed even more loudly, throwing his arms wildly about him.

'So the important Lord Edward Clancy couldn't wait! He has spunked into a kerchief, and now must spunk into his breeches like a common servant boy who sees a lady's white flesh for the first time and cannot control his emissions!'

'I swear I'll see you to your grave, Harold!' Edward tensed his arms. Although he was of slim build, he was strong and muscular and his biceps showed through his jacket.

'Really? The timid worm threatens!' Harold suddenly jumped forward and grabbed Edward by the neck. 'You misbehave again, Eddie dear, dear Eddie, and you shall be punished.' It was time Harold put Edward in his place and he took a risk: 'I'm sorely tired of your girlish tantrums. If you must behave like an uncontrollable strumpet, then you shall be treated as such and whipped thoroughly.'

The cowardly Edward quaked in Harold's iron grip and a tear dripped from his eye, trembled on his cheek, and slowly ran to the corner of his mouth. The thought of receiving pain at the hands of his brother was a frightening prospect. Harold had never gone this far with him. 'I, I shall accede...'

Harold had gained ascendancy over Edward, and he would now add the final humiliating insult: 'Behave like a wench again and I shall force you on your knees not only to beg forgiveness but to take my virile member in your mouth and milk it like a whore until my ballocks are fully emptied!' He shook Edward roughly and that, combined with a sudden jolt as the coach ran over a rut, caused the brother to burst into a flood of tears.

'Hal, dear Hal, I shan't oppose you.' Edward gasped for breath. 'Just let me know when I can have the girl, I'll be content with that. But you can't make me suck your... you can't! It is so enormously proportioned it would kill me. I'd die from lack of breath.'

'I can do as I please, dear Eddie, and you know that. Do not provoke my anger.'

Edward shook, and his terrified eyes took on a pleading expression. 'I could not swallow it, Harold, indeed I could not! Please don't make me!'

'I'll let you off the hook for now,' said Harold, thinking it would be a most pleasant way to humiliate his brother, 'providing you behave with the utmost decorum.' He let go and Edward rubbed his sore neck. 'You may help me prepare the young lady for her visit to Madame Farquar's!'

Edward frowned sulkily, wiped away his tears, and tossed his head. 'You do not do me justice,' he whined doggedly. 'I have the title, and as such I should be in charge.'

'Eddie,' Harold glared aggressively, 'unless you have something useful to say, be silent, else mother shall hear how you've been spending her money behind her back. She will not be pleased! You'll be banished to Clancy Towers again.'

'Death and damnation! A pox on the woman!' Horror contorted Edward's face as he contemplated the awful thought of managing the Irish Estate. Situated in the most inaccessible position, it was a wild, windy and bleak place inhabited by peasants and sheep.

'Eddie,' Harold laughed, 'your coarseness is insulting,' he mimicked.

Edward sighed heavily. 'I could not bear it!'

'Then keep your teeth away from the girl and have patience!'

'I suppose I must.' Edwards shoulders heaved as he capitulated. 'I shall be most gentlemanly towards the lady!'

Whilst the brothers had been arguing, Betty had curled herself even smaller and squeezed her eyes tightly. She was not naturally vindictive and her jealous, vengeful feelings had abated. But since she no longer cared for William her first love, she must find another. Of course there was Adam, the groom. He said he loved her, and though he'd been the cause of her first punishment, he'd been too cowardly to oppose her husband. He hadn't even tried to save her from the water. Of course there would be plenty of gentlemen at Madame Farquar's, but that seemed a distant prospect. Why wait? Betty was in the company of two gentlemen, both of whom desired her. But who was it to be? Harold or Edward?

Edward's earlier talk of cruelty had excited Betty but he seemed cowardly at heart, afraid of his brother's anger. Harold, however, seemed fearless, dominating and powerful. His recent outburst had simultaneously frightened, aroused and intrigued Betty, and she began to think that perhaps she could love him and submit herself to his sexual will. But she'd have to let Harold know of her feelings without incurring the vicious attentions of Edward.

Edward moped into a corner whilst Harold turned Betty over and gently uncurled her. Still feigning sleep, she offered no resistance and flopped heavily against him. He'd meant to leave her alone, but her voluptuous beauty was far too inviting. Placing his ample lips over a nipple he sucked it deep into his mouth then pulled away, gently joggling the chain connected to the ring in her cleft. Betty could bear it no longer. She opened her eyes, mouthing the words: 'My love, my love...'

Harold smiled gently, but since Betty had been given one of Zillah's herbal remedies, he couldn't be sure she was aware of whom she was speaking to. For his part he would love Betty, but she must come to him willingly, not under the influence of a potent drug.

Edward glared maliciously. He'd have liked the delicious fruit to himself, drug or no. 'Such innocence must be ravished thoroughly.'

'Not by you, Eddie. If anyone is to possess this beautiful angel, then he must love and cherish her.'

'But I thought you didn't care much for the "peasant".'

'I'm beginning to change my mind.' Harold ran a finger over Betty's cupid's bow and between her lips, whereupon Betty began to suck. 'She is just a child. She sucks like a baby.'

Edward rubbed his growing erection. 'She is fully eighteen and that is old enough. Think how those ruby lips would work upon your cock, or mine, sliding down from the head to nibble the ballocks and suck them into her mouth.'

'Control yourself, Eddie!'

'Then I warn you not to bait me, Harold, or I shan't be responsible for my actions.' Edward's voice became shrill with frustration as he rubbed his tormented groin. 'Oh, to enter each orifice until her stifled cries for mercy become cries of wanton desire! Harold, I would fuck her now!'

'Not possible, dear Eddie. Your constitution does not allow it. Remember the surgeon's advice: "Restrain from all vices, in particular those of the flesh. Drink no strong liquor. Douse the virile member with a strong solution of borax. Ice-cold baths followed by a tincture of toads' blood..."'

'Do not remind me. I shall change surgeons and find one to give me advice more suited to my disposition.'

'Well, there are leeches a-plenty willing to administer their poisons to fools such as yourself. But meanwhile, my dear soft brother, safeguard your health and play the foil. We must wash and dress her before she wakes. Pass me the flannels.'

'I wish you would not treat me like a lackey.' Sulkily, Edward brought out a wooden box containing some soft cloths soaking in a perfumed emollient. He then took various articles of feminine silk clothing from a carpet-bag and shook them out by turns.

'If you didn't behave as a whinging lackey you'd not be treated as such! Hold her still.'

Between them the brothers prepared Betty's toilet, wiping away any remaining strands of seaweed and sand that stuck to her skin. They removed the remnants of the bridal veil, which had clung tenaciously to her skin. Like a rag-doll, Betty deliberately flopped this way and that, occasionally murmuring as she was dressed in her finery. First the cream silk stockings with lacy tops and pretty frilled garters. Next a delicate crushed silk camisole with matching trim. Then the corset, tight-laced to accentuate Betty's tiny waist and the firm swell of her young breasts and hips. Over these were placed layers of petticoats, each with a convenient slit at the rear. Lastly a cream lace dress, similarly slit and with an extremely low décolletage such that her breasts could not help but be exposed. All was beribboned and trimmed with tasteful decorations.

Edward knelt on the floor and slipped a pair of cream court shoes on Betty's tiny feet whilst Harold placed elegant combs and ribbons in her hair. A few touches of rouge on her cheeks and lips, then scented oils on her wrists, neck, the back of her knees and the crease of her arse. At last she was ready, propped up against the bolsters again, her golden hair tangling prettily over her white shoulders.

'Now for the final touch, Zillah's unctuous cream. She is by all accounts a lusty wench, and these oils will merely exaggerate her own inclinations.' Although Harold wanted Betty for himself, he was also driven by sexual jealousy. Thus he both tempted and repelled his twin. 'When she arrives at Madame Farquar's she will be trembling with unsated passions. Her lust will know no bounds. Edward, arrange her petticoats.'

Edward lifted the rich silk cloth. Both men stared lasciviously at the vision before them. Half-naked Betty had looked beautiful, but half-dressed she appeared more highly erotic. Her legs were slightly parted to reveal a creamy expanse of thigh above her stockings and between a darker triangle of blonde hair barely curling over the delicate pink gash of her cunt. Her petticoats, rumpled carelessly around her hips, added to the voluptuousness of the sight.

'Let me poke her, Harold.'

'Later, perhaps. You've had your hors d'oeuvre. Now for mine.' Harold dipped his large forefinger in the pot, and parting Betty's outer lips with two fingers he began to rub the mixture into the crack. Then he pulled gently on the chain connected to the gold ring which pierced the tiny hood above her clitoris, making sure that a goodly quantity was rubbed over the rising organ which began to peep from its hiding place.

Harold's attentions were the perfect cue for Betty's performance. As if in a fever, her eyes began to dart under her lids and she began to murmur: 'Bless me, Father, for I have sinned! But I ain't really bad, Father, an' me cunny do feel so nice...' Betty's hips trembled as, with a subconscious action, she pushed herself onto Harold's hands so that her delicious spongy spot might receive his attentions. At first she'd thought to merely make an impression of lustiness, but the friction inside her cunny served to excite her passions. With a juddering motion she began to give way, and without thought for the consequences, her hips bore downwards in a pushing movement. Harold naturally responded by wriggling his fingers and rubbing furiously on the delicate spot just inside the upper part of her delicious cleft.

'Oh, father, father, I can't help meself, oh my, oh my, if you do tha' I shall spray all over yer hands. Oh, oh, I shall spray, I knows I shall!' Betty let herself go and the juices poured from her cunt, wetting Harold with a fair deluge, her tiny arse-flower dilating and twitching as she orgasmed.

'Ah, Edward, the girl is spending enormously. Such a torrent of juices is a rare gift. Why, the wench's cunt is a fountain! My hand is quite, quite wet.' Harold licked at the running juices covering his hand.

'I thought as it were mother I were kissing... I din't know as I'd be punished... Why do I love him so, Candace...? Giles, where is William...? Oh, Father,' Betty's hand searched under the petticoats for her cleft, '... me cunt is all wet with spunk...!' her fingers explored. 'What if I were to give birth...? But I ain't done nothin', Father. He came atop me an' he hurt me but I love him... I ain't so bad, Father... Why should I have to wear this horrid belt...?' Betty fingered the gold chain.

'What, in damnation, is the girl saying? Let me touch her, Harold.' Edward edged nearer, but Harold had pulled Betty's petticoats over her legs. The coach was now travelling over rough ground and the sound of the wheels almost obliterated

Betty's mumbling.

'Enough, Edward, is enough.'

'Muttering about William, about spunk.' Despite his earlier emissions, Edward was beside himself with frustration. 'Her bawdy talk is more than I can bear. If I cannot have her now she must frig me.' Edward loosed the buttons and his hardened cock sprung out, the red head gleaming wetly as the foreskin slipped back. Edward's member was of average proportions, being neither long nor short, neither fat not thin, but it was rigid with sexual passion. He looked appealingly at his brother.

Harold, who was by no means unexcited himself, relented. 'She shall frig us both. Sit the other side of her. When you are ready to spunk make sure you do not soil her dress.' He brought out his cock, which was larger than Edward's but very slightly softer, grabbed hold of Betty's small hand, and applied her fingers to it. Edward followed suit, uttering a deep sigh as he did so.

Betty's fingers gripped around the instruments of pleasure and slowly moved up and down their length. Her eyelids fluttered and a pleasurable smile played about her plump lips as she picked up speed and was soon vigorously frigging the frustrated brothers.

'Oh, William, darling. I din't know as you 'ad two pintles. Whatever made you grow another? I never know'd a man wi' two afore.' Betty kissed each prick in turn. 'Why, they's different tastes, but they's both nice. This one is red, an' this one is purple. Oh, William. You 'ave four ballocks, too, an' they feels all fat an' full o' spunk!' Betty squeezed her tiny hands around the sacs.

Edward was the first to reach his climax. 'I am coming. Ah! I am coming.' Pinching his foreskin over the glans in an attempt to slow the ejaculation, he drew aside and spunked into the kerchief again.

Now Harold could avail himself of Betty's two hands. He placed the free one under his ballocks.

'What are you doing, sir?' Swaying slightly, Betty opened and closed her eyes.

'Nothing, my dear. You are only dreaming... dreaming of William... dreaming of taking William's spunk. Ah my dear wife, are you ready to swallow your husband's vital fluids, the essence of manhood?'

'You should have let me...' Edward whined.

'Be silent, else *you* shall swallow my spunk, not Betty!' Harold's face had reddened even more and his breath came in short pants as he reached his climax.

'But it's not fair...'

Ignoring his brother, Harold crouched over Betty in what must have been a very uncomfortable position. Grasping the strap hanging from the roof and bracing his legs against the seat, Harold pushed his cock between Betty's parted lips. Her willing mouth closed upon the rigid member, sucking it in deeply.

'Swallow your husband's spunk, and be thankful your Master lets you off without a whipping.' With a brisk action Harold thrust forward, but the movement of the coach drew Betty tantalisingly away, so his pubic hair merely brushed her face. To compensate, the reverse movement suddenly ground them together. Betty opened her eyes and pulled her mouth away, having ingested only half of the seminal fluid, the remainder spurting onto her hair.

'Why, sir. You are not my husband! You are... surely not Lord Clancy? No, you are dark, whereas he is fair! Who are you, sir? How dare you?' Betty touched her curls. 'Oh, sir, you have spunked in me hair!' With that Betty's eyes closed and, thoroughly exhausted now, she fell into a faint.

'Edward is mine, dear black one.' Zillah stroked the cat. 'He has a heart of stone! But as for Harold, we shall see, we shall see. Man's lust is a powerful force!'

'We'll soon be at the Cock and Whippet.' Edward rubbed

his hands gleefully. 'One night in a comfortable bed and the girl is bound to be ready for us!'

'Brother,' Harold had been watching Betty closely, and was now worried about her condition, 'we cannot take Betty to the inn in this feverish condition. She must have suitable rest and care. We should travel to the nearest hospice.'

'Then take her to the Sisters of Nommerci! The convent hospice!'

'Excellent! She'll be safe in the hands of the nuns.'

Chapter Four

Low Life at the Bawdy House

An odd couple – Parslow's toolleywag well used – Dreams of beating Betty – Nipple clamps – Ferocious humping – Ill-assorted lovers – A plot to seize the fortune – Impersonation – The plotting of nuns

Liza and Parslow sat each side of the kitchen fire munching toasted muffins and speaking between mouthfuls. They made an odd couple. He was probably no more than seventeen, though he didn't know the year when he was born so could not have said exactly. She admitted to being just under fifty.

Liza rubbed butter from her mouth onto her hands, then her pinafore. She looked sideways at Parslow. 'Well, Snips, ain't yer got summat fer me, me beauty?'

The young man was hardly a picture of desire. He was beaky-nosed, spotty and scrawny, and his clothes hung loosely about his thin frame. But as far as Liza was concerned he had one saving grace: an enormously huge cock, totally disproportionate to his body. And that was the 'beauty' to which she referred.

'What'll you gimme if I 'ave?'

'A farthing. An' don't look at me wi' that face. It's all yer getting today. Now hurry up if yer knows what's good fer you.'

Parslow sighed, untied his breeches, and reluctantly brought out his prick. It lay pink and flaccid in his palm, but was nevertheless a formidable object. It was indeed so large that many a maiden had balked at the size of it. But not greedy Liza. Today, however, it refused to rise.

'What's this poor soft thing, then, dearie?'

'It's me snake, ma'am.' Parslow shook his floppy cock from side to side. 'I'm tryin' to wake 'im, see.' The boy had been happy at first with satisfying his youthful urges in Liza's capacious cunt or arse, but her demands had become outrageous and he was flagging.

'But it's only a little grass snake. Can't we get it a little bigger?' She licked her lips lustfully and a drip of spittle ran from her mouth onto her hairy chin.

'If yer rubs it ma'am, p'raps it'll turn into an adder, an' bite yer!' *An' I wouldn'a mind if it killed yer!* Parslow had intended to stay with Liza until he'd saved enough money to leave. Then he'd be off like a pistol shot! Meanwhile, it was getting more difficult to satisfy the greedy woman.

Liza hoicked her skirt up to her knees, seized his manhood, and skilfully began to pull the foreskin back and forth whilst Parslow lay back and allowed her to get on with it. 'Now me dear, where shall us put little snakey? Back or front?' She stood over the young man, tucking her petticoats out of the way. 'We'll soon make 'im stiff as a stile-post.' She bent over and sniffed. 'Snakey's got a nice smell, dearie, an' what a sweet little eye a-winking at me.'

'Snakey ain't well today, ma'am.' Parslow smiled crookedly. He had no inclination to satisfy her lust whatsoever, and though he didn't particularly want to annoy Liza, he couldn't help teasing. He'd been pocketing Liza's money ever since arriving at the manor. He'd followed her to London, and it would not be long before he had enough to stand on his own and run his own group of fancy 'ladies'.

'You know, Liza, I fancy meself in a gennelman's coat. In charge o' me own cunny-warren, like.' He grinned maliciously. 'Them young hussies be bound to want a taste o' me cock!'

Liza gave him an angry glare. 'Arter all I done fer you, Parslow!' She let go of his prick, sat heavily over it and rubbed back and forth. 'Gettin' them girls fer you an' all.

Now make a poor ole widow woman happy!' She rolled up her sleeves as if she meant business, and pulled her skirts aside. 'I reckon me clitty's bigger'n yer toolleywog!' It wasn't true, but nevertheless Liza did have an exceptionally large clitoris, so large in fact that she'd been taken for a boy at birth. 'In fact, I reckon I could a-been a gennelman, no mistake.'

Parslow refrained from saying what he thought: *You got the hairs to prove it!* At puberty Liza had grown breasts like other girls, but her underarms sprouted more densely and her stomach was covered with an excess of pubic hair that joined the thatch at her cleft.

She began to rub her elongated bud, and though Parslow didn't mention it, he was beginning to think that perhaps Liza was a man after all. 'Come on Snips, me pet. I'm right randy and right wet and...' Her hips juddered as she spent on her hands, spraying juice over Parslow's prick. She then slumped heavily on his groin and rubbed her cunt lips furiously against it.

Apart from her rather masculine appearance, Liza had been neither pretty nor ugly before the ravages of pox, work and time had taken their awful toll. However, the grimace that attended her orgasm was nothing short of horrific. She scowled, her lips twisted this way and that, her mouth dripped with gobs of saliva and guttural noises gurgled from her throat. Not that Parslow cared one way or the other about that. It was not Liza's appearance that put him off, but rather that she did not satisfy his sadistic urges. To please him, Liza had procured a couple of serving girls, but the word had got around and even those of the lowest order, desperate for money, recoiled from taking part in his nasty practices.

'Tell me the plan agin, Liza,' Parslow urged, making a couple of thrusts with his hips. 'Snakey wants to hear.' Despite his prick's reluctance, the inevitable happened. Liza's weight had acted as stimulation and Parslow's mind did the rest. 'See, Snakey's a-coming up nice now!'

'Well, Snips.' She pulled him to her and put his matted hair against her shoulder. 'Well, me darlin', you gotta find Betty an' we'll put her away, like, an' shame her.'

'Wot yer mean? Put her away?' Parslow's cock stiffened as he imagined lovely, fresh Betty imprisoned and at his mercy. 'Where shall us put the trollop?'

'Shut her in the dark hole! The hole where no one'll find her. '

'Where's that then, ma'am? We ain't got no proper dungeon like the manor. Tha's what she deserves! Chains, an' whips an'...' He clenched his fists in anticipation.

'The cold wood cellar. She can go down there fer a week or two.'

Parslow grinned wickedly. 'Arter that, I reckon she'll do as she's told. We'll give her bread an' water, but not too much! An' make the trollop drink it from a trough like a little piggy porker.'

'She won' like them spiders and bugs as gets down there.'

'An' the rats! Don't forget the rats!' Parslow smiled in an ugly way and jiggled his hips. 'An' how shall us shame the hussy, eh Liza?'

'I thought on that a lot. And I decided, me dear, I decided to let you loose on the trollop!'

'To do as I likes? Well, Liza, you is sweet, me dearie. Ain't yer jealous? Mind you, she ain't nothing to me!'

'Oh, no, Snips, me dearie. So long as you gives me bubbies a nice feel and I gets a-rumping with yer lovely hard toolleywag, I ain't complaining.'

Parslow began to hump up and down in his seat, and Liza rode him as hard as she could whilst thinking at the same time how she'd get the money back off him.

'Tell us more dirty talk, Liza. Tell us about naughty Bet.' He thrust his hips upwards and then in a quick circular fashion.

Liza squealed excitedly, like a cross between a baby's cry and a suckling pig. 'You keep a-humpin' then. Now, we'll put the trollop in the woodshed wi' no clothes on...'

'An' we'll frighten her wi' talk o' ghosties! An' in the night a nice big ghostie will come to her, smack her little bottom, an' stick summat hard up her cunt, eh, Liza?'

'She'll beg us to let her out. She'll be standin' there, all naked, her little titties all a-sticking up wi' cold. She'll be beggin' and a-beggin' us.'

'An' we won't, will we Liza? We won' let her out. We'll put cold water on her instead.'

'An' then I'll let yer fetch the box o' tricks!'

'I'll get them screws out...' At the thought of the nipple clamps Parslow's prick grew even stiffer and Liza let out a fart and then a couple of loud groans as he began to hump ferociously.

'You do that, me dearie. That's right, Push up nice an' hard like.' Liza pulled her large breasts out of her corset. 'An' give me dugs a tickle.'

'An' I'll put the screws on her nipples right hard.' He humped harder and twiddled Liza's huge brown nipples. He'd liked to have tweaked them very hard, but didn't dare. 'I'll screw 'em tight till she screams an' pees herself wi' fright.'

'You do that, dearie. Come on, hump up harder! It's no more'n she deserves, the bad girl.'

'An when I done that I'll smack her silly face and beat the chit black an' blue...'

Hump!

'I'll beat her bare backside...'

Hump!

'I'll thump her arse an' whip her teeny little bubbies...'

Hump...

'Until she cries "Mercy", but it won't do no good.'

With a final thrusting Parslow ejaculated and his hips shuddered fearsomely. Liza held onto his tangled hair and thumped herself up and down on him, increasing the friction to extract as much pleasure as she could. 'Oh me darlin', me darlin' Snips. I'm a-comin' agin.'

Exhausted, the odd couple tidied themselves, sat back and contemplated their future in the fire. Liza thought of the money to be made through prostitution and how one day she'd have enough to set herself up as a society lady. Parslow thought of how he'd milk the old hag dry, then run off with the money, taking Betty with him. He'd keep her prisoner and make her do exactly what he wanted. Every day. Every day for the rest of her life.

'What happened to them papers? Eh, Kit, Eh?' Grace shoved her elbow painfully into Kit's ribs.

'How should I know? Summat must have the buggers. Last time I looked under the sink they'd gone!'

'A likely story! Well we'll go and look together.'

'I'll be quicker on me own, Grace. The horse'll go faster if you ain't in the cart.'

'Why, you cheeky son of a pig's pizzle!' Grace gave Kit such a shove that he fell backwards and sat rubbing his arm. 'I don't trust you to go a-looking fer 'em. You'll get away from me an' you'll be arter Betty agin. Then who knows what would happen? Kit knows just where them papers are, Liza!'

'It ain't no use you two lovers a-quarrelling agin.' Liza glared angrily. 'Grace, you get on back to the mansion and find them papers on yer own.'

'An' then wot?' Kit was sulking.

'I told yer. Don't it sink in yer thick 'ead. Parslow will fetch Betty an' take her to the secret location.'

'Where's that then, Liza?' Grace folded her arms and glared.

'It wouldn'a be no secret if I tells you as well.'

'Why can't *I* go an' find Betty, 'stead o' Parslow?' Kit was beginning to tire of Grace and would relish the chance to meet Betty again.

'Not likely!' Grace's face was red with jealousy!

In fact, the two ill-assorted lovers had begun to fall out of favour with each other and were constantly bickering. Grace had taken on rather superior airs since she'd been set up as a fancy woman in Liza's bawdy house. Furthermore, her enormous carnal appetite was more than fully satisfied due to the number of clients she entertained; at least forty a day. As a result she was less interested in Kit and more interested in securing an income for her old age. However, she wasn't going to let Kit go easily, especially if the beautiful Betty were involved.

'If you two don't stop a-quarrelling there'll be hell to pay.' Liza glared viciously. 'I'm running a proper house fer gentry an' I don't wan' no problems. Jus' you go an' find out what Giles and Adam are up to, Kit, an' leave Parslow to get Betty.' She folded her arms decisively. 'Grace you go an' look fer them papers.'

'I'm off then. Give us kiss, Gracie me dear.' Kitson pecked her on the cheek and ran out before she could say anything.

'If he goes arter Betty, I'll friggin' kill 'im, so I will!'

'Grace, come here.' Liza pulled the girl to her and sat her on her huge lap. 'Tell me, what do you think o' Betty?'

'I reckon she's a jumped-up trollop. Thinks she's so fancy. Better'n servants. Why, she's a peasant herself!'

'Well, I have a little job fer you.' Liza smiled encouragingly. 'Do you think as you could impersonate the girl?'

'I might, on'y I don't know what yer mean. What's "personate"?'

'Pass yerself off as Betty. Dress up in her clothes. Make sure you find them papers an' keep out o' the Master's way.' She winked. 'There's money in it.'

'What'll I do arter I got 'em?'

'All you have to do is to take them papers, pass yerself off as Betty, go to the magistrate, an' prove yer right to the fortune.'

'An' I'll be a proper Lady?'

'Oh, yes me dear, a proper Lady wi' servants an' all. There ain't no doubt about it.'

Grace smiled. In truth, it was not a nice smile but it was the best she could do. 'An' what o' Betty?'

'Leave that side o' things to me, dearie. Leave it to me.'

'You wouldn'a really harm her?' Grace was jealous and a liar to boot, but she lacked the immoral fibre of Liza. She was also frightened of authority. 'We don't want no trouble wi' the beadle.'

'Have no fear, me dear. Have no fear. The chit won' get no more'n she deserves.'

'So long as I gets 'er to lick me clitty every day. Las' time...' Grace rubbed between her legs at the thought. 'Las' time...'

'You're a one, you are, me dear!' Liza gave Grace a sloppy wet kiss on the cheek. 'Yer worse than I were at your age. You ain't got no time fer that.' Liza took Grace's hand away from her crutch and pushed her to her feet. 'Now fer Betty's old clothes. Look in that bundle, Grace, an' put 'em on.'

Grace pulled out the very items of clothing that Betty had worn on arrival at the manor. 'I don't know as they'll fit me Liza.' Grace began to remove her own soiled clothing. Although she no longer wore a servant's uniform she had not improved her personal habits. The pink silk dress was spotted with greasy marks and her underlinen was grey and streaked with foul-smelling stains.

'This camisole's small.' Grace pulled the material over her ample breasts and buttoned it. Since her arrival in London she'd lost some of her puppy fat and the garment just about fitted, albeit tightly.

Although Betty was much smaller than Grace, the skirt and petticoats could be gathered over a slim or large frame simply by adjusting the ties in the casing. Grace loosened the waistbands and stepped into the petticoats, then the skirt.

'Put on the jacket, me dear, an' the shawl.'

Grace obliged. She looked a pitiful sight swelling out of

Betty's clothes. 'Do I 'ave to wear this?' She put on the cambric cap. 'It ain't half itchy.'

'You must cover yer hair, dearie. It's the wrong colour.'

Grace tied on the bonnet. 'Well, what does I look like? Does I look like Betty?'

'Why, me dear. You looks lovely. The picture of innocence. Now make sure you keep them clothes clean. Don't let them whites go grey, else you won't look the part.'

'Huh, I don't know why Bett's so fussy. She's no better than she is.'

'That's as may be. But you don't want to be found out.'

'What'll I do now?'

'Listen, dearie, an' I'll explain the rest o' the plan.'

Grace sat on a stool and leaned her elbows on the kitchen table. She listened thoughtfully, and occasionally an almost pleasant smile played about her mouth as she dreamed of riches and a position in high society. She'd have beautiful silk clothes, the finest shoes and hats, handsome admirers, and best of all, she'd have Betty to do her bidding.

'Here, you list'ning?' Liza shoved Grace in the ribs.

'I were thinking, Liza, when I got the money an' the land an' all, you can be me "aunt", an' that toad Betty can be me lady's maid. She won't be so fine an' la-di-da if she's to serve me!'

'She'll 'ave to do as you say, won't she dearie? Everything you say.'

'I'll do jus' as I like, won't I? An' if she don't obey, I'll whip her so 'ard, I will!' The thought of giving Betty a thorough beating stirred Grace's loins and she put a hand up her petticoats to fondle her cunny. 'She can serve you an' all, Liza.'

'Thank'ee me dear.' A ghastly leer crossed Liza's face as she remembered the indomitable fire in Betty's eyes. 'I never did like the chit! Too full on herself. I'll pay her back fer being cheeky, so I will!'

'We'll get 'er to lick our cunts clean as many times a day

as we likes, till 'er tongue fairly aches!'

Liza and Grace folded their arms simultaneously as if the matter had been decided.

'Mother Superior,' the old nun bowed her head respectfully. She'd carefully tended Betty during her illness and having befriended her, was eager that the virgin should be allowed to stay in the convent. However, she was worried that Betty would become involved in the less religious side of the nun's activities, namely their lesbian pleasures. 'Betty's condition has greatly improved over the weeks, but the fever is still in evidence and she seems to have developed an illness pertaining to the womb.'

'I am not sure of your meaning, sister. Explain yourself. Have you noted the time of her monthly cycles? You have much experience in these female matters.'

'Firstly, I believe she has not reached the menarche. Secondly, it appears that the girl's womb is overheated. A dripping ague has set in, caused perhaps by the strange ring piercing and the chains she wears about her intimate person. Her, em, "areas" are always wet. She should be left alone.'

'Left alone, Sister Ignatius? What *do* you mean? Please speak forthrightly!'

'She should not be interfered with.'

'To what do you refer?'

'I refer to the "pleasures", as you call them. Though why they *should* be called that, I do not know! It does not seem natural to me! We are brides of...'

'Good Heavens, sister, it is our tradition! No man will be present and we remain virgins! Why, you have even taken part yourself.'

Sister Ignatius folded her arms and spoke grimly. 'A long time ago! And I did not like it one jot!'

'The convent would be empty if we did not allow it!'

'Betty is far too young!'

'Pish and nonsense!'

'Mother, you may inspect the rags. There has been no blood.'

'That signifies little. As you well know, sister, an exhausting fever may temporarily stem a girl's flow.'

'Perhaps we should call the physician for his opinion.'

'What in Heaven's name are you thinking, sister? No man is permitted within these sacred walls!' The young Mother Superior folded her arms. 'Besides, we'd have to pay highly for such services and our finances are, to say the least, in danger! Betty is perfectly well and we shall go ahead with the ceremonies.'

'It would go against our promise to the Clancy's to keep her unsullied.'

'She will remain a virgin. I see no deception. We have been paid well and will keep to the letter of our words and satisfy all parties.'

Sister Ignatius frowned. 'The letter of your word is not the spirit!'

'God's passion, sister! It is gold, not scruples we need. How else shall we honour our debts? The coffers are empty! The remainder of the prince's gold has not arrived and perhaps never will. We cannot afford to eat much longer.'

'Surely a little gruel is nothing.' Sister Ignatius sighed.

'I must satisfy all parties.' Mother Superior steepled her hands thoughtfully.

'Who are these parties demanding satisfaction, Mother, and how exactly do you intend to satisfy them?'

Mother Superior looked angry but controlled herself. 'Sister Ignatius, I value the wisdom of your ripe old age, but your lack of trust is irritating. And these are modern times, remember.'

What was far more irritating to Mother Superior was the fact that the convent depended on an income, albeit small, from Sister Ignatius's family. It would not do to cross the woman.

The crafty nun smiled and took the old woman's hands in

hers. 'Trust me, sister. I fully respect your concern for Betty, but I cannot disappoint the powers that be. If I confide in you, will you promise to keep silent on the matter and take it no further?'

'You can rely on my absolute discretion.'

'It is a strange history and far too complicated a web to untangle. Suffice it to say that according to a most peculiar will, Betty is to inherit a fortune if she gives birth to a child but remains a virgin.'

'What madness is this?' Sister Ignatius sat heavily on one of the hard oak seats and crossed herself. 'Is it not against both God and Nature?'

'Against God? How? Even the Church of Rome has its own fine example in the Mother of the Saviour!'

'I do not think the Church meant the Virgin Mary to be emulated! The Devil must be at work here! I will have nothing to do with it!'

'Let me finish!' Mother Superior frowned. 'I will tell you a little of Betty first. She is not the innocent you imagine. The girl has always been lusty. At the tender age of sixteen, her stepfather, having failed to prevent her from constantly masturbating, hauled her before the parish priest.'

Sister Ignatius threw her hands in the air in horror. 'Mother, I had no idea, the sin of onanism in one so young! And little Betty guilty!'

'I tell you, it was common knowledge that she could not keep her hands from her parts! Naturally she had to be punished. Her penances were apparently long and arduous, involving much work on the part of Father Loughran, who spared no effort to cure her of this mad sickness. But no amount of confession and praying would stop the trollop!'

'Trollop! Strong words, Mother.'

'Indeed and so, sadly, it was necessary to pierce her with the ring of shame!'

'No! The ring and chains of shame! I wondered what they signified! I'd heard of such devilish things but never thought to set eyes on them! But they do not prevent her from a-watering all over the sheets!'

'Exactly. Can we keep such a Devil's child within these walls? She must leave as soon as she is well. Meanwhile, as with many a herbal remedy, we must treat like with like. She will be made to pleasure each and every nun, including you, Sister Ignatius! Perhaps a wetting of your dried up and withered cunt will teach her a lesson she won't forget!'

Sister Ignatius fell speechless to the floor.

'How'd you get here, Em?' Betty sat up weakly, drew the thick woollen night-shirt away from her legs, and tried to get out of the high bed. 'I never thought as I'd see you agin.'

'I come 'ere arter I escaped from the mansion. Now get back, silly.' Emily pushed her friend's shoulder and Betty fell against the pillows. 'Stay where you are. I'll come up there.'

Betty rolled over. 'I must be a-dreaming agin!' She rubbed her eyes.

Emily hitched up her heavy novices habit, climbed up and tucked herself under the covers next to Betty. 'See, me darling, you ain't a-dreaming'. We *are* together.'

The girls embraced lovingly. They had missed each other's company, the good times together and the sufferings shared.

'Why you a-wearing the habit? You ain't a nun, is you?'

'Not likely. I on'y done the novices part. I ain't a-staying, I can tell you! I done the initiation. I ain't staying longer else they'll bring in Zillah.'

'Zillah? But I already got me gold chain an' the ring over me clitty!'

'They gets up to all sort o' tricks. You don't want to stay here!'

'But they been kind to me, Em.'

'On'y fer a reason. Don't trust no one 'cept Sister Ignatius.'

'Come with me to Aunt Rowena's.' Betty kissed Emily. 'She'll be wondering where I am. You come too!'

'We can't leave straight away. Not tonight. Anyways, I got other plans. I worked it all out, see. You go through the "Pleasures" tomorrow.'

'What'll they do? I heard about whipping an' all sorts.'

'Them ole nuns likes to get hold on a virgin from time to time. They won' whip you hard nor nothin'. They jus' likes to set you a-thinking mad thoughts so's you go off men.'

'Why'd they call it the pleasures, then?'

'You pleasures them an' they pleasures you, till they stand it no longer.'

'They gives you a little spanking, then sets you to work a-licking all their cunnys.'

'Well, you know I done all that stuff afore at the mansion.' Betty laughed. 'Remember Grace's fat cunny, and Liza's great long clitty. It were so huge I thought it were a pintle!'

'And the Mistress Emma, don't forget.'

'I shan't forget that nasty, scheming triple-turned whore in a hurry! She'd have poisoned all on us if she could!'

'Forget the old life, Bett. You can't change things. Think on the morrow.'

'I am,' Betty suddenly giggled, 'but there's over fifty o' them nuns!'

Emily laughed. 'It takes ages. Arterwards, if yer good, they tickle yer clitty an' rub yer bubbies, an' put little candles up yer cunny. They give you a good time so as you wont leave an' run off with a man. They knows jus' how to drive a girl mad.'

'I thought they's meant to be brides o' Christ, not lewd minxes.'

'Oh, they's all virgins. Well, most on 'em, anyways. An' they don't do nothing with men, unless it be the gardener. An' he's so old an' shrivelled he don't count, 'cept sometimes he brings his nephew, an' he's well hung, but Mother Superior don't know that. She's inspected him an' all!'

'How'd the boy get away with it, if he's so well hung?'

'When he was a tiddler, he had a funny habit of poking

his pintle up his bum.'

Betty's eyebrows lifted in astonishment.

'Oh, only when it were soft like. So when he first come 'ere he popped it up inside an' drew the curls over so just his balls hung down. Then he put a bit o' dung on his bum so as Mother Superior didn't want to come too close, an' it fooled her. Since then he's growd a bit. In fact he's growd a lot!'

'Well I never did!'

'Oh yes you did!'

Betty laughed this time. 'Oh, Em, I's so glad yer here. Let's cuddle up.'

'I'll stay till dawn. Sister Ignatius said as she'd watch out fer us. She's a bit strict an' she don't like us girls a-kissing, an' she never attends the pleasures, but she's got a good heart. Now listen to me, them nuns love a new girl. We'll fool 'em to think you like it here, then when we gets the opportunity we'll be off to Madame Farquar's.'

'Madame Farquar's? Why go there? Ain't it a bawdy house?'

'Oh, Bett, you silly, o' course it is! But that don't mean they's all bad there! I been there afore an' I tell you it ain't at all bad. When you see the fine clothes they wears...'

'It's not fine clothes as I want Em, not really.'

'The ladies don't half eat well, Bett. They don't want fer nothin'.'

'I'll come with yer, but I ain't staying there.'

'Let's talk in the morrow. You look tired, Bett, me dear. Shall us kiss yer cunny, me dear?'

'Oh do, Em, do, an' I'll kiss yours arter I spent.'

Emily crept under the covers and wriggled her body into position with her face directly over Betty's luscious motte. With her hands, she gently parted her lips and buried her tongue to the hilt. But just as she did so she felt a little tickling on her leg which caused her to jump up. 'Oh, Bett, we ain't a got fleas?'

'Course you ain't. It's only me.' The blanket was off.

'Why, Timmy, how'd you get in?' Emily tapped him on the hand. 'You naughty boy to startle us so rudely!'

'I come up the drainpipe,' the gardener's nephew grinned cheerily, 'an' in the winder! Easy. What you a-doin' of?'

'You know very well what we're doin'! Ladies things.'

Simple Timmy was a strapping lad, only just sixteen, over six foot tall and very gentle. His complexion was ruddier than usual and his fair hair tousled in all directions. He'd undone his breeches and was cradling a massive erection in one hand, the other fondled his meaty ballocks.

'Who's this then?'

'I's Betty.' She smiled and her eyes lit up. Even though he sported the largest member she'd ever seen on a young man, it was obvious by his gentle bearing that he posed as little threat as an oversized puppy who wanted to ride his master's leg. 'Em told me you done a clever trick with yer toolleywag. Don't suppose you could do it now.'

'No, but I knows another trick I *can* do now. A very clever trick!'

'He's full o' silly tricks, ain't you, Timmy?'

'It ain't silly,' the boy pouted, and a tear formed at the corner of his eye.

'Don't be wet, Timmy.'

'Don't call me silly. I don't like it that's all. An' I don't like you wearing that dress, neither.'

'Well then, I'll take it off! Shall I?'

'Oh, Em! Will you?'

'Any case it's not a dress, it's a habit.'

Timmy giggled at his own joke. 'It's a funny habit thought, ain't it?'

'Do you want to see me starkers, in the flesh?'

'Oh, Em, will you show us yer bubbies. I loves yer bubbies.'

'I'll show you more'n that. You can see everything I got!' With a saucy expression on her face, Emily pulled off the different layers until she stood stark naked in front of the boy. 'What do you think o' me?' She posed provocatively, hand on hip.

'I think you's lovely, Em. Them bubbies is so round, an them teat's so pretty.' Timmy's lip quivered in anticipation as he began to frig himself, drawing his loose foreskin back and forth over the bright red tip. 'Can I touch 'em? They's like little rosebuds.'

'Later, Timmy. Jus' show us yer trick. Bett ain't seen it yet.'

Timmy giggled and worked more furiously on his oversized member, whilst Betty stared in disbelief as he suddenly shot a stream of spunk right across the room. The sperm took a great arc and landed neatly in a large goblet on the table.

'Now drink it, Timmy!'

'Do I 'ave to?'

'If you wants yer rumpy-pumpy, you do. Put yer dangler away fer now!' With some difficulty Timmy tried to tuck his male equipment into his tight breeches, but since the rampant member would not reduce in size, he gave it up as a bad job and left all hanging loose.

'Won't go in, Em! I's too big an' I got too much spunk in me ballocks!' He tried again in vain. 'Can I 'ave a bit o' rumpy-pumpy wi' Bett, an' all?'

'Not likely!' Emily frowned and Timmy followed suit. 'Drink up! If you ain't good, you won't get nothin'!'

Timmy took a small sip. 'Oh, Em, I loves you. Here's to you!' He lifted the goblet, swigged and swallowed. 'An' you, Bett, I loves you, too!' Another sticky swig.

'You loves all the ladies. Now finish yer drink an' put yer bits away, I say!'

'But you's *all* lovely.' A last swig. 'I can't help meself! Why, the ladies in all the world they's all *so* lovely, lovely as flowers!' Timmy set the goblet down and began to dance around the room, his cock in one hand, his ballocks in the other. 'Shall us sing you ladies a song? I know lots o' bawdy rhymes.'

'Shush, you'll wake someone. Now Timmy, be a good boy and wipe the cup clean with yer finger and finish it off!'

Betty smiled at Timmy. The young man was most engaging. He'd make a fine husband for one of the village girls, or perhaps a fine manservant for her when she became a lady. 'Timmy, would you like to be a ladies' manservant?'

The boy's eyes lit up, but before he could reply Emily spoke up. 'Course he would, an' he's been well trained. He does everythin' a lady likes, specially if'n she ain't got no husband to please 'er. I trained him all by meself! Try him! He's got a lovely strong tongue!'

'Would you like to pleasure me, Timmy, with yer tongue?'

'Oh, missy, there ain't nothing I'd like better,' he quickly glanced at Emily to see her reaction, 'except to lick Em, o' course. She's me mistress, see. An' I do just as she says, whether I likes it or not. But I usually likes it, see. An' if Em says to pleasure yer little cunny, why I shall, whether I likes it or not, but o' course, I should like it!'

'There, I told you he was willing, didn't I Bett? Let's to bed, all three.'

Chapter Five

The Nuns' Pleasures

Cunny kissing – Dreaming of the priest – Plan of escape – The humiliations of Sister Humility – The Wheel of Shame

'Wake up, Betty.' Emily pulled on Betty's arm until she sat up in a wobbly sort of way. She shook her somewhat roughly, but as that failed to wake her friend, she wound her arms around her shoulders and caressed her gently. 'Come on, give us a kiss, Bett! Oh, *do* wake up!'

Betty rubbed her eyes drowsily and pouted her sleep-swollen lips. 'Ain't yer mouth sore arter all that cunny-kissing last night?'

'No! That's what mouths are made for. Fer kissing friends.'

'Well, mine's right sore,' Betty inspected her cunny-lips.

'If yer not careful I'll kiss yer cunny agin, an' then you won't never want to leave the convent!'

'Oh, Em, I quite forgot we was here. I were dreaming we was at the mansion...'

'You was, was you?' Emily grinned. 'I should think it were more like a nightmare than a dream!'

'I s'pose it was. We was both in the chapel waiting fer Father Loughran to hear our confessions. We was whispering. Neither on us had done nothing wrong so we decided to make up stories.'

'Why'd we do that?'

'Cos we hadn't got nothing to confess and he wouldn'a believed us. Anyways, you went in first – it were so real Em – and you told him a pack o' lies and he punished you with his toolleywag!'

'He never!'

'It sounds funny now, but it weren't funny in the dream. He pulled his toolleywag out o' his cassock and suddenly it became long as a pea stick, only thicker, and he ran round the chapel, his robes a-flying and beating you with the big stick!'

'What happened nex'?'

'I went in and did the same, only this time his nob had grow'd and grow'd. It grew so long it poked out o' the winder, so we went outside and pulled on it and tied it up to a post. And there we left the priest!'

'Funny you should dream o' Father Loughran.'

'Why? He ain't never far away from me mind.'

'Oh, I heard tell he comes to hear the nuns' confessions tomorrer, arter the "pleasures". He has to come then, else the poor innocent souls'd have nothing to confess. He comes once a year an' they pay him but it's not the money he comes fer, it's the humiliation, see. He supervises all the penances.'

'I thought as men wasn't allowed in the convent.'

'He don't go right inside. He 'as a special confessional in the Chamber o' Contrition where the nuns' penances take place. That's the only time they's allowed out the convent, or to see a man. Mother Superior lets 'em, see, because she knows the priest won't tup 'em.'

Betty's face lit up unexpectedly. 'Is Father Loughran *really* coming here? I ain't been to confession for, I don't know how long, and I got much to confess!'

'You doesn't want to confess to Father Loughran does you?'

'Yes I does!' Betty went red with embarrassment and turned her head away to hide her face from Emily. 'I can't help meself, see. He's a man o'...'

'A man like any other, Betty. He has the self-same tools, the self-same fleshly desires.'

'I know that, Em, but he's still a man o' God with the power to turn the bread an' wine into flesh, and the power to forgive! There ain't nothing on earth, nothing, not even excommunication, takes away that.'

'Yer too religious fer yer own good, Bett. Still, it won't do no 'arm, an' if'n it makes yer happy, why not? Now fer the plan? We was going to make a plan fer escape!'

'Do we have to? I ain't never made a plan afore.'

'That's half yer trouble. You allus wait till it's too late an' then yer done for. Listen, you stay for the pleasures an' then think o' summat to do that's bad so's the nuns won't want you to stay much longer, not even Sister Ignatius.'

'Why'd they want me to stay any case?'

'Mother Superior thinks to make money out o' you. Sister Ignatius is so holy no one 'ardly likes 'er. She ain't got no friends. As fer the other nuns, they're hysterical with womb fever. They think o' nothin' else but the pleasures o' the flesh, nothin' else at all.'

'What's the use o' that if there ain't never no men?'

'They pleasure themselves!'

'I know, Em, and that can be *so* lovely, but it ain't the same as having a big pintle to suck, and a master's fingers and tongue on yer parts.'

'Mm. 'Specially Timmy's. I think as I could love the boy. He's well hung, an' he does exactly what I says, only he ain't got much in the way o' smartness.'

'That don't matter, Em, he can learn.'

'I don't know as 'e can, Bett. Now, listen. Arter the pleasures, you can go to confession and arter you finished you'll swoon into a fever an' play as if yer mad. Mother Superior will be scared o' scandal, so she'll put you to bed in the care o' Sister Ignatius. Meanwhile I'll 'scape with Timmy and send word to the Clancy's, tell 'em yer ill.'

'And what if they don't get the message?'

'I'll make sure as they do. I'll speak to 'em personal-like an' convince 'em they shouldn'a left you 'ere. Me an' Timmy will meet you at Madame Farquar's.' Emily gave Betty a resounding kiss on the cheek. 'What do you think o' that?'

'What about me? Don't I get to run away?'

'There ain't no need. The Clancy's will take you to

Madame Farquar's in any case.'

'Why don't you come with us?'

'Cos I want Timmy to 'scape wi' me! Now Bett, give us a kiss an' then get yerself ready. Sister will be here soon to take you to the Palace o' Pleasures.'

'Sister Ignatius?'

'I doubt it. I 'spect it'll be Sister Humility. Listen carefully. This is what you must do...'

'Will it be long afore we get there? Me feet's cold.' Naked and barefooted, Betty followed Sister Humility along a seemingly endless corridor which led underground and into the hillside where the Palace of Pleasures was located.

'You are not to talk!' The nun took out her rosary and carved a tiny notch into the first of the large wooden beads. 'A punishment for talking!'

'You never said!'

'And another!'

'What punishment? I ain't done nothing wrong!'

Sister Humility sighed deeply, shook her head and cut another notch. 'Every novice who joins us has done something wrong and we aim to beat it out of her. That's why the sisters are here, to atone for both their sins and the sins of the world.'

'I ain't done much, except,' Betty tried to think of something shockingly bad, 'I sucked two men together... I sucked two pintles, both at once. I stuffed them deep in me mouth and they both spunked right down me throat.'

'Two pintles?' Sister Humility stopped short next to an oak bench situated in a dark alcove. 'I must sit down a moment. Now Betty,' she tapped the seat next to her and then surreptitiously slid a hand onto her own clitoris, 'tell me all about it.'

'Why, yes, sister!'

'Tell me, what were they like, these pintles, these virile members? Were they long, or thick with pendulous and juicy plums? Did the veins throb with passion? Tell me, Betty, tell me. You have much to confess and you may as well tell me first! It will create the right frame of mind.'

Betty tried not to show her surprise as she told her tale to the curious nun, and urged on by the nun, describing the relevant parts in great detail.

'So now you knows it all. I can't think Mother Superior will want me as a novice now.'

'On the contrary. She will enjoy bringing a sinner to the fold.' The nun lifted the skirts of her habit. 'And I shall enjoy it too! Kneel Betty, kneel before me. I am not called Sister Humility for nothing!' The nun opened her legs wide to display her cunt. She was not a young woman, but all was neat. Dark hair, with only the slightest hint of grey, curled around the orifice. 'Lick me, Betty. Put your little tongue upon my clitty, and remember when you are spinning on the wheel of shame, that it is I who hold your destiny in my hands.'

'I ain't going to lick yer clit now. No I ain't!'

'But you most certainly are, unless you wish to be incarcerated in the dungeon below.' She drew back a sliding door in the panelling. On the other side Betty could see a young woman, stark naked, standing on a plinth and caged in a wire birdcage. She looked unhurt but very bored. 'See, her sin was an attempt to fly the nest. Therefore her punishment fits the crime.'

Betty knelt, took a deep breath, and buried her face in the woman's cunt.

'Ah, ah, I am spending. Drink my cunny-juice and live!' Betty lapped at the woman's cunny to receive the spurting juices.

'Well, that's that. But do not tell! Else you shall find it will not be to your advantage. Come. Follow me.'

The first room in the Palace of Pleasures was decorated to imitate a brothel. Red tapestries hung on the walls and the furnishing, mainly huge cushions, stools and low settles, were upholstered in rich velvet.

'This is the room of temptation! It is here that we begin the "Pleasures". You must wear suitable clothing, such as a whore might wear.'

Sister Humility gave Betty a pair of brown leather boots, a pair of drawers, and a short camisole. 'There, put these on.'

'Is this all?'

'It is. Perfect! Now lean over the settle, and turn your head to one side. Oh, not like that!'

Betty was being deliberately difficult, and she earned several notches on the rosary. Sister Humility was concerned to place Betty in such a position that she could be seen through the peepholes. Unbeknown to the other nuns, apart from the Mother Superior, she made a small fortune from selling tickets to view the "Pleasures". Behind the panelling were several gentlemen who had paid highly to see the latest virgin and her humiliation.

'There, Bett. All is correct. Await your preliminary punishment.'

Betty knelt at the settle, her white rump exposed. She trembled a little with anticipation and excitement.

'Remember you must not flinch, else you will remain longer on the wheel.'

'What is the wheel?'

'More questions. Another notch for you, Betty!'

After a few moments the nuns filed into the room, each one grasping the instrument of flagellation.

'Take that!' A gentle swipe. 'And that!' Another. 'And that!' A harder one.

'It ain't fair, I ain't done nothing!'

'Liar! You are sinful, and as such must be whipped and humiliated thoroughly!'

It was the Mother Superior. She had not allowed the nuns to beat Betty hard. If anyone was to do that, it would be she.

'On the floor and crawl behind me, wretch. You may hold my hem in your mouth as a token of your abasement. Grovel!'

'I will not!'

'Oh, but you will! Another notch, sister!'

Betty made as much fuss as she could without incurring too many notches, and after a few minutes they entered the inner chamber. Here all the nuns, including Sister Ignatius, were assembled around a huge wheel.

'Here, Betty, the wheel of pain and pleasure is before you. Face each nun, bow before her and beg forgiveness for what you shall do. Feast your eyes on the scene before you are blindfolded. Climb up.'

Betty's eyes were blindfolded and her body spreadeagled. She was affixed on her back to the wheel with her feet dangling. The wheel was constructed in such a way that her body was available from all angles. It could be turned right over or spun in a horizontal position. It could be tipped so that she was upside down.

'May the pleasures begin! Sister, spin the wheel!'

Suddenly Betty felt herself turning, faster, faster. The wheel began to take all angles and after but a few seconds she was totally disorientated. At last it stopped, and at that moment two nuns stepped forward. The nun at Betty's befuddled head stood astride her mouth, forcing her cunny over it. The other used a feather to tickle her cunny.

'Suck, Betty, suck… but beware! Do not allow the devil's milk to come, else the strictest punishment will ensue!'

Betty sucked hard on the anonymous cunt over her mouth. It was difficult to breathe, since the cunt was pressed down hard and was sliding all over her face. Meanwhile the feathers constantly tickled at her own cunny, driving her to distraction.

'Lick harder, Betty, and resist the temptation at your lower parts! Spin, sister, spin!'

Suddenly there was a new cunny over Betty's face, and a face instead of a feather over her own, searching for her clitoris, titillating and rubbing. Betty tried to hold back. The feathers, followed by the licking, had driven her mad and her frame began to shudder as she muttered, 'Oh, oh, I shall spend... I shall spend!'

'No, Betty, no!' The face withdrew and a cold piece of ice was placed over her cleft. 'Spend and you shall be whipped!'

The tremblings in Betty's groin subsided for a moment, and then the torture began once more. The wheel was spun, and each time Betty felt a new cunny on her face, a new pair of lips at her mouth. She tried desperately not to spend, but it would be impossible, for the nuns were practised at their craft and knew exactly what they were doing. Time and time again they brought her to her peak then allowed the waves to subside. But Betty was not in control, and she knew that if they had their way she would spend and spend and spend.

'Ah, Mother, I cannot help meself, ah! Ah!' And the first of her orgasms reached its peak.

'Untie her!'

Betty was placed over a stool, her bottom high. Mother Superior, her hand raised aloft, stood behind her. 'You are a sinner, are you not?'

'Yes, Mother.'

'And you allowed the devil's milk to flow?'

'Yes, Mother.'

'Then take this!' A series of sound blows belaboured Betty's tender arse. 'And this! And this!'

'Oh, oh!'

'And now for the wheel of the withered cunts.' Mother Superior took off the blindfold. The younger nuns had all disappeared, and there remained only the older ones.

'See, here are the nuns you have so disgraced by your lewd behaviour. They have watched your shameful performance, the way you relished each nun's parts and sucked and licked without compunction. The way you tempted all to sin, hoping to draw the devil's milk and drink it for yourself. You must be chastised, and what better way than to treat like with like! Kneel before each sister. Kiss their feet humbly, licking them as you do so, and beg forgiveness for what you are about to do! Beg forgiveness, before you wet each cunt with your seemingly eager and insatiable tongue!'

Betty was blindfolded and tied to the wheel again, this time face down. The older nuns were allowed to sit in chairs which were at a convenient position for Betty to perform the cunnilingus, which she did so, urged along with several stinging smacks across her rump.

'Spin the wheel!' And so the performance was repeated. At last it was Sister Ignatius's turn, and Mother Superior had decided to make it extra humiliating for them both.

'Sister Ignatius, you have been concerned about the devil's influence on Betty. Now is your chance to rectify that situation. You will drive the devil from its deepest hiding place!'

At first the old nun did not realise what she had to do, but when Mother Superior bent Betty into a crouching position, her arse high in the air, there was no doubt. 'I must poke my tongue there, Mother?'

'Yes, sister.' The nun was thoroughly enjoying herself. 'Poke it right up Betty's hole, else you must seek the devil in each and every orifice of the entire convent. And if you fail you will be excommunicated!' She had not meant to say that last word, but it had slipped out. 'However, as you know, God is merciful!'

The old nun began to work on the humiliating task of licking Betty's arse. Scared of being thrown out of the convent, she made a good job of it, and soon Betty was squirming and wriggling. 'Oh, sister, oh!'

But Mother would not, of course, be satisfied. 'Lick harder, sister. You know the penalty if you do not obey. And Betty,' she smacked her bottom, which by now was quite red, 'do not wriggle so. It will be your turn soon.'

Soon the positions were reversed, and Betty was a-licking at the old nun's tight and puckered hole. 'Lick harder, Betty, put your tongue up!'

Betty did her best and Sister Ignatius, who at first was appalled and ashamed to think that one so young should perform such an intimate task on her ageing carcass, slowly started to enjoy it. Her ancient hips began to buck and Betty slipped her tongue now at her arse, now up the cleft to her cunt.

Mother Superior was watching closely. Perhaps she had made a mistake in allowing Sister Ignatius to avoid the pleasures during her sojourn. She might be old, but she was flesh and blood. The Mother spat on her fingers and slipped her hand between Sister Ignatius's legs. Seconds later the old nun orgasmed for the first time since she'd joined the convent. Her pent-up lust knew no bounds, and she screamed in pleasure and horror. 'Ah, ah, I am coming! The devil's milk descends... ah! Ah!'

'And now you too, sister, are mine!'

Sister Ignatius dropped to the floor. She had been unable to resist the devil. 'Mother... Mother, I beg you forgive me. I have sinned, and despite my life of abstinence the devil is within me. Help me,' this time she rubbed at her own cunny, 'help me drive him out!' She threw herself at Mother Superior's feet, took her hem between her two remaining teeth, and bit with such force that she loosened them both.

'Then tomorrow, with the assistance of Betty, you shall drive the devil from each and every orifice in this convent! It is about time these sisters were cleansed of their filth!' Mother Superior looked down at the grovelling nun. 'And I have another idea.' She was thinking of the men behind the panelling. It would be easy to drill some holes for the purposes of fellation. 'I think, perhaps, the devil's member itself could be brought to bear upon the matter. For unless the evil spirit becomes flesh, how are we to drive it away?'

Betty lay exhausted on the wheel. She was tingling all over. As might be expected, the pleasures had served to excite her passions and prepare her for the natural activity she had so far denied herself. Betty longed to be plugged to the very core. Her cunny was dilated as wide as it would go, and her body ached for penetration. 'William,' she murmured. 'William…'

'Sister, the girl must be cleaned. Lick her entire body and when you have finished, she may do the same to you. And then for good measure, for I am overheated now, you both shall do the same for me. Untie her!

Chapter Six

The Cock and Whippet

December 1778 – No place for modesty – A very hairy cunt – Lingering cunnilingus – The priest's spunk – Heiress to the fortune – Betty's virginity discussed – Inspection of a cunny – Ellen's treachery – Story of the Bishop's pintle – Lies about Mary

Betty lay fast asleep, propped amongst the soft pillows of a homely farmhouse bed belonging to the "Cock and Whippet", a hostelry situated in a country area en route to London. Since she'd been collected from the convent by the Clancy twins, she'd lain for two weeks in a fever. And under strict instruction from Dr Maidment, the local physician, had been constantly cared for by Mary, the lowest of the serving maids. Trustworthy Mary had been chosen in preference to Ellen since she was the more gentle and kindly of the two. Besides, the physician, having encountered Ellen intimately, well knew of her scheming, avaricious nature. He'd examined Betty, in a strictly professional manner of course, established her virginity using the usual method, diagnosed hysteria and prescribed bed rest, manual stimulation of the female parts to be carried out at a later date, and the consumption of various herbal remedies.

The brothers had spent the fortnight abstemiously, at least to their thinking, eating of Mrs Biddle's simple fare of roast meats and vegetables and partaking of large quantities of country ale. Jealously, they watched over Betty, neither wishing to leave her in the company of the other, nor trusting the prescription of Dr Maidment. They intended to leave the inn as soon as Betty was well enough to travel, and though she was not yet recovered, she seemed so much improved they'd decided to leave the following morning. Thus, each in a good mood since they both hoped to take Betty for themselves, they'd begun to celebrate.

They were now enjoying a well hung grouse with plenty of claret to wash down its greasy home-cooked accompaniments. Encouraged by Harold, Edward had decided to ignore his own doctor's recommendations for abstinence. Though he'd drunk less than his brother, the alcohol had taken effect quickly. Unbeknown to each other, both brothers had employed Ellen, the senior maid, to carry out various personal services. Au fait with the ways of the world, she was up to any trick.

Harold had paid the girl generously, ostensibly to wait on Betty, but in reality to divert Edward's attention away from her. Edward had paid Ellen a stingy sum to get his brother drunk. He then thought to gain her assistance in the deflowering of Betty. Crafty Ellen had her own ideas, involving the acquisition of as much money as possible combined with the usurping of Betty's place in the brothers' affections.

'I done washed her, sir. She has such pretty curls.' The plump little maid curtseyed, her bosom spilling over her neckline since she'd deliberately untied the lacing of her dress. 'And she's ate her gruel, though she ain't woke up proper yet... an'...' she hesitated, making a pretence of being intimidated in the presence of two fine gentlemen.

'In that case you may go.' Edward winked then held out a farthing, waving at the door as if to dismiss the maid.

'Begging yer pardon, sir.' The girl curtseyed lower, hoping that her bosom thus displayed would tempt the Lord to love her rather than the beautiful Betty. She cast her eyes downwards submissively. 'Begging yer pardon...'

'Yes, what is it? You may speak, girl.'

'Well, sir,' she twisted her hands together, fluttered her

eyelids artfully and turned to Harold, 'may I stay an' look arter the lady. She do look so tired an' I can attend to her person...'

Harold looked at the maid, then at Betty who lay peacefully sleeping. 'If you promise to make yourself useful to the lady.'

'Indeed I do, sir,' Ellen smiled shyly but knowingly.

'She is very tired and may need much assistance,' Edward interspersed. 'Personal services may be required.'

'I do now 'ow to please a lady,' she fluttered her lashes, 'an' a gennelman, too. And the lady do look so sad.' The girl sighed. 'She's pretty ain't she, sirs?' There was a slightly jealous look to her face. 'In them fine night clothes.'

'But you are pretty too, my dear, and need no finery to display your charms.' Harold pulled the maid to him, kissed her fully on the lips, fondled her large breasts and lifted her petticoats to reveal her cunt. 'Such lovely dark hair.' A faint smell of sweat and the tang of a ripe girl's cunt wafted upwards. 'What think you, Eddie?' Harold coaxed, then turned Ellen and held her arms so that his brother could take a good look at her semi-naked attractions. Ellen crossed her sturdy legs in mock protest, pressing her damp thighs together until they dimpled.

The maid's fleshiness was certainly to Edward's taste and his groin stiffened, but he liked to play the Lord. 'Brother, spare me the indignity.' Edward curled his lip scathingly, tipped his head as if to consider the proposition, then from an arm's length flicked at Ellen's nipple with his thumb. 'She is but a lowly servant and somewhat coarse to boot!'

Ellen smiled in appeal and cocked her head to one side, trying to look neither disappointed nor insulted, but her lip quivered and she flushed angrily.

'Nevertheless, a gentleman may wish to make use of such artless, peasant charms to assuage his raging passions.' Harold rattled the loose coins in his pocket then whispered aside. 'These girls can be bought cheaply enough. A sovereign is a fortune to a peasant!'

'I suppose you are right, Hal.' Edward moved in closer and laughed to himself, for he'd only given Ellen a threepenny bit. 'Such creatures are for the use of needy men such as ourselves, and for a trollop she does not seem too used up.' Edward forced his hands inside Ellen's dress and roughly pulled out two large breasts, each voluminous mound taking the shape of his cupped hands as he squeezed rather too hard. 'So, you know how to please a man!'

Ellen bit her lip and glared at the brothers reproachfully. Harold hadn't told Ellen of his brother's sadistic tendencies. He'd merely suggested she must allow him any liberty. Still, the large payment he'd offered would buy her silence. Harold settled in his chair and watched the tears well as Edward squeezed harder, but Ellen did not flinch.

'I *do* know as 'ow to please, sir. I don't need no persuading like. Oh sir, please let go, sir, yer hurting me.'

'First uncross your legs, my dear. There is no place for modesty here!' With a last squeeze of the soft plump flesh Edward took hold of her nipples. 'I assume you are expecting money.' He nodded towards Harold and raised his eyebrows. Ellen did not deny the charge. 'No doubt you would do anything for a coin or two, so let us not pretend otherwise.' Edward rolled Ellen's fat teats between thumb and finger and began to pinch tightly. 'Well, do you object, young lady?' Ellen did not reply. She blinked and Edward noticed with satisfaction the large teardrop that ran down her cheek. Slowly he inspected Ellen's belly from her naval to the cleft where her black hair grew in great profusion standing out in curly tufts, almost like a bush. 'What a great hairy cunt you have, my dear!' Letting Ellen's breasts fall heavily, he placed his hand between her thighs just above the knee and wedged her legs apart. A slight moan hissed from Ellen's lips. She wasn't used to being hurt, but was excited despite herself.

'Oh, sir.' Ellen wriggled free of Edward's grip, wiped away her tears and held up her heaving breasts for inspection.

'You ain't half pinched me dugs! See! See yer fingermarks!'

Ignoring her protest, Edward slid his hand to her inner thigh where the sweat and freshly running juices had made it slightly sticky. The girl wriggled, clamped her legs together modestly, trapping his hand, then allowed it to creep higher until it was on the hairy mound itself. 'Yes, a very hairy cunt indeed. Try it for yourself, brother.'

Ellen recovered herself. She liked the feel of Edward's hand groping at her motte and she wriggled her hips to increase the friction. 'All the better to swallow you up, sir.'

Harold had infinitely more desire for Betty than the maid, but being a sensual creature, he could not pretend total disinterest. 'What delicate hair, like threads of the finest silk.' He pulled Ellen over to him then tugged at her cunny curls, slipping an exploring finger between her pink labia. 'And beautiful soft juicy lips.' He pinched one, then winked at Edward. 'You have the luscious figure of a lady, my dear. What a lovely specimen of girlhood, eh brother?'

'I does anything, sirs, anything you like.' Ellen panted heavily and a bead of sweat dripped from her shiny red forehead.

'Indeed.' Harold twiddled his fingers gently, then lifted the girl's chin and winked as he wriggled his fingers between her fat cunny-lips. 'You are very wet, my dear.' The maid blushed as he took his hand away. 'What think you, brother, would you like to fuck this pretty cunt?'

'An admirable cunt, if I may say so, dear Harold, but a cunt is only so much flesh! Let me inspect her more thoroughly. Over here, girl.' Edward stood Ellen before him. 'Open your legs, girl. Pull your cunny-lips apart. I wish to see precisely what you have to offer.'

Ellen stood, her legs apart, and obeyed his directions.

'That's better. Yes, good.' He inserted three fingers inside Ellen's passage and began to make deliberately rough stabbing movements, at which the maid winced. 'Well, my dear,' Edward hissed in Ellen's ear as he continued to maul her, 'I thought you said you'd do anything! Perhaps more money would induce you?' He slipped a half-crown in her pocket.

'Oh sir, oh sir, fer a sovereign I does the lot! Anything as you say, kind sir!' Ellen deliberately opened her legs wider, allowing another finger inside.

'A thumb, my dear, a thumb as well.' And in it went. 'Such capacity, Harold. I believe the wench could take my whole hand!' As he spoke, Edward tweaked a nipple and then proceeded to suck the other.

Ellen breathed heavily. 'Oh, sir, I am spending,' and Ellen shook heavily as the juices flowed.

Since Edward had been imagining that he was touching Betty, the prime object of his desire, he was now thoroughly aroused and determined to involve her. 'Of course, being flesh and blood, a lady can be made wet too!'

The maid winced again. Edward's fingers were hurting her now and she would be glad of a reprieve. 'I take yer meaning, sir.' She pulled away from him. 'May I?' Saucily, she placed a kiss on Edward's cheek, climbed up on the bed, put her arms around Betty, and kissed her on the cheek too. 'I don't mind what I does, kind sirs, so long as...' Ellen looked up at the two men. 'I know as 'ow to please the lady.' Betty heard but did not stir.

'Take care, Ellen,' said Harold, hoping to divert the girl's attention from Betty. 'Take care to please your masters, too, especially Lord Clancy. He is most influential and powerful. T'would be wise to please him, personally. He has a fine member. As you can see it is bursting to be satisfied. Your plump lips would suit admirably.'

Ellen cast her eyes down deferentially. She must please both men, playing them against each other. That way she would make a deal of money.

'You will be well paid, have no fear.' Edward dug into his pocket and placed another coin on the table as he poured another drink in Harold's goblet.

'I don't mind what I does. I can entertain ladies an' gennelmen.' The young woman smiled in an enticing manner as she pocketed the coin. 'Though I likes to serve gennelman best.'

'Be quiet and stand still. We are not interested in your prattling or what *you* like best! Come here.' Edward twizzled Ellen around and bent her over a stool so her bottom was high and her breast low, almost touching the floor. 'You are paid to serve and will do so whether you like it or not! Now let's see what you have to offer. Show me your arse.'

Ellen pretended to be shy. 'Oh, sir, you can 'ave a feel, but I don't know as you should *look* at me bum close up. It ain't half rude.' She was frightened of Edward, but sensing his impatience she lifted her petticoats and pushed her bottom up as high as she could. 'There, sir. Now I done it for you. You can see all I got.'

'She certainly has a magnificent arse!' Harold patted her rump gently and slid his palm over the soft flesh.

'Then she must show us more.' A sharp slap from Edward caused the white orbs to flush pink. Yes, the maid's large posterior would certainly take a beating well, particularly in the sensitive cleft! How pleasurable it would be to torture such flesh, to pinch it black and blue, to restrain the stupid peasant and force her to submit to a host of voluptuous humiliations. Perhaps he would fuck her. Edward cracked his bony knuckles. How much more satisfying if Betty were in his power too! 'Part your cheeks, girl!'

'Oh, sir. I ain't done that afore!'

'I thought you were much experienced and knew the ways of men and their desires. You have hardly earned your coins. Perhaps Mary would be more willing...'

At the mention of Mary, Ellen suddenly lost her modesty. 'Like this, sir?' Quick as a flash, she parted her bum cheeks and wriggled her arse about, displaying the private folds of puckered skin as if it meant nothing shameful to her. 'Do you want to see me cunny an' all?'

'The chit has no shame!' Harold laughed as Edward gave her a sharper slap on the rump, leaving a red hand-shaped mark which raised up and then grew darker after a second or two.

'Excellent skin for whipping, don't you think Hal?'

Ellen gasped. 'Don't whip me, sir. Please don't. Why, yer hand hurts enough.'

Edward would have liked to deal with Ellen's plump posterior straight away, but he reckoned it would be better to get Harold drunk first. That way he could have both girls to himself. 'Attend to the lady and make sure you perform well. Else the whip...'

Ellen practically leapt up on the bed, and the mattress heaved under her weight. She snuggled up against Betty and caressed her lovingly whilst keeping one eye on the third coin Edward had placed on the table. The men proceeded to attack the claret, both with the intention of reducing the other to an incompetent wreck. Their feet went up on the table, empty bottles were thrown about the room, their faces got redder and the laughter and carousing got louder. From time to time Ellen would leave Betty and give her attentions to Edward, who took all sorts of liberties with her, fondling her voluptuous flesh and urging her on with salacious talk. Since she was practised in the art of cock-teasing and had been well paid by Harold, she made a good job of exciting Edward's member whilst returning to Betty to give an interesting sapphic performance.

For Betty, the events of the previous days had merged into one long dream interrupted by various strange nightmares. Now, having benefited from Mary's tender care, and the gruel she'd been fed, she was gradually coming to under Ellen's slow caresses. She was about to sit up when Ellen slumped right on top of her, rubbing her hips against Betty's and crushing her mouth with a hard kiss. Fairly squashed under the dead weight, Betty could not protest.

'What pretty curls.' Ellen smiled at the men, belying her

jealous thoughts: *I'd cut 'em off wi' me knife so I would. Yer no lady. I'll learn you!* She kissed Betty on the lips again and tried to poke her tongue inside her mouth.

Betty opened her eyes and stared straight into Ellen's crafty face.

'Shush an' listen,' Ellen whispered. 'I'll wake you, slow like, an' you's to let me tickle yer cunny-lips with me tongue. You can have half the money,' she lied, nodding to indicate the coins gleaming on the table. 'Do as I say, an' if you don't I'll...'

Betty didn't notice the threat in Ellen's voice. 'I don't mind if you do nice things to me. I learned about that afore. I wish you'd get off. I can't hardly breathe. An' I don't want no money.'

'Right, you pretend to be asleep. Go on yer back first, then roll over, draw yer knees up, an' I'll lick yer cranny from behind. Wake up gradual, an' we'll give 'em a cunny-arse show they won't forget in a hurry.'

Edward's plan to get Harold drunk and take advantage of Betty with Ellen's assistance hadn't taken into account Harold's constitution. Harold had inherited his mother's tolerance for alcohol, and though he'd drunk considerably more than Edward, he was less affected. Edward was now in such an inebriated state that he'd lost his impetus and had become extremely suggestible.

'So, dear Eddie,' Harold gulped a slug of claret straight from the bottle and began his delaying tactics, 'you are unaware of William's attempt to take Betty's virginity on the altar!'

Betty started. Her recollection of the wedding day was still piecemeal and her mind flooded with dramatic but disconnected images. Blood rushed to her face. By now the maid's hand had found its way up Betty's petticoats and between her legs.

'Yes, tell me how he took her, I should like to know.' For a split second Betty's petticoats flew in the air, treating

Edward to a glimpse of pink flesh. 'Ah, there is the very cunny William poked.' Edward's reawakened concentration was torn between listening to his brother and watching the maid as she played with the body of her semi-conscious victim. 'And there it is again, so pink, so fresh!' Edward nudged Harold in the ribs. 'Imagine... if it were a virgin cunny... mm... and rubbed by a lowly maid! How delicious! The very thought...' Edward fingered the buttons on his breeches. 'It looks tight enough to me. What I should like to do, Harold, is push something very large inside.' Edward began to shake in his excitement. His dealings with the maid had fired his sadistic imagination, and now if he could only make Betty his own, to do with as he pleased. 'Something very large indeed! See my hand, Hal.' He waved it in front of his twin. 'My fingers are most aristocratic, long and slim. They would easily slide into the girl – aah, if only William hadn't taken her – and once the fingers are in, well the thumb and the wrist naturally follow...' Edward leaned over in his chair, then suddenly jumped up as Harold's words took effect. 'Did you say something about Betty's virginity?'

'Control yourself, Eddie, concentrate and listen. It is a most amusing tale involving Father Loughran, mad dogs and copious quantities of William's spunk. I'm astounded you'd not already heard.'

'Ud's pity, brother, you know I've been running around Mother. I've had no chance to see anyone, not even Emma's foul butler, Grubb. He usually tells everything for a coin or two. God's bodkin, look what the trollop's doing now!' He undid a button and a second one popped off and pinged onto the floor.

'No doubt Grubb's been too busy carrying out that evil woman's plans. I'll say something to Emma's credit; she's not as tight as you, Ed, and she pays well. Grubb has always been most faithful to the highest bidder!'

Edward's face took on a detached air. The alcohol was playing havoc with him, but for a moment he seemed sober.

'Grubb's had plenty of my gold in return for intelligence.' Edward's hand delved inside his breeches and he fiddled with his floppy cock, but the claret had done its work. He sniffed pompously. 'And I have to say some of the information has not been sound.'

'More fool you! He's a liar as well as being the most avaricious servant I have ever come across. I tell you...'

Edward's face sunk into a gloom, and then suddenly brightened. 'But Harold, did you say "attempt"? Is the girl still a virgin? What luck, eh?' The thought sent tingles through his groin but the failing cock would not rise.

By now Betty had rolled over on her back and flung her arms and legs open like a young child dreaming. She was trying to eavesdrop, but the maid had her head up Betty's skirts and was bobbing up and down over her groin making particularly loud slurping noises. All that could be seen below Betty's waist was her delicate ankles and the lower part of one leg.

'Why did you not tell me before? It is hardly surprising her cunt felt so tight!' Edward's energy renewed and his face lit up with delight as a lace stocking top and garter came into view. 'What luck! What luck!' Nothing would please Edward better than forcing the virginal Betty to suffer at his hands, to lick her virgin juices as he whipped her into submission. 'God's lid! Wake up little man!' But Edward's prick refused to rise. 'How come the most lecherous and lewd man in Christendom did not take the little flower by force and fuck her to the waist? Was the size an issue? Such a large member as he is said to possess would surely split a defenceless girl's tender cunt.'

At this point the maid, who was doing her best to listen to the conversation, lifted her head to expose Betty's cleft to full view. Betty's muscles tightened. The conversation had confirmed what she hoped for, that her virginity had certainly not been taken. Suddenly she saw a bright image of the hounds. Blood. Men shouting. Dogs barking and biting as she lay half-naked on the altar. William spunking between her thighs as he drew away. As usual there was an enormous quantity of spunk, but this time far more than usual, too much for one man. She'd felt it with her hands and rubbed it in her cunny thinking that if she could not have William, she might have his child this way.

Suddenly a new series of forgotten images half-filled Betty's consciousness. First there was Zillah bending over her and whispering strange words. 'Take the devil's seed, dearie. Rub it in well. Rub it in well! The Black Prince shall fertilise you!' Betty heard the cackle of the old gypsy and then she saw the priest looming over her. Around his head was a bloody bandage and he was smiling. It was a strange, triumphant smile. In his hand he held a large glass phial and he began to pour the warm contents between her legs. 'Take my spunk, Betty. Take my spunk and may the stronger man's seed fertilise the virgin bride!' Betty's hips shuddered as she orgasmed.

'Oh, sir, the lady don't half taste nice! She has spent all over me tongue. Her cunny is fair sopping with juice. Won't you gennelmen join me an' come atop...? You'd slide in easy. I could wet her tight little bumhole for yer, too.'

Betty was too busy concentrating on her orgasm and the bizarre memories that had been resurrected to hear Ellen's suggestion, but Edward responded by grabbing Harold's arm. 'Why not, brother? I am tempted beyond endurance.'

Harold laughed. 'Your cock is hardly up to the task!' Harold adjusted his own prick, which had caught in an uncomfortable position as it swelled in his tight breeches. 'Lick her clean, Ellen. That will satisfy us for the time being.'

Betty lay back, exhausted again. She was more puzzled than frightened and what she needed most of all was to be comforted. Innocently, she wound her arms around the maid's fat body. 'Won't you hold me, dear?' Betty spoke so quietly that the men, engrossed in loud conversation, did not hear. 'I need a friend, and one day I might become a rich lady. Would you serve me?'

Ellen kissed and caressed Betty for a while. Perhaps there was more money to be had if she was clever. Betty seemed agitated, and when she sensed the girl was calm she attended to the cunnilingus, first slowly, then with greater enthusiasm. Feeling better, Betty whispered sweet compliments to the girl: 'Oh, you *are* a dear. If I were a real lady, an' I might be one day, I'd *so* love a maid like you.'

Yer a jumped up trollop, no mistake! The maid thought. 'Let me turn you, me dear, an' I'll lick yer bumhole nice an' slow, like.' Betty allowed Ellen to push her over and arrange her legs so that the maid could reach her arsehole with her tongue. She relaxed into the pillows, allowing Ellen free rein. It was not long before Ellen's expert touch tickled Betty to distraction until she had to wriggle out of reach. 'Oh, me dear, how sweet,' Betty whispered. 'Let's be friends!' The young women exchanged a hug, Betty thinking she'd found an ally and the maid pleased that she'd discovered a dupe.

'How can I serve you, me lady?' Ellen's face was serious, but underneath she was laughing.

'Lead the men on with more bawdy talk. Tell them more o' what you do. Anything you like to keep them from taking what ain't theirs to have. I shan't appear to wake yet.'

'I'll do me best, me lady. I'll take 'em right near the brink, then draw 'em away. It's me trade. I ain't a maid as such, if you get me meaning, an' I knows the ways o' men, 'specially gennelmen.'

Meanwhile, Harold continued his explanation. 'You know that William's virile member is reputed to be enormous, of such gigantic proportions that many a maiden has fainted at the mere sight of it, but that was not the reason for the lack of consummation.'

'So, Betty is still intact. What luck, eh?'

'Exactly. And that is the very reason she must not be defiled.'

'I don't see what difference it makes to us. She is married

to William. If Betty gets rogered, he'll take another virgin bride. What of it?' Edward took a large swig of claret. 'I say, Harold. Look where her tongue is now.'

'For heaven's sake, Eddie, you're drunk. It's simple enough. Listen carefully: According to the ancient will, Betty, *the female in line*, will inherit if she has a virgin birth, otherwise the fortune will be lost to Rome.'

'I know. I know. You don't need to go over all that nonsense about the Bishop and the nuns and the Church of Rome. I've heard it all before! Why can't we just watch and relax...'

'Edward, I warn you to be silent, else I shall not be responsible for the violence of my actions. You are not listening properly. Betty is married to William and she is still a virgin. The marriage has not been consummated so it could be annulled, thus allowing her to marry another.'

'But why would anyone want to marry Betty?' Edward was nonplussed. 'She is a mere peasant.'

'Not so!' Harold shook Edward. 'Listen carefully. She may have been reared amongst farmhands but by a quirk of fate Betty is the female in line. There is no male heir. Do you get my meaning at last?'

A look of wonder crossed Edward's countenance. 'You mean, the fortune will come to Betty? I don't understand. How? What has Betty to do with the Squire's inheritance?'

'It's a long, complicated story...'

'Not too long, I trust?'

'The story goes back a long way and is mostly irrelevant, but I'll outline the main points: According to an old will, the Squire's family could keep their fortune if the heir was born of a virgin. Of course we know that is impossible, but nevertheless the family had to keep up the pretence by resorting to a particularly painful and barbaric deception.'

'Such as?' Edward's eyes lit up as his imagination set to work.

'They would sew the girl's cunt tightly and she would then give birth as a virgin. Of course the practice died out...'

'Pity...'

'But the fact is, that if Betty's virginity is taken the fortune will revert to the Church of Rome.'

'The Church of Rome is barely legal. How is this possible?'

'The rich and powerful have their methods!'

'But how is Betty the female in line? Surely Squire Rogers...'

'The Old Squire married twice, the second time bigamously. Betty's mother, Rosamund, was the offspring of his secret marriage to Wilmott, Betty's grandmother. Records show that Rosamund kept her virginity and, to this date, the same is true of Betty.'

'And what of Squire William? Surely a marriage between him and Betty would be incestuous?'

'Yes, except for the fact that William is not the legal heir. Maud, Squire Rogers' wife, took a lover and William was the result of that liaison.'

'I see.' Edward tapped his fingers against his cheek in contemplation. 'So I could marry the trollop and there is still the possibility of the "virgin birth" required by the will. We could sew her up as they did in the old days. Oh, how I should like to stitch her lips...'

'There'd be no need for that particular cruelty! There are other ways...'

'Perhaps, and as long as William is taken care of... I know a ruffian who'll stop at nothing for gold.'

'I have a better plan which we'll discuss later. Meanwhile, let us enjoy the products or Mrs Biddle's excellent wine cellar and frig ourselves into the bargain. Your good health, Eddie, and success to our endeavours!'

'Yes... I concede you are right, as always! I'll open another bottle. Your good health, Harold! A toast to you!' Edward lifted the bottle and swigged. 'But if I cannot poke her,' *and I shall,* 'neither shall you.'

'I have no intention of doing so!' *Not yet awhile!*

Ellen had half listened to the conversation but had not

caught the main gist of it. She continued with her caresses whilst the brothers continued to drink, each one hoping to outlast the other and thus have Betty to himself when she awoke properly. At last Edward staggered drunkenly to the bed and peered between Betty's legs. The maid held Betty's cunt open for inspection. 'Now, my dear.' Edward swayed and touched the maid's hair with an expression of faint repugnance. 'What do you think? Is the lady a virgin, or no?'

'She is fairly tight, sir, though she's lucky enough to have a small hymen. I'd swear that no man has entered this little place, though she may have worked herself with her fingers. You'd be the first, sirs, to put yer pintles up, I swear it.'

Betty kept stone-still. The treacherous maid was doing the reverse of drawing the men away. She felt Ellen's finger under the small pocket created where her hymen joined the perineum. 'See here, sir,' she smiled wickedly, 'this tender piece o' skin ain't broke yet! Mind you, she's right juicy. I'm sure she'll stretch to take the biggest member. An' I think she could be fucked without bleeding if the man were not too large.' She smiled, pleased with herself. 'Then there's 'er little arsehole. What a sweet little rosebud she has, sirs. Why it's so tight an' puckered. Ain't nothing been up there neither, 'cept me tongue.'

The young woman looked expectantly from Harold to Edward and then back again. 'Shall us wake 'er? Or does the gennelmen want 'er out cold, like, so she don't feel nothin' when you come atop 'er and give 'er a good fucking right up 'er cunt and 'er arse?'

Betty was tempted to jump up and scream, but Ellen's next words made her think better of it. 'I can tie 'er, sir,' the maid persisted, 'an' sit on 'er face while you put yer toolleywags up 'er cunt. No one'll hear if she screams. The master is deaf an' the mistress is out... I don't mind what I do to entertain you, sirs. The Bishop o' London comes regular...'

Edward interrupted. He was now extremely drunk and had completely forgotten their earlier decision. 'What do you think, eh, Hal, dear brother?' His speech was slurred as he put his arm around Harold's neck. 'Shall we fuck the girl, eh brother? Shall we both fuck her? You take her cunny, I'll poke her arse and then we'll swap. The girls can lick us afterwards, poke their tongues wherever we order.'

Though he'd imbibed large quantities of alcohol, Harold was in control. 'Listen, Ed, we must preserve her virgin state. She is far more valuable intact. Wash your face and sober up. Go on, get out.' He shoved Edward across the room into the adjoining chamber, then he addressed Ellen: 'So you have been honoured by a visit from the Bishop? Tell me more.'

'Why only last week Bishop come arter another gennelman, though don't tell no one. A great fat man is the Bishop, an' his pintle is very small, so small I could hardly find it in the rolls o' flesh no matter how I poked me finger around. An' it would *not* get big, sir, whatever Mary did. So we hit upon a plan. I lay on the bed with the bishop atop me. He weren't half heavy too. I sucked his ballocks – they were big enough – an' tickled his toolleywag with me tongue and Mary, she's a big strong girl, smacked his bum. Well, that weren't good enough so off she runs an' gets the riding crop an' gives the Bishop a good whipping. He didn't half spunk down me throat arter that!'

Judging her salacious talk had had little effect, the maid thought of another idea. 'You gennelmen would like me friend Mary. Why the dirty girl likes to lick bumholes clean. The sweatier the better. She ain't half good. All the gennelmen say so. She has a long tongue, see, 'an she puts it right in the little 'ole and she twiddles it about. There's no one better'n 'er. She don't charge much, neither.'

'You are here to look after the Lady. Help her into her nightgown but do not disturb us. And take good care she does not sleepwalk.'

'But, sir, Mary don't mind eating eggs, neither. I knows. I seen 'er do it. She only charges—'

'Be silent girl! That's enough of your filthy prattle. We are English gentlemen, not debauched followers of the French Marquis.' Harold glared, removing himself to the anteroom as Ellen shrunk back to the bed, muttering to herself:

'Never heard on him. Who is the Marky, anyways? I 'spect it's a dirty foreign gennelman up to no good milarky!' Ellen twined her arms around Betty. 'Come on, then, milady.'

But Betty shrugged her off. 'If you think I'm a-making friends with you, you've got another thing coming!' She glared angrily at Ellen. 'Leave me alone, else I'll scream! I'm going to sleep.'

'What, in them pretty clothes?'

'Yes. You keep off. I hate you!' And Betty turned into the pillow and burst into soft tears.

Chapter Seven

Betty Bites Back

A Fortune for a virgin – Fiddling with a foreskin – Virgin's blood – Ellen exposed – Threat of the riding crop – Betty's pretence – A cunny dilated – Chaste kisses – A swollen clitoris – Edward spunks again – The sin of fellation – A solemn promise

The brothers relaxed in the anteroom. Edward had sobered up a little and they were discussing Betty and her fortunes again. 'So, I could legally marry the trollop. Hm.' Edward stroked his chin thoughtfully.

'Your worries would be over.' Harold grabbed Edward's hand and squeezed. 'To think, no more relying on Mother or distant aunts for money. The mansion and lands would all be yours. And the "East India" capital too!'

Of course it had occurred to Harold that he, himself, was in a position to marry Betty. Self-centred Edward had not even considered the possibility, and Harold did not suggest it for he knew that Edward would then lose the incentive to preserve Betty's virgin state.

Edward's face was a picture of complexity. 'Think how it would thwart Mistress Emma! Ha! Ha!' He suddenly started laughing as he remembered the birthday celebrations at the mansion. 'Did you hear how the Squire confounded the old hag's plan for her party?'

'Of course. Which brings us back to the original matter. The Squire discovered Emma's anniversary party had been planned expressively to violate Betty's virginity in a most debauched manner. It was not merely an excuse for dissipation, revelry and gross indecency.'

'If only he had not returned! I should have had my share of the girl then! Her humiliation was a delight to behold.' Edward fiddled with his foreskin. 'The business with the cucumbers was excellent entertainment, the maiden twins were as ghastly as ever – they could not keep their busy, lecherous hands off Betty - and Emma was about to set the grooms on the girl...'

'Stop babbling and listen. Whilst you were leaving with mother, Squire William rode off with Betty to the chapel and... What the devil...?'

The maid came running into the room. 'Sir, oh, sir. She 'as bitten me! Oh! Oh! The lady's bitten me.' Her eyes widened. 'Oh! Oh! She's drawn blood! I shall die!' With a dramatic gesture she fell unconscious onto the floor.

Leaving the luckless maid to her own devices, both Harold and Edward hurried into the bedchamber and to Betty's side. Deadly pale, she was lying peacefully on the bed, a red stain at her mouth and on the counterpane.

At that moment, as if it had been rehearsed, there was a loud banging at the door and Mrs Biddle, the Innkeeper's wife, accompanied by Mary, came rushing in. 'I heard a bang, sirs, an', begging yer pardon, thought as I better investigate.' Mrs Biddle looked around the room as if she knew what to expect, but noticing Betty she looked genuinely surprised. 'Oh spite! Is she done for?' Mrs Biddle glared angrily, then quickly changed her expression to one of compassion. 'What *has* that trollop done now? I'll see she gets it! Mary, attend to the lady. Ellen, where are you?!' Strong but muffled words came from the antechamber. A few minutes later the woman returned, dragging the screaming maid by the ear.

'I ain't done nothing. I on'y did what you...'

'Shut yer mouth!' Mrs Biddle glared at Ellen venomously.

'She bit me,' the girl wailed.

'It's the old trick, sirs! Or at least a version of it.' She slapped the girl soundly around the ears. 'She were up to summat, I guessed it. She never does as she's told.'

'That ain't fair! You tol' me to...'

'Don't you contradict me, you hussy!' Another series of slaps. 'The girl's a plain liar, sirs, an' that's the truth.'

'What the devil is going on? You will pay dearly for this business, Mrs Biddle. If Betty is harmed you will have to answer for the consequences!'

'Mistress, she's sleeping quiet enough.' Mary stroked Betty's brow with a wet cloth. 'She ain't hurt. It's the virgin's blood on 'er mouth, sirs.'

Perplexed, the men looked at Mrs Biddle for an answer.

'I can assure you no real harm's been done, though this trollop must get her punishment and I leave it up to you, kind sirs. Do as you wish with her and use whatever method of correction you see fit. She has her notice. I presume you gennelmen are in possession of a riding crop!'

'Please, mistress, don't let me go, oh please don't let me go! Don't let the gennelmen whip me. I'll be good. I promise. I can't bear a whipping! Why, I already been smacked on me arse! I'll do anything.'

'I've had enough of yer tricks.' Another resounding slap. 'If you don't shut up I'll turn you out naked as the day you were born!' Mrs Biddle shook Ellen violently. 'An' you know them goblins an' ghosties is about!'

Ellen threw herself on her knees, buried her face in Mrs Biddle's groin and sobbed silently, her fat body wobbling in distress.

'Would you be good enough to explain the matter?'

'Well, milord,' Mrs Biddle rubbed her hands humbly then grabbed hold of the maid's hair and pulled her face into view. 'Ellen keeps a phial in her pocket, just in case one o' the gennelmen wants a virgin. An' if all goes right, she clamps 'er legs together, screams blue murder an' empties the blood between 'er legs. The gennelman is satisfied an' Ellen gets 'er full money.'

'And was that trick planned for us today?' Harold grinned mockingly. 'You hardly think...'

'Oh no, sirs. That would not do with you gennelmen, being men o' the world who knows a hussy when you sees one. No, sir, when she saw Betty was a virgin she reckoned on a different scheme, an' that was helping you gennelmen get atop her. An', in truth, most gennelmen would've obliged.'

'Then they would not be true gentlemen. Pray continue, Mrs Biddle.'

'When that partic'lar suggestion, an' all the bawdy talk she could think of, came to nothing, she thought as she'd make out the lady bit 'er, so you'd pay up all the same. An' see, she's gnawed her own arm to prove it!' She grabbed hold of Ellen's arm to show the bite still dripping with blood. 'Look! I'll bandage her up and send her to you when she's ready. She deserves a good whipping, no mistake, the scheming liar!'

Harold glared angrily at the woman. 'How do I know she has not poisoned my little lady with her bloody concoction? The poor young woman is recovering from a drowning and is already weakened by the surgeon's prescription. I tell you...' Harold wagged his finger.

Mrs Biddle let go of Ellen and wrung her hands. 'Have no fear, sirs.' Her expression belied her words. She did not want to lose her reputation for running a quiet house. 'We'll wake the young lady.' Mrs Biddle went over to the bed. 'Play yer flute, Mary. Wake the girl with a little tune. We'll soon see if there's harm done or no.'

Mary took a small flute from her pocket and began to play *Greensleeves*. She had a natural ability and the tune flowed sweetly and softly, in perfect pitch. Mrs Biddle stroked Betty and Ellen stood stock still, pressing the bite with her hand, scared out of her wits.

In her contrived sleep, Betty began to hum along to the tune and then to sing softly: 'Alas my love, you do me wrong to... Oh! Oh!' Betty's arms and legs began to thrash about.

'She's delirious. Change the tune Mary. She don't like this one. It's giving her nightmares.'

Mary did so, whilst Mrs Biddle sat Betty upright and shook her gently.

'How are you, little Betty?'

'Where am I?' Betty rubbed her eyes. 'I were in the water. An' the seaweed were all around me legs. An' I went under. I don't remember no more. Is this Heaven?'

'Indeed not.' Harold signalled Mrs Biddle away and sat on the bed next to Betty. 'Though you were nearer to Heaven than you know, thanks to that chit!'

'I thought as I heard an angel.' Betty's eyes focused on Mary, who was still softly playing the flute.

'That's no angel!' Mrs Biddle laughed. 'Now, sirs, if yer satisfied, I'll be off, an' leave you gennelmen to yer business. There'll be no charge for the room. It'll be comin' out o' that trollop's wages. An' if any time you wish fer extra services, there'll be no charge neither. I tell you, that hussy will be made to pay for her tricks!'

Mrs Biddle and the maids left hurriedly. The door slammed shut and for a moment their footsteps could be heard drumming the staircase. Likewise Ellen's screams as her mistress boxed her ears soundly.

Edward had picked up another bottle, slugged deeply, then thrown himself into an armchair in the corner of the room. His head flopped heavily on his arm as he tried to keep awake.

'Where am I?' Betty looked at her surroundings with a pretence at surprise. 'What happened?'

'You nearly drowned in your attempt to escape from the mansion. I saved you, dear child.' Harold knelt by the bedside, took Betty's small hand in his and kissed it. 'I pulled you from the icy water,' he exaggerated, 'warmed you and brought the breath back.'

Betty smiled, half in a daze as if she'd not quite come to. 'Like a prince in a tale. I thank you, sir. I ain't never worn silk afore,' Betty smoothed the cloth of her skirt thoughtfully, 'though I know its feel.' She thought how pleasant it would be to wear the finest silks constantly. Certainly this man had the money to keep a woman in such luxury.

'And you are the princess. I shall call you Princess, my dear.'

'I ain't dressed like one.' Betty crossed her arms over her breasts. 'Why, I'm half naked! Me titties is all a-coming out.' Betty covered herself with the sheet.

'But you are beautiful as you are. You should not disguise your beauty, Princess. To show a woman's charms is all the rage in Paris.'

'But I ain't a whore, nor a strumpet from the streets o' Paris! Any case, who are you, sir? I ain't seen you afore.'

'But you have, my dear. At the mansion, if you care to remember. Emma's scandalous party must be the talking point of the parish by now, dear Betty.'

'Is that me name? Betty? That's pretty.'

'Do you remember nothing before the rescue?'

'I don't know, sir.' Betty blushed as she lied. Though she'd planned to declare her love to Harold, his physical presence and boldness confused her. 'I dreamed, all sort o' strange things... wild things... and things I cannot speak on.'

'What troubles you, little Princess?'

'It were the dogs. They came and they was biting. I were frightened. Oh, hold me, sir, please do! I feel the fear come upon me again.'

Harold was only too willing to oblige, and he held Betty tightly to his chest. 'Could you love me, Betty?'

She trembled, hot and feverish in his arms. 'Oh sir.' Betty opened her eyes, only to see those of Edward staring at her from across the room. She gave a start as he loomed drunkenly from the shadows. 'Oh goodness! Who's that? Why, if it ain't Lord Clancy!'

Harold relaxed his hold on Betty as Edward flopped heavily on the bed, the bottle at his lips and claret dripping from his chin. Drunkenly he pulled the sheet away. 'Your body was made...' he pawed eagerly at Betty's flesh, '...made for gentlemen to admire. Why hide its glory?'

Grabbing Edward's wrists tightly in one large hand, Harold drew a dagger from its sheath. 'Desist, wretch, or your red blood shall surely stain these sheets alongside the virgin's blood.'

Betty tried to cover her naked bosom, but the linen had tangled with their bodies. As she pulled on the cloth her breasts shook and her pale pink nipples stood up defiantly. 'Lord Clancy, indeed!' She was enjoying her performance. 'Why, he don't behave much like a gennelman, pulling off me clothes an' all!'

'Yes, Betty, you are right. This pathetic weakling is the great Lord Edward Clancy! Observe his slobbering and be thankful that you are beholden to me, Harold, his twin and the rightful Lord, not this whimpering idiot.'

'I have given you rare jewels, Betty,' Edward whined, 'pink diamonds fit for a queen.'

'It ain't true?' Betty fingered the choker and turned to Harold for confirmation.

'In a manner of speaking,' Harold scorned. 'The generous Lord Clancy thought to give you paste, my dear.' Harold turned to Edward and spoke in an undertone: 'But I swapped the necklets!' He laughed at the horrified expression on Edward's face as he turned back to Betty.

'Ain't they real, sir?'

Harold avoided giving a straight answer. 'The original jewels are diamonds, once belonging to Lady Clancy herself, a wedding gift.'

Jealous and angry at his brother's betrayal, Edward closed his jaw and stared weakly. 'My dear Lady, of course the jewels are real...' But Edward was out of his depth. Incredibly drunk, he'd remember nothing in the morning. Despite his inebriation his prick had risen at last and he'd have given anything at that moment to have Betty, but he dared not cross his brother. He tried another tack. Suddenly standing up, he became drunkenly eloquent, waving his arms about as he spoke: 'I have saved you from all manner of sexual excesses at the hands of Father Loughran, a fate far worse than death by drowning, for it would propel you into the fires of Hell!'

But Betty was not listening. Harold had pulled her closer, pushed her into the feather bed and whispered endearments in her ear.

Edward strutted around the room speaking into the air: 'Imagine if you were at the mansion now,' he hissed, 'in the power of the evil priest...'

'Oh, sir.' Betty's breathing became heavier. Harold slid his fingers around Betty's tiny waist and over her rump. 'Oh, sir, do not tempt me, I beg you... Oh, sir, you are hot!'

Edward, seething with jealousy, kept on muttering: 'But not as hot as the priest who would have forced himself upon you, taking no heed of your anguished cries. Did he not wish to split that other, darker passage?'

But Betty and Harold were oblivious to Edward.

'Oh, sir. I love you, I love you. I can hardly bear it, and yet...' Betty's breath came in short spurts as she wriggled in Harold's grasp.

'Think of the vile, unnatural acts Father Loughran wished to subject you to!' Edward persisted. 'The Church of Rome has much to answer for!'

But Betty wasn't listening to Edward's ramblings. 'Oh sir, sir, I shall faint. I shall faint with pleasure. Oh, how love hurts!'

'I would not hurt you Betty, my sweet darling.'

But I would! Edward watched jealously as Harold's hands roved over Betty's clothing. He imagined dipping the tip of his own finger between her cunt lips then sliding it, wetted, just inside her arse. He imagined forcing his prick into her anus, stretching her delicate flesh.

'Oh sir. Your embrace weakens my resolve.' Betty's cunny relaxed and dilated as if to receive a welcome guest. 'I am powerless to resist. Oh, sir...'

'Then think yourself lucky,' Edward was determined to interrupt the couple and he was almost shouting, 'lucky to be rescued by gentlemen!'

By now they had rolled over, and seeing Edward's hangdog look, Betty was reminded of the puppy who'd played a part in her rescue from the mansion. 'Why, sir, that's the name o' the little dog. It were Lucky, the little dog, oh, sir...'

'Yes Betty,' Edward leered, thinking he wore a pleasant expression. He wanted to regain ground and make a favourable impression. 'The dog, the pup who rescued you from the priest, 'twas mine!'

'Yours, sir. I had no idea. I thought Lucky were Giles's dog.'

'So now you are beholden not only to Harold, but to me.'

'Am I, sir?' Ignoring Edward, Betty snuggled into Harold's warmth, then covered his cheek with kisses. 'If I am beholden to you both, sir, then I thank you. I thank you for saving me and will be ever grateful.' Another series of warm kisses on his cheeks.

'My child, you thank me with pretty words, a fluttering of your dark lashes and numerous chaste kisses, but that is not enough. If you love me, as you say...'

'I don't know what you mean, sir.' Betty smiled innocently as she rearranged the bedding, plumping the fat pillows up. Now the brothers sat either side of her, Edward leaning drunkenly.

'We shall take care of you, dear Betty, I promise.' Edward wiped his sweaty brow. He'd been fully aroused by the freedoms Harold had taken, but the claret had addled his brain. He was finding it exceedingly difficult to stay upright, let alone awake. 'I shall feed you titbits with my own hands and no one shall be allowed liberties with your body.' He laughed pathetically. 'Not even you, dear brother.' He made a weak attempt to push Harold over, and by now was breathing heavily in Betty's face.

'I thank you, sir, for your consideration.' Betty looked Edward straight in the eye, trying not to inhale his wine-laden breath. 'But it would not be a liberty if I were to allow it. Would a kiss on the lips suffice to thank you, sir?'

'A kiss, my dear? A kiss on the lips? That is... that is... what is it brother?' Edward looked around the room, confused. One of his hands fondled the now dwindling bulge in his groin. For a minute he'd forgotten where he was.

'A kiss, I'd say, is the preliminary exchange of vital juices, Eddie. And far too good a prize for you, so keep away.' Harold pushed his brother into the pillows. 'I shall teach Betty the proper method of thanking her master.' Harold took Betty's small hands in his and stared at her half-naked breasts. 'The etiquette involved is simple. After all, if I am to take care of you...' He put Betty's hands on his erect manhood and held them there. 'Your tiny hands, your mouth, those beautiful ruby lips...'

'Oh sir, I don't know...' Betty's sex throbbed, her swollen clitoris had hardened, growing hot and firm between her thighs. 'I don't know as I can do what you want.' Betty shrugged her shoulders and her breasts wobbled. She said the first thing that came into her head: 'My husband is a violent man.'

Now that Betty was awake her charms became more apparent. Harold was eager to have the girl service his cock with her lovely mouth. Edward desperately wanted to join in but Bacchus was winning the contest. Eyes half closed he spoke in his most lordly, drunken voice: 'All we desire is for you to please us, don't we, Hal?' His smile twisted into a grimace.

Harold ignored his brother and his eyes sparkled as he spoke to Betty. 'Surely it is not an onerous task to thank a gentleman in the usual manner?'

'Oh, sir, I would not have you think I'm ungrateful. I know that I'm helpless in your hands and as such entirely dependent upon your goodwill.' Betty looked at Harold appealingly. 'I don't know what's the usual way to please a gennelman, but I'll try my best. I can cook and sew, clean and dust, and I can sing too.'

'Betty, Betty...' Edward sat up, swaying. 'There are few ways...' he patted her shoulder, 'few ways in which a penniless woman can show her appreciation to a gentleman.' He patted her shoulder again and smirked, but his eyes had started to close again. 'One of them, Betty, one of them is to... to...' Suddenly Edward slumped into the pillows. The claret had caught up with him at last.

'By Jove! Your charms were too much for him, Betty! He has spunked in his breeches again! Ha!' Harold pushed his brother off the bed, whereupon he rolled over on his face.

'Oh, sir, you'll hurt him.'

'Fear not. He'll go into a daze for a while, might even sleep till morning. Now, my little one, I have you to myself at last.' Harold played with one of Betty's curls, winding it around his finger. 'A prize, indeed! Such beauty should be worshipped.' He kissed her cheek gently, thinking how she would play her part so well at Madame's. Thinking, too, that he was truly beginning to love her.

'You flatter me, sir.' Betty smiled, a puzzled expression crossing her face. 'I ain't never been worshipped afore. That's fer princesses, and ladies, and angels and...'

'But you are more beautiful than any lady I have set eyes upon. More beautiful than any heavenly angel.'

'Oh sir, you don't want to say that afore the priest!'

'Priests are men, Betty, liable to temptations of the flesh. Why else must you confess in the dark, if it is not to remove the provocation?'

'I never thought o' that afore.'

'Men will throw themselves at your feet!'

'I don't know, sir, as I want that. I ain't used to it, see.'

'Priest, bishops...'

'It be more nat'ral, like, the other way round. I learned to kneel afore the priest, and me feelings... oh, I can't explain.

Father Loughran, the priest, see...'

'Betty, listen carefully. You have been reared with your allegiance to the Pope. Father Loughran practises his faith illegally. It is not safe to be seen with him. Why else do you think he must now pass himself off as the Squire?'

Betty clasped Harold's large hands in hers and gazed into his eyes. 'There ain't nothing comes more nat'ral than to submit myself to a man.'

'In that case, the time has come for you to submit to your benefactor.'

'Sir.' This time Betty spoke with lowered eyes. 'Tell me, sir, how you wish me to submit to you.' She kissed his hands reverently.

'I do not require you to sacrifice your precious virginity, nor to sully your fair hands, merely to put yourself under my protection...'

'I done that, sir.'

'And once in my protection, to please me in small ways. You have a beautiful mouth, Betty, ruby lips and a strong tongue by all accounts.'

'Sir, I have always tried to please and...'

'Shush.' Harold put a finger over Betty's lips. 'I hear that you are well versed in ways to accommodate a man, that you have been and are willing to comply, excepting only in the giving of your virginity and the entering of the forbidden passage. Is that correct?'

'Sir, I said many times afore, my chaste state is precious to me. And the other place is too tight.'

'But your mouth is not so.' Harold leaned nearer and kissed Betty full on the lips, thrusting his large tongue deep into her throat. 'Put out your tongue.' He bit it gently and kissed her again. Betty reeled. Harold was strong, his muscles rigid against her frail and tiny frame.

'Sir, what must I do to please you best?' Betty drew away and smiled enticingly.

'I hear you have managed to accommodate a number of

male members within this soft cleft, including one that is reputed to be abnormally large.'

'Oh, sir, your fine words confuse me.'

Harold put a finger in Betty's surprised mouth. 'In other words, you have fellated.'

Betty looked puzzled for a moment, and then suddenly remembering the priest's accusations at the mansion, drew a quick breath. 'Oh, sir!' Her eyes grew big. 'Father said as it were a sin!'

'And did you commit the "sin" of fellation, Betty?' Harold grinned, highly amused. 'Have you taken a male member within your soft lips, sucked on it, swallowed and ingested the fertile juices?'

'Well, sir,' Betty reddened, 'it is true that I have taken such things inside me mouth, and I did it to please the Master, Squire William.' Betty wriggled. She was excited and embarrassed at the admission. 'But I been to confession with the priest, so me conscience is clear.'

Suddenly there was a movement from the floor, and some incoherent mumbling followed by a sudden outburst from the half-conscious Edward. 'So the pretty Betty has been a-cock-sucking!' A stream of saliva dribbled from the corner of his mouth and his eyes gazed randomly. 'Ha!' He laughed madly. 'She admits as much! Ha! She has been a-sucking pintles and swallowing spunk!'

'But sir,' Betty grew even redder, 'I thought you said as he wouldn'a wake. And now he knows what I done too!'

'The rogue is tougher than I thought, my dear! He'll forget by morning.'

Edward's speech slurred as he tried to rise on his elbows: 'Harold, you are not the only one who can take his drink! Hic! And Betty, you think William cares for you? Hic! Even now he's enjoying Sarah's plump charms.'

'It can't be, sir.' Betty looked at Harold. 'Surely not my sister!' She was surprised. 'Why, Sarah don't like men!'

'I hear, hic, that William is so full of spunk that ten women a day cannot satisfy his lust. How is he to be rid of these fertile juices unless he takes as many women as he can?'

Harold stroked Betty's yellow hair. 'My brother is jealous, Betty, and would make you jealous, too. That way he thinks to take you for himself.'

'I know'd o' William's dalliances, but better me sister than a harlot!'

'See, Edward, the Princess is not jealous.' Harold held one of Betty's hands in his for a moment. 'How charmingly tender you are, my dear.' *So innocent, so loving.*

'Sir, I *were* jealous at first, but now I no longer love William.' Suddenly Betty burst into tears. 'I hate him! I hate him with all me heart! He betrayed me for a whore! I served the Master faithfully and took his beatings willingly. Now my wish is to be revenged upon him.'

Betty's outburst took Harold by surprise. If she knew about William's affairs why was she so angry now? He lifted Betty, holding her tightly as she sobbed for a full minute. Then, slipping from his arms, she slid to the floor and knelt before him with her head lowered again. 'Sir, I could love you,' she whispered, 'and serve you well, if you would master me.'

Harold stroked the tangle of golden curls. Unlike his brother he was not naturally sadistic, but a surge of lusty power thrilled his blood as her vulnerable head nestled into his lap.

'Do you give up the Squire willingly?' Harold placed his hand on Betty's neck where the blonde curls were dark and wispy. *So delicate, so fragile!* His prick hardened against Betty's cheek.

Betty wound her arms around him and squeezed, breathing the manly scent as she nuzzled into his groin. 'Yes, master,' she whispered, excited to the core. Submission: the keenest of thrills, a sharp-edged blade, cutting, cutting to the quick.

'Then swear to renounce him and to take me as your common-law spouse.' Harold lifted Betty's chin. The pressure of her cheek against his organ was becoming unbearable.

'But I cannot, I am legally married to William!'

'In a popish ceremony. That is hardly legal.'

'But in the eyes of God, surely...'

'No, Betty. In the eyes of God, and the Church too, a marriage that is not consummated is in name only. It is null and void.'

'So it would be no sin?'

'Betty you are free to marry!'

'Then I swear to God I give up William as me husband and take you instead as me common-law spouse. And may I be damned to Hell if ever I betray me word!'

Chapter Eight

A Score to Settle

Edward well inebriated – Ellen offered for punishment – Sins remembered – A large breast exposed – A pinched bottom – Reminded of a whipping – An enormous erection

Harold caught his brother's astonished eye. He knew there was nothing that Edward would like more at this moment than to have Betty swearing allegiance at his feet! Edward's mouth hung open and a drip of spittle gobbed onto the floor.

'God's bread, Harold, I can't move. Get the girl to come here and satisfy me. I would have her tongue upon my cock, not yours!' If Edward had been capable of standing he'd have stamped his foot like a naughty child. Instead, his leg twitched pathetically. 'She should be mine! Mine! I should marry Betty.' His voice rose to a squeak, leaving Betty in no doubt that the brothers knew her secret. 'It is I, it is I who should have the fortune!'

'Get up you fool, and get out!'

'Why can't the girl come here?'

'Betty is mine, you idiot, and no longer for the taking! She has sworn herself to me!'

'You only want her for the money,' Edward muttered. 'Why not admit it?'

'Get out before I hit you!'

'Bring Ellen. Bring Ellen.' Defeated, Edward began to whine. 'Let the maid satisfy me. You said I could have her, brother.'

Suddenly there was a knock and Mrs Biddle came creeping in dragging Ellen behind her. She'd been listening at the door, waiting for a suitable opportunity to arise. 'Begging yer pardon, sirs, I brought the maid to you.' Ellen stood hunched over, apparently terrified. 'Perhaps, sirs, you wan' to give the chit 'er punishment she so rightly deserves.' There was a nasty, vicious look in the woman's eye.

'Please, mistress. No!' Wailing and sobbing Ellen threw herself on the floor and clasped Mrs Biddle's ankles. 'Don't let 'em! I can't bear it!'

Harold was not sure whether Betty had heard Edward's remark about the money, but he decided to ignore it and take charge of the situation. 'Ellen, you will satisfy the natural urges of Lord Clancy. If you do well, then perhaps your punishment will be lightened. Mrs Biddle, you will leave the room. Ellen, get up and do as you are bid.'

Immediately the crying stopped and Ellen stood up and curtseyed. 'Yes sir.' There was a crafty look on her face and her dry eyes flashed jealously as she made up to Harold. 'Shall I suck his Lordship's knob? Or shall I tickle his balls, or is it a licking he fancies?' She twisted on the spot and spoke out of Edward's hearing. 'Sir, I know all sorts o' tricks. I can satisfy you first, if yer likes.' She cast a jealous look at Betty.

'I do not like. Attend to my brother, else the whip...'

Ellen rushed over to Edward, knelt down and began to slobber over his wilted prick, poking around with her tongue to give it renewed life.

'Keep him happy and out of my way, do you hear?'

'Yes, sir. I'll pull him into the other room.' Without compunction Ellen rolled up her sleeves, braced herself, then grabbed hold of Edward's legs, dragging him through the archway and out of sight, his head flopping limply behind.

'Oh, sir, she'll hurt him!'

'Nothing of the sort, Betty! The important Lord Clancy is far too drunk to feel a thing! As I said, he'll remember nothing in the morning. Well my dear,' Harold tilted Betty's chin upwards, 'will you be happy as my wife?'

'Sir, I am happy to serve and please you, and you alone. Yet I cannot help but think sadly on those I left behind.'

'You still have a soft spot for William?'

'I don't know, sir.' Betty sighed and her heart seemed to fairly leap out of her breast. Too much change, too much strong emotion: love lost, love found. And lust, lust, lust! 'I wish I knew what happened to all me friends. When I left the mansion Father Loughran had taken the Master's place and William had gone. Giles and Adam said as Lady Clancy would help.'

'Mother has agreed to take care of your dear girlfriends.'

'Candace? Emily? Gita? All of them?'

'Every one, my dear. You shall meet up in good time. We planned to reunite them all at Madame Farquar's.'

Kneeling at Harold's feet, Betty took one of his coarse hands in her tiny one and kissed it tenderly, the moisture on her lips wetting the dark hairs on the back of his hand. 'Oh, sir, I must thank you.' Betty pressed its firmness to her ruby lips over again, kissing the rough hairs. 'You have saved us all from a most evil fate! I am truly in your debt, but there is another thing...'

'What is it my dear, innocent child?'

'Innocent?' Sadness suddenly welled in Betty's eyes. 'If only that were so!' Betty's sense of sin weighed heavily and she could not pretend otherwise. 'I cannot truly serve you as your wife unless me sins is forgiven by God.' She continued to kiss the hand, and Harold placed the other on the back of her neck. 'I must make a good confession. Father Loughran...'

Jealously, Harold grasped the dark hair at her nape, turning Betty's head so she must look into his eyes. 'And you wish to confess to the evil man who would have ravished both virgin passages?!'

'Oh, sir. I can't hardly explain meself, but I must see the priest,' Betty trembled, pushing feebly against the hand that held her.

'Betty, the flesh is weak, and like any other the priest is made of flesh and blood. Do you miss his evil attentions?' Harold bent over and gently kissed her. 'Even whilst you have sworn to be mine?'

'Sir, I am yours but I am so confused. I have a need to attend the confessional and seek advice. I can feel the Devil grow within me again and I must confess, else I shall go to Hell.'

'For heaven's sake, Betty, what do you mean?'

'When I first bowed my head before the priest, thinking only to confess my sins, I felt the devil's teat grow large between my legs, and no amount o' rubbing by Father Loughran would make it go away. It just growd and growd and I grew wetter.'

'Indeed, so the priest has it all ways, the crafty hypocrite!'

'Father said as I was a temptation to good men. And I done a heinous sin. And that's why I must wear the chains and the ring. And then he rubbed me like I done meself.'

'So, Betty, first you must confess your sin to the priest, describing it in detail, no doubt. Then you demonstrate your sin to the priest. Then he must test your innocence using the self-same method. Then you express your contrition and receive God's forgiveness!' Harold's grip on her hair tightened and his cock visibly strained against his tight breeches. 'Where exactly did he rub you?'

'Just there, sir, in the cleft below the mound where your hand suddenly rests.' Betty gazed dreamily at Harold, making no attempt to push his exploring hand away.

'Why, dear child,' his eyes glazed over at the thought of the priest's finger on Betty's beautiful cleft, 'you are indeed a temptation to all men.'

'Sir, 'tis true I sinned since I were a small girl, but only with meself. Felan, that's me stepfather, caught me at it and made me show the priest what I done.' Betty caught hold of Harold's finger and circled it on her palm. 'I done it like this, sir. It's such a nice feeling. And then my husband,

William, taught me a little of what I should know in the ways o' the flesh. And that was afore I married him, so I suppose that were a sin, as well. And now... surely I must confess before I take the full vows and swallow the body and blood o' Christ at Holy Mass?' A tear ran down Betty's cheek. 'Otherwise, sir, I should not be worthy of God, and me soul will be stained forever.'

'You are most worthy, dear, for what you see as carnal sins are the natural reactions of the flesh. I would not have my wife otherwise. For a frigid woman to marry is a sin against both mankind and nature. And truly, Betty, your beauty must be allowed to reproduce itself in nature. Well, if you must confess to a priest, I can arrange it, but meanwhile you must put the past behind you.'

'Do you promise you will hold nothing against me?'

'Why, of course, my dear.'

'I just wish I been born a Lady.' Betty pouted, but now she had Harold's assurances she would soon brighten.

'Betty, your bloodline is honourable, despite your lowly upbringing. You have the fire, the demeanour, the beauty of a born Lady.'

'Sir, you flatter me!'

'It is time we celebrated.' Harold raised his voice and called the maid. 'Ellen, go fetch a magnum of champagne from the cellar. We are to drink a toast.'

Ellen was eager to make reparation for her earlier behaviour. 'Just a-comin', sir.' Scufflings and whisperings emanated from the anteroom. A few moments later Ellen appeared through the doorway slowly adjusting the lacing of her dress. Her hair had fallen out of its cap and hung lankly on her shoulders. One of her large breasts was exposed and she seemed in no hurry to cover it up. It hung pendulously to her waist, its huge brown nipple in stark contrast to the white flesh, oddly beautiful.

'I done a good job, sir, fer his Lordship.' Ellen licked her lips, cupped the huge tit and played about with the nipple.

'Why, I licked his pintle so good he done woke right up now an' its as big an' firm as a cowcumber.' She smiled her crafty smile. She was obviously aroused by fellating Edward, but had had little satisfaction for herself. 'An' his Lordship,' she lied, 'says as he wants Betty there to suck me titties like a baby an' lick me clitty to make me better. He done pinched me hard.' She lifted her skirt to show two purple marks on her white bottom. 'But I don't mind cos he give me more money.' She rattled the coins in her pocket. 'An' his Lordship give me claret, too,' she boasted. 'I ain't never drunk it afore! Well?' she said, rudely looking straight at Betty. She'd gained confidence by her own lies and those Edward had been spinning. 'Are yer goin' to lick me clitty?'

Betty glared. 'No I ain't!'

'You didn't mind it afore when I done yourn! Huh!' She put her hand between her legs. 'Lord Clancy said as he loves me an' he'll see me any time, an' he asked me if I were married an' I said no. His Lordship wants me to—'

'Quiet Ellen!' Edward appeared in the doorway, leaning heavily against the jamb. It was quite remarkable he was able to stand at all, but he was now driven by his plan to outwit Harold and gain possession of Betty. With the help of the avaricious maid, he would fetch a whole case of champagne and drink Harold under the table. 'Stop fiddling with your cunny and assist me to the door. We must join the celebrations.'

Ellen, her breast still hanging out loosely, put one of Edward's arms around her shoulders and helped him through the doorway. 'Oh, yer Lordship, you ain't half a caution. I reckon as all the village girls, an' the ladies, come arter you.' She reached up to whisper in his ear and the pair of them, laughing heartily, went down to the cellar.

Some while later Edward, leaning heavily on Ellen, swayed into the room followed by a manservant struggling behind a large case of champagne. Harold and Betty had been kissing and touching gently. Now her shoulders were uncovered again and her pert breasts peeked out at the neckline.

Ellen had been plotting to avoid her punishment by urging Edward to punish Betty instead. It was a ridiculously transparent plan that would be sure to come to nothing. In between sharing a bottle of champagne with Edward she'd been frigging him in the cellar, and his erection was as hard as it could be under the circumstances.

'It seems that Betty must be punished, not Ellen, for she tempts men beyond endurance. She must be thoroughly punished, brother, whipped into submission. Ellen will hold her down.'

'Well, sir, I ain't a-doing it on purpose!' Betty shook her head. 'And Ellen ain't a-holding me down neither!' She was back to her usual lively self. 'I can't help me looks, and I can't help this low dress, it don't cover me titties, and I confessed to Father Loughran and...' Betty broke off as she saw the manservant winking and gesticulating.

'The girl ain't half got pretty curls,' the man said loudly, then very quietly and evenly so only Betty should hear: 'She's like a flower, an' if I were a bee, I'd fly over hills for her.'

Betty's heart thumped and she gasped, covering her confusion with a cough. Was it really Adam, the groom whose love for her had been the cause of her first whipping?

'What are you muttering about, you dolt?' challenged Edward. 'By Jesus, put the case down, open a bottle and get out!'

'I were on'y saying, sirs, like,' the cork popped and the man handed the bottle to Edward, 'if I were you I'd...' Adam stood square in front of Edward and thrust his hips forward. His insultingly enormous erection stretched his coarse breeches tightly.

'"If I were you" Ha! The presumption of the idiot!' Edward pushed Adam in the chest, nearly falling over as he did so. 'Haven't I seen you somewhere before?'

'No sir, first time I set eyes on yer, sir.' He met Edward's glare and held out his palm in anticipation. The lord, who'd been fiddling in his breeches, put his hand in a pocket.

'Be off with you.' Edward threw the farthing into the spittoon. 'Or it'll be the beadle and the stocks followed by a horsewhipping.'

'Thank you, sir,' Adam nodded his head, 'I won' trouble you no more.' He bowed and winked at Betty, who lifted her eyebrows and winked back, mouthing the word 'Adam'. Leaving the money in the spittoon he left the room. Quick as a flash, Ellen had retrieved it, wiped the slime on her apron and secreted it in her pocket.

As the door quietly closed, Edward spoke to Harold. 'See how Betty flirts with the lowest of servants. How can you expect me to restrain my manly feelings when she flutters her eyelids and tosses her head in provocation? Come Ellen, assist me to the bed. I am tired and need a little comfort. I am not feeling my usual self!'

'But you won' punish me, sir?' Edward's sharp tone had startled her.

'Later, your punishment will come later, my dear, if at all. For now you can show me your bubbies. I should like to kiss them.'

Ellen settled on the bed with Edward on his back. She'd undone her lacing and both breasts hung dramatically over his face. 'Does me bubbies please you, sir?'

Edward gazed upwards as Ellen lowered her breasts, almost smothering him with their soft droopiness. Edward closed his eyes, transported. He loved large breasts, their softness, their pliability, and as he sucked on the huge teats he imagined how he would bite them, pinch them, constrict them in torturous screws, pull them, squash them, shape them as he wished. As he dreamed, he could not resist biting. Ellen pulled back but his teeth held hard.

'Yer hurting, sir. Oh! Oh! Oh!' Suddenly her teat plopped out, swollen and bright red. By now Ellen was thoroughly excited and she pushed the other nipple forward for Edward to suck on.

Meanwhile Betty's blood coursed with adrenaline. She'd recognised the young groom who'd fallen in love with her and her heart had leapt in fear. She too was thoroughly excited, and prattled on desperately as her mind raced. 'I don't mean to be a bad girl and a temptation to men, but I can't help meself. I don't know as why it should be bad to take pleasure, any case.' Betty twisted a lock of hair in her finger.

'An' you don't mind a-taking pleasure in yer looks neither.' Ellen pointed at Betty's neck as she bucked up and down over Edward. 'Dressing up like a la-di-da lady an' all in them jewels.'

Betty felt the choker. 'The diamonds?' She didn't know whether they were real or not but she was childishly excited. 'Oh! I never saw them proper. Can I see? Have you a glass? Ain't there one on the dresser?' Ignoring Ellen, she jumped up to look for the glass, and holding it at arm's length posed to her reflection. 'Why, they's so pretty. They's all pink!' She fingered the jewels. 'I could be a real lady and go to a real ball.' She ruffled her curly hair and smiled, tipping her head this way and that. 'Oh, but the priest would say it were the sin o' pride.'

'Betty, come, sit on my lap and listen.' Harold encircled his arms around Betty. 'You must think of yourself as a lady. Now, do you wish to confess, dear Betty?'

'Sir, it is the only way I shall have me peace o' mind.' She bounced on his lap.

'Then it shall be arranged as soon as we reach our destination. The Bishop of London is a well-renowned confessor, and many ladies of high rank receive his ministrations and do penance under his auspices.'

'Why, thank you, sir, thank you.' Another shower of kisses. 'But I don't know as I can confess to another man. Father Loughran has been me confessor since I were a child. He knows me ways.'

'The Bishop is a man of God. He is elderly in years and very experienced in the ways of the flesh.' Harold drew back thoughtfully, resigned to the fact that he must indulge Betty in her strange taste for the confessional. 'He will guide you in spiritual matters. He is the very epitome of discretion. Have no fear.'

'Sir, will you kiss me?' Betty threw open her arms to receive his embrace, and whispered in his ear. 'I love you, Harold, and your will is my command. I am at your mercy, but pray do not take what is most precious to me. William has gone and I cannot live without a man to master me, but if I lose my virginity I lose everything.'

Harold drew Betty close and whispered in her ear. 'Then you must help me to thwart Edward. He would break your hymen if he could. We cannot trust him to leave you alone, Bet, unless we can help him satisfy his lust.'

'Well he has Ellen now!' On the bed the bizarre couple were entwined. First this way, then that.

'It will be short-lived,' Harold continued. 'Edward finds his utmost satisfaction in cruelty. It is his passion, and if he sates himself in this respect he'll have no energy left for other pastimes. If you assist me in the punishment of Ellen...'

'Oh, sir, gladly. She's as nasty and treacherous a piece as I ever met. Shall we? Shall we teach the maid a lesson she won't forget?' Betty's eyes illuminated. 'Shall we now?'

'In the morning, Betty. In the morning you may do whatever you will with her. I see you have a score to settle. Meanwhile...'

Chapter Nine

Whipped into Submission

Ellen's humiliation – Betty tastes the whip – A punishment well-deserved – Anilingus – Tickling a cunny – A reddening bottom – An unwanted orgasm – Cunt lips smacked – Trussed like a chicken – Riding a cunny – Redcoats – A coward's funeral

Ellen's red, tearstained face looked pleadingly at Harold and Betty as Mary pushed her forward into the room. Making a great show of herself, she wiped away a teardrop with the back of her hand, threw herself on her knees and pressed her hands together. 'Oh, please sir, don't whip me. I cannot bear it and the mistress has smacked me black an' blue all over.' She appealed to Mary. 'Stop 'em, oh do!' Then to Betty: 'An' you me dear friend, don't let 'em, I beg you.'

'Yer a lying deceitful hussy and deserve everything you get. I seen you ain't got no bruises. You wouldn'a cared what happened to me, long as you got yer money! You ain't no friend o' mine!' Betty pushed Ellen's shoulder.

'But me lady...'

'Me lady, is it now?' Betty laughed, smacked Ellen's face, and then hissed in her ear: 'You deserve to have yer clitty bit right off!'

Shaking with fright the girl burst into tears, but they had no effect on her audience who merely waited until she'd composed herself.

'Oh, sir?' Ellen moved on her knees and settled before Harold with her hands clasped together. 'Won't you have pity?'

Harold was stern though not unkind. 'Ellen, have you, or have you not, misbehaved?'

'Well, sir, I din't mean...'

'Answer the question. Have you, or have you not, misbehaved? Well?'

'Sir, I done wrong an'...'

'Exactly,' Edward interrupted as he walked through the archway. 'And now you must suffer your just punishment.'

Ellen threw herself on the floor and kissed Edward's boots. 'I thought as you would let me off, sir. Arter what I done las' night, I thought as...' her voice trailed off as she knelt up and gazed helplessly, first at Edward, then Harold and Betty, then back to Edward. 'Didn't I please yer, sir?'

'If you think your performance last night has spared you, Ellen, you are mistaken, for the very opposite is true.' Edward spoke haughtily. 'You may slobber at my feet as much as you like, but that will not change what you are.'

'You have shown yourself to be a liar and a cheat, to give yourself only for money not for love.' Harold glared. 'You deserve to be thoroughly chastised.'

Ellen bowed her head. 'Yes, sir.' She did not believe she should be punished, and she was trying to think of a way to get out of her predicament.

'Betty, would you like to choose the method of discipline?' Harold watched the girl he loved. She seemed highly excited. Her eyes had brightened and there was a rosy tint to her delicate cheeks.

'Indeed, sir, for I know what hurts most!' Betty narrowed her eyes. Ellen reminded her of her sister, Sarah; selfish, cunning and treacherous.

'Excellent!' Edward rubbed his hands gleefully. 'We must give her as much pain as she can tolerate, or more.'

'I was thinking, sir, of the humiliation, rather than the pain. It's not only the cut of the whip that hurts!'

'Good girl!' Harold ruffled Betty's hair. 'And afterwards?'

'She shall be comforted,' Betty laughed softly.

Ellen peeped through her fingers. So Betty had a weak spot. Good.

'Comforted?!' Edward snorted.

'If you comfort her a little she'll be more willing, sir, for her feelings will be confused, and she won't know whether she likes it or not. Then we can disgrace her afresh. Why not add to Ellen's humiliation by bringing Mary into it? I should like to see her perform in front o' gennelmen such as yourselves.'

Whilst Betty was speaking, she imagined Ellen licking at Mary's cunny, licking at her arse. She laughed wickedly. Ellen's confused but horrified expression could be read like a book. Although she'd caught everything Betty said she clearly didn't know what to think of it all. A look of utter dismay washed across her face. Her jaw dropped open and her cheeks grew pink with embarrassment as if she'd read Betty's very thoughts.

'Betty is more clever than you thought, brother!'

'And we can whip her if she spends! She can lick Mary till her tongue fair drops off. Then we can bring her to the very brink and send her packing!'

'Excellent.' Edward rubbed his hands as Harold enfolded Betty in his arms and kissed her.

'And when we send Ellen packing, we'll tie her so as she won't pleasure herself.' Betty laughed with relish at the thought of Ellen, frantic for sexual release, excited to the point of madness and unable to achieve her orgasm. A fitting punishment for the cheat who would have sacrificed Betty's virginity purely for money.

'So, Betty, what punishment do you choose first?' Harold spoke so sternly that the maid shook with fear.

'Sirs, I should like your permission to do as I please with Ellen. I have ideas a-plenty to satisfy all of us. If you would be seated and observe for a while...' She gestured with a flourish of the hand. 'And Mary, perhaps you will watch and learn.'

Betty addressed the maid. Her cheeks were flushed, her eyes bright with mischief. 'Here, take the whip, Ellen. You are to start the proceedings. Don't look so surprised. You're to punish me first. Well, do you agree?' Betty smiled at Harold, who nodded.

Ellen was confused. Betty did not seem like a religious penitent. But then she'd heard of girls who actually liked being whipped, rather than merely tolerating it for money. Perhaps Betty was one of these. 'I suppose I don't mind.' She shrugged her shoulders.

'This is the idea, Ellen. You whip me bare arse. If you can make me cry for mercy then you are let off, if not you must undergo the same from me and more. Well?'

So, that was the game. Ellen was certain sure she had the strength to make Betty cry out with pain. 'Gimme the whip, skinny. You won' be laughing arter I finished with you.'

'Don't be too sure, missy.' Betty lifted her skirts and petticoats dramatically, then bent over a convenient footstool so that her bare buttocks were in full view of Harold and Edward. Ellen stood to one side, holding the whip somewhat pathetically at first. The sight before her eyes, combined with the men's approval, stimulated her jealousy to the point of madness. Betty's beautiful arse was lifted high and the petticoats frothed around the white skin to make a lacy frame. From behind, her tight arsehole could be glimpsed and the slit of her cunt with its dark blonde curls was just in view.

'What luck, eh Harold? Such a smooth rounded arse deserves to be whipped. What a joy to behold. No marks and just the tiniest of dimples. Ah, she is lovely! Go ahead, Ellen, else I shall start on your voluptuous behind.' The evil glint in Edward's eye spurred the girl to action. Betty had bitten her arm, though everyone was convinced she'd done it to herself. She'd make the wench pay.

The twins settled themselves onto the couch and relaxed.

'Now, milady, brace yerself.' Ellen cracked the whip sharply in the air, then flicked Betty's bare flesh.

Betty was impervious to the punishment. 'Ha! What a weakling you are Ellen. Are you tickling me with feathers?'

The maid pulled a face. 'I'll learn you.'

Another crack of the whip and Betty's flesh turning pink, but she showed no sign of feeling pain and laughed raucously, taunting the maid. 'Do it again, Ellen. It tickles me so!'

Suddenly Ellen became furious with rage. She lifted her arm as high as she could, and gritting her teeth, delivered several vicious blows to Betty's arse. 'Cry milady, cry!' Betty would not cry, but burst into peals of laughter. Ellen suddenly realised that she was to receive exactly the punishment she was meting out, and more. With a piteous howl she was on her knees behind Betty. 'Oh! Please milady forgive me, I din't mean to hurt you!'

'Then, Ellen, if that is true you will do me a favour.'

'Anything, miss, anything.'

'Go down on yer bended knee before Mary and kiss her feet!' Mary had been watching the whole scene with obvious relish. Now her eyebrows lifted with amazement.

'I will not!'

'Oh no?' Betty jumped up and seized the whip. 'You will and you will beg to lick her arse!' She paused, her hand upraised. 'Go on. Do it! Do it!'

Ellen looked at Harold and Edward. Their expressions were merciless. Edward lifted one finger as if to indicate the severity of her position. 'Milady, I will... I will!'

Though Ellen had agreed to take her punishment, she was still looking for a way out. She was very fond of forcing her artless friend Mary to do the most unspeakable deeds, but she was not quite so fond of humiliating herself.

'An' if I do, will you let me off...?' But Betty's face was so furious, so fearsome, that Ellen was immediately on her knees before Mary, kissing her feet and sobbing out the humiliating words.

And in but a few moments, Mary was over the stool, her skirt around her neck, her plump pinky rump exposed, a look of intense triumph on her soft features. Behind her knelt Ellen, shaking and tearful. Tentatively, she put out her tongue.

Edward was enjoying the scene immensely. 'Mary, you will part your buttocks. You must lick her thoroughly, Ellen. Wriggle your tongue on the dark flesh. And wet it properly, else the whip...'

Ellen lunged forward with an expression of distaste, but she dared not refuse. And behind Ellen stood Betty, beautiful Betty, flushed with appetite. She knew only too well how the maid would feel, utterly humiliated, desirous and deeply afraid of the pain to come. But part of her felt envy. She glanced across at Harold, her co-conspirator, and knew too that he admired the way she had taken Ellen's whipping, knew also that she could take more, much more, from the man she loved.

Betty stood poised ready to inflict the corporal punishment upon the deserving servant as she lapped helplessly at Mary's tight puckering. 'Does she satisfy you, Lady Mary? Or does the hussy need a little urging with the whip?' Betty tapped gently across Ellen's waiting buttocks, and then slipped the leather between her legs, pressing on her cunt lips.

Quiet, sweet Mary had always been the victim of the maid. How delicious that she could now enjoy the bully's humiliation. For once the tables were turned so, given this opportunity, she was determined to extract the maximum pleasure. 'Why, Bett, she ain't working at all. I can't hardly feel 'er tongue on me arse!'

'That ain't true,' Ellen wailed as she took a breath of air. 'I'm trying me best!'

'Be silent, you lazy thing!' This time Betty struck sharply, causing Ellen to cry out in pain and rub her posterior. A bright red stripe gradually appeared on both arse cheeks.

'Back to work with yer tongue! And keep yer hands away.' She lashed the maid's hands and the girl withdrew them speedily. 'Do as I say, else it'll be the worse fer you!' And then the whip softly between Ellen's legs again, tickling at her cunny, maddeningly.

Lounging on soft cushions, both Harold and Edward watched Betty in admiration as she roused Ellen's sexual response. By the time Betty had finished with her she'd be begging for a man to plunge his member deep within, but that pleasure was to be withheld. As for Betty, perhaps she would relish a further taste of the whip to excite her passions.

Ellen, frightened of too much pain, and thinking this might be a way to avoid it, began to work assiduously with her tongue and lips. Whilst she did so Betty urged her on with rhythmic strokes upon her reddening bottom, each time finding a fresh white section to beat.

Meanwhile Mary called out her instructions. 'Too slow, twirl faster, you lazy chit!' Another stroke of the whip.

'Put your tongue inside, hussy, an' push it right up!' Another stroke and then a flick between the legs. Ellen wriggled.

'Ellen, you are not licking hard enough.' Another stroke. A meaner flick upon her cunt lips. Mary had pulled her arse cheeks wide apart and Ellen's face was so deeply buried she could hardly breathe. A little cry was forced from the maid's throat.

'Kiss me properly with your lips! Suck! Suck!' Another stroke, and then a vicious flick between the legs as Ellen tried to follow orders by sucking at the tight hole. Her cunt had naturally begun to open, and the outer labia had parted so that the delicate inner petals were showing.

'Harold, see how Ellen's lips curl apart. Why, she needs a man to satisfy her lust, the dirty trollop. How dare you show yourself so shamelessly!' And Betty began to belabour every inch of the maid's arse-flesh, finishing with a final cut that clipped her clitoris, causing the girl to spend in pain. 'I should like to beat the trollop till she bleeds!'

'No, mistress, no! Please spare me!' Ellen shuddered with her unwanted orgasm. She was angry that the pain gave her pleasure, and though she'd been determined not to cry, the tears had sprung to her eyes. Two large streams ran down her face.

'She has spent! The hussy has fairly spent all over herself!' Betty shoved a hand between Ellen's legs. 'She is disgustingly wet. Why, her thighs are a-running with juice! She must be punished right here!' And Betty wriggled her hand on Ellen's sopping cunt. 'Oh, you are a dirty wicked girl, Ellen. You don't deserve no mercy.' Betty gave the maid's inner thigh a resounding smack with her palm. 'You deserve a right hard whipping, you do, right betwixt them tender lips!'

Ellen turned to the men in horror. 'Please, kind sirs, please spare me. I don't know as I can take no more beating, an' not on me tender parts, not on me tender cuntal parts.'

Edward spoke first. 'If you wish to avoid a thorough beating of that eminently punishable area, then you must first attend to the lascivious demands of the present company. If you do well, that is if you give maximum pleasure, you will only be whipped lightly. If you do badly, then I am afraid the punishment will be more severe.'

'Yes sir, yes sir. Thankee sir.' Ellen had crawled over to the couch where the men were seated, and began to fawn over Edward's feet. 'Anything to please you, sir.' She kissed his boots over and over again. 'Shall us suck yer feet, sir? Shall us lick yer arse?' She crawled over to Harold. 'An you too, sir, I'll do anything you please, on'y don't let 'er whip me cunny hard!'

'You have done well, Betty, in bringing this over-proud creature to such an abject state.' Harold smiled. 'You seem to have a natural facility. The chit is as clay in your hands.

'I know as how it feels, sir, and how pain and submission promote desire.'

Ellen glared at Betty, thinking how she would love to humiliate her, love to feel Betty's tongue upon the dark regions of her own anal flesh!

'And do you desire to be at the mercy of Ellen?' Edward interposed, thinking to add another twist to the scenario.

'Why no, sir, it is Harold I would serve, for I think of him now as my master.'

'But if I wished it?' Harold stared into Betty's eyes, and she lowered her lashes deferentially.

'Sir, I've relinquished William and given myself to you. I offer you all rights over me. I will obey your every command.' Betty threw herself on her knees beside Ellen. 'If you wish me to serve the maid, I shall, fer your sake, sir, even though I do not wish it fer meself.'

'Betty, my love, my exquisite darling, not for the world would I have you place your tender kissing lips upon this treacherous servant's guilty arse! Rather the reverse!'

'Why not, brother? She has offered herself to do as you command. The beauty is entirely at your mercy.' Edward rubbed his groin. His member had grown hard and the swelling stretched the cloth of his tight breeches. 'No doubt she would suck this rod,' he pulled out the throbbing object, 'if you ordered her to do so!'

'Dear brother, do not attempt to anger me. True, Betty is mine and therefore at my command, but not at yours. Remember that or it will be to your cost. Your skill with the sword is sorely lacking, and as for pistols, well...' Harold rolled his eyes in deprecation.

'Why, brother, it was a mere suggestion,' Edward squawked in his usual cowardly fashion. 'But the whipping has excited my little man,' he fondled his penis, 'and he must obtain satisfaction.'

'Oh, sir.' It was Mary. She'd become excited by the anilingus and further excited by seeing Edward's rampant cock. 'Sir,' she spoke to Harold, 'may I attend to Lord Clancy?'

'What say you, dearest Betty?'

'Sir.' Betty reached out tentatively for one of Harold's hands, which she then clasped in hers. 'I say yes to that, but as for Ellen...'

'You think she must be castigated further? She is shaking with emotion.'

'Master, Ellen shakes with consternation and fear, but she still has a certain glint in her eye which bodes ill. I do not think she has yet been a-mastered. And I think as she must be tied and set to watch the pleasure o' the company.'

'Excellent! And how would you have the maid tied?'

'Trussed like a bird with all her parts a-showing. That'll learn the chit!'

'Excellent! See to it dearest girls.'

Betty and Mary seized Ellen, removed every stitch of her clothing and lay her, naked, on her back. Before she could protest she was tied up, as near to Betty's description as was possible with human limbs, trussed like a chicken. They'd wound twine around and under her breasts to emphasise them, and secured her arms around her folded legs, the slit of her pink cunt and the dark hairs of her bottom totally exposed for all to see.

Edward leaned into the cushions and Mary settled herself before him, taking his steaming member between her lips.

'Now for you, my darling.' Harold turned to Betty. 'What is your pleasure? Would you like to rub your darling cunny upon Ellen's face?'

'Why, sir, apart from taking yer own sweet member within me cunt, and that I cannot do, there ain't nothing I'd like better!'

'You can settle yourself over Ellen and take me in your darling lips at the same time.'

Excitedly, Betty pushed Ellen nearer to the couch with her head against it. She then sat heavily upon the maid's embarrassed face, at the same time nuzzling her own face in Harold's groin as he lay back to receive her ministrations. Poor, miserable Ellen was almost suffocated in this position, but a few muffled groans told Betty she was breathing.

'Ellen, you miserable maid, I shall ride your face until I

spurt all over you.' And whilst Mary gave Edward what was to be his last sexual pleasure on this earth, Betty rode and rode harder and harder, forcing her cunny over Ellen's chin and nose, rubbing it back and forth delightedly. 'Lick Elly, lick, lick me cunny!' The unwilling girl, tasting Betty's essences, was now driven madder than she could have dreamed, until at last she was overcome with the desire to please the beautiful girl she so hated. She put out her tongue, flickered it expertly between Betty's lips, and sought her clitoris which she sucked between her lips and nibbled, thus urging Betty to give her best service to Harold's cock. Wild with the mad pleasure, Betty sucked, licked and titillated the powerful genitalia before her. Rubbing her face on Harold's ballocks, she sniffed his manly scent and then gently took each orb between her lips and sucked, wriggling her tongue on the soft, hairy sacs. At last she could contain her own fertile juices no longer, and just as Harold spunked deep into her throat, so she orgasmed all over Grace's face and into her mouth. 'Ah! Ah!' Betty murmured. 'So beautiful, the sins of the flesh! Ah! Ah!' And her body shuddered in repeated spasms as the spunk flowed deep within her.

Betty stood up and recovered herself. But Ellen lay whimpering with unsatisfied passion. 'Milady, please milady...' she begged.

'What is it? The trollop is so demanding!'

'Please may I spend, milady?'

'No you may not! That is your punishment you stupid girl!' Betty picked up the riding crop and brought it down in Ellen's cleft, just hard enough to cause a little pain. The girl squirmed, but the cut of the whip caused her to come to orgasm and her juices began to flow copiously, at which point Edward spunked down Mary's throat.

'Ellen, you are done for! I told you not to spend!' Betty untied the knots binding Ellen and pushed her into a kneeling position. She began to beat her arse furiously, and Ellen, now entirely submissive, allowed it.

Just as Betty was about to deliver the final blow, there was a hammering and banging upon the oak doors of the downstairs hall. Shouts and dogs barking, the sound of men's voices and women's screams. Loud steps on the stairs and imperious thudding at the bed chamber door. Ellen and Mary screamed simultaneously and Ellen clasped both hands over her sore rump. Betty dropped the whip. Harold took control.

'Edward, retire to the other room.' The coward was only too willing. 'Girls, under the eiderdown.' More thumping on the door. Harold strode to the door and opened it wide. 'What is the meaning of this? How dare you!'

The two redcoats were not perturbed. 'A warrant for the arrest of Lord Edward Clancy.' He waved the parchment in front of Harold.

'Let me see. Hmm. A warrant for the arrest of Lord Clancy, is this possible?' he said over-loudly whilst perusing the document. 'It seems in order.'

'I understand Lord Clancy is residing here.'

'Indeed? And how did you come by that intelligence?' Harold was stalling.

'It is not within my province to say, sir.'

The second man sneered: 'Are you his Lordship's valet?'

'Indeed not.' Harold ignored the insult. 'I am Harold, his brother.' He raised his voice again. 'What is the charge against Lord Clancy?'

'A serious number of crimes, sir. Defrauding, smuggling, avoiding revenue, and lastly, treason!'

'Treason?! I cannot believe my brother to be capable of such an act! He is entirely devoid of brains, in other words, stupid!'

'But, begging yer pardon, sir, perhaps not as stupid as you think!' The man grinned insolently. 'Perhaps the Lord is merely a conniving traitor, ready to sell himself to the highest bidder, and it is you who lacks the—'

'I shall have your guts for garters, man!'

Suddenly there was a crash, a movement of furniture, the

sound of a shutter opening and banging shut, the report of a musket and a horrifying scream. Then, silence. The redcoats rushed out and the girls, silent until then, emerged from under the bedclothes, dishevelled and frightened.

Betty held Mary's hand, rushed to Harold's side, and they both clung to him. Ellen slipped out of the room. She'd had enough punishment and was about to find one of the grooms to satisfy her throbbing cunt.

'I must find my brother.' Harold led Betty and Mary down the narrow staircase and into the muddy yard.

The company assembled outside. Mrs Biddle, dressed in her nightgown with her crippled husband leaning on a pair of sticks, the servants, grooms, and other guests half-dressed. Surrounded by a ring of redcoats, Edward lay in the muddy yard. His unseeing eyes were turned to the cloudy sky. A red stain coloured his white linen shirt and seeped into the lace at his neck. For a moment his hand shook, trembled, and then lay still, forever.

'Ashes to ashes, dust to dust. Lord, I commend to you this spirit...'

At last the ceremony was finished, the fancy coffin lowered into the hole, and the few mourners dispersed, leaving only Betty and Harold at the graveside. Betty wiped away the tears. Her face was red and blotchy with crying, and though in her short life she was used to death, it always came as a shock. The sky had misted over and it had begun to drizzle.

'Come, my dear, you'll take cold. We must go. We are delayed over a week. I have business to attend to and Mother is expecting us within the hour.'

'Goodbye, Edward.' Betty removed her black veil and gloves and placed them on the fresh grave. 'May you rest in peace.' She turned, and smiling weakly, wiped the single tear that fell from Harold's eye. 'So you loved him a little, sir?'

'He was my brother, Betty, and half my blood, even if the

tale of my birth is true.'

'They do say that blood is thicker'n water.'

'Are you ready, my dear?'

'I am. I mourned a little and said me goodbyes. I done the proper thing.'

Harold and Betty alighted on the steps of the waiting coach and hastened inside. The driver pulled on the reins, shouted an instruction, cracked the whip, and they were off.

Chapter Ten

Out of the Frying Pan

Fortune-telling – Escape – The angel strips – Nipples pinched – Pintles a-plenty – Double fellation – Youthful scents – Pink diamonds and a ruby stolen – A pack of lies – Gentleman Jim and One Ballock Billy

Inside her hovel, Zillah bent over the unscrubbed oak table, two fingers delicately holding a thin shard from the crystal ball. After staring intently at the splinter for some while she began to rock back and forth, a strange moan emanating from her throat. 'Ah! Past is past! I see Edward in a pool o' blood an' a coach racing, racing. Damn it, the fools have killed Edward! Present calls! I see Betty. Good girl she is a-sucking pintles, a-swallowing spunk. Ah, suck Betty, suck! She has two men. The figures are dark. Hereafter beckons. Ah! The picture dims. It dims! Damn Kitty-cat, where are you?'

The black cat shook its tail, squeezed its yellow eyes into narrow slits, arched its back, and then it was gone.

The coach had been travelling for near on an hour and by Harold's reckoning they should soon reach their destination, the Clancy mansion. The conversation had naturally been subdued, and Betty had descended into one of her glooms. The shock of Edward's untimely death had shaken them both into thoughts of mortality and the fragility of human life. But they had done their duty by him, and after all said and done, even though he was Harold's twin, Edward had not been the nicest of persons. He'd been selfish, avaricious and cruel, so although they had both mourned at the loss of human life, their feelings would inevitably be short-lived.

Betty cast her mind back to recent events, her marriage, the loss of her husband, her escape, and then she looked at Harold. Yes, he was handsome. Yes, if he would master her she could love him. But *would* he master her? Betty sighed and thought of William. He had known how to make her his. He had known how to make every fibre of her body cry out for the cruel lash of his whip. Would Harold do the same?

'What are you thinking, my dear? You look so sad.'

Betty sighed. 'I don't hardly know. I was a-thinking o' William.' Betty sighed again. She'd loved him so deeply! And now she'd given him up for another man, and she couldn't help but feel a certain sadness akin to mourning.

'He is in capable hands, my dear, being cared for by his sister, Mistress Emma.' Harold smiled.

'Emma!' Betty's eyes widened with horror. 'But sir, I thought as he'd gone to a whore! Oh my, what shall I do? He is with Mistress Emma?'

'My dear, why should that trouble you?' Harold stroked Betty's face gently.

'She will surely give him belladonna.'

'Why should she do that?'

'Why? Why? To weaken him until...' In her heightened emotional state, Betty tried to control her tears. 'Sir, the Mistress Emma entertains a false belief that she will inherit a fortune when William dies. She will kill him. Oh take me to him, sir.' Distraught, Betty grasped Harold's hands. 'Oh please do. Take me to him, sir. I do love him!'

'Betty, you cannot love two men.' Harold felt a burst of compassion mixed with love, anger and jealousy. 'You have sworn to renounce him and give yourself to me.'

'But I thought as he'd gone to a whore...' Betty was beside herself. Her beautiful face was flushed and her lovely white bosom, encased in the black dress, trembled with passion. 'Oh sir!'

Harold gazed possessively at her loveliness, and his rampant desire overcame his softer feelings. 'You have sworn and must abide by it.'

'I cannot! I cannot!' Betty covered her face with her hands.

'So, you are still in love with William?' Harold shook Betty's shoulders, took her hands away from her face, then tilted her chin so she must look into his eyes.

'Oh! Oh! What shall I do? I must go to him. He must be saved!' Betty threw herself on her knees before Harold and pleaded with him. 'Please sir, oh please sir. Do take me to him.'

But he would not be moved. Rigid with love and jealousy, Harold could not let his newly won prize go. 'If you wish to see William alive you must do exactly as I ask.'

'I must go to him!'

'If you go to him, you go to the devil. You said as much yourself.' Harold was not about to relinquish his prize, but he could not take Betty to his Mother's country home in this state of disaffection. 'I will arrange for you to see William at Madame Farquar's in the presence of a chaperone, after which you must vow never to approach him again. He must disappear from your life!'

Of course, it would fit in with Harold's plans admirably if Squire William were to "disappear" altogether, perhaps at the evil hands of Emma, but Harold was no murderer, nor would he condone it. There would be another way. Perhaps the press-gang could be engaged.

'I thought as I weren't to go to Madame Farquar no more.'

'Betty, you have promised to be my wife. I would not take you there under any other pretext. We are to put up there, nothing more. Madame has letting rooms, comfortable apartments, and you will be safe in her hands.'

Betty was not convinced. 'But I heard you and Edward a-talking on it. You said as I must enter into the household of Madame Farquar, a great lady of wealth and position.' She frowned. 'And I know what that means. You take me fer a whore!'

'No, Betty, no! That was before you had sworn your love.'

'You said as she "quietly entertains society in a private capacity and is in need of female companionship." You said it!' Betty glared at Harold. 'You don't want to marry me. Yer arter me fortune. I knows it in me bones. And Edward said it too!'

'Betty, my love, Betty!' But how could he convince her? She'd remembered every word.

'You said as she entertains Gentlemen and Ladies on a reg'lar basis and must keep them fully amused. You said as I must submit to yer gentle attentions.' By now Betty was distraught. She had worked herself into a passion and was almost hysterical.

Harold took hold of Betty's shoulders and shook her roughly, but she would not be calm. And then he did something he had not intended to do. He lifted his arm and brought his palm crashing against Betty's cheek. Betty stared with a look of shock on her face. Her cheeks began to glow and the tears came at last. 'Oh sir, oh sir, what am I to do? I see I cannot go to Lady Clancy as yer wife. And I must see William.'

'You will be safe at Madame Farquar's.'

'And the visit to Aunt Rowena? She been expecting me fer near on two weeks.'

'You may entertain your good aunt, and anyone else you please, in your very own private chambers at Madame's residence.'

'Will you rescue William for me? Truly?'

'Indeed. I shall arrange for him to be removed from Emma's cruel protection.' What Harold did not disclose was that he intended to send William abroad in the care of His Majesty's navy.

Betty was utterly subdued now. She did not believe Harold's protestations. How could she have been so stupid? 'Then I am willing to submit myself to you, sir. Whatever you desire is my desire.'

'Your virgin prize too, Betty?'

Betty bowed her head sadly, but did not reply.

At that moment the cart suddenly swayed violently to one side, almost as if by design. Harold and Betty were thrown immediately together, and then higgledy-piggledy to the floor.

'What the Devil...?'

Running over a rut, then another, then another, the cart jolted to a halt deep in mud and twisted at an angle. The coach door opened spontaneously and Betty, together with the servants from atop, was tossed into the mire.

'Odds bodkin, get yer finger out me eye!'

'An' get yourn out me arse, dogbolt!'

'Hey, look to the lady.'

'She ain't no lady, she's a trollop!'

Suddenly the sound of horses' hoofs pounding, a loud whinny as the rider grew near, and the sharp report of a pistol. 'Stand and deliver! Yer money or yer life!'

Betty sat up, too surprised to be afraid. She was covered in filthy mud, the beautiful ebony silk of her mourning dress ruined, her golden hair streaked with leaves and dirt. Suddenly she was lifted into the air by strong arms, and before she could protest she was riding away from the scene, clinging desperately to the highwayman in front.

The horse galloped away and Betty knew she must stay astride. She'd escaped Harold without hurt, but he was sure to chase after her. He'd probably want to marry her in secret, seize the fortune and be rid of her. In his eyes she was obviously not fit to be a real wife, to meet Lady Clancy in society and become a Lady herself. In the distance behind she heard shouts, oaths and the sound of a chase. She must find a way to rescue William herself.

'Faster, go faster!' Betty held on tightly and snuggled up to the man's broad back. 'He's a-coming to get me!' The wet had begun to soak through to her skin and she shivered with cold. The winding trail led through thick woods and the trees, close each side, hung low overhead, every so often swinging down and sweeping over the two figures. Gradually the noises of the chase ceased and their pace slowed.

'Won' be long, Bett. Won' be long!' The voice sounded vaguely familiar, but as it was distorted by the wind rushing past her ears, Betty could not place it.

At last the horse came to a halt. The rider jumped off, lifted the exhausted Betty into his arms, and carried her over the threshold of a small cottage hidden deep in the forest. 'Here we be.' Without removing the scarf tied over his face, he set Betty down next to a roaring fire and put a warm blanket around her. 'There's hot milk in the jug afore the fire, a little loaf, see, baked special, dry clothes in the closet, an' clean linen on the bed. You be safe enough here. Oh, an' there's a jug an' fresh water a-warming in the kettle fer washing. Giles will be back soon.'

'Giles?' Betty blinked in surprise. 'And who are you, sir?' She smiled. 'Don't go!'

But the man had already gone. The horse's hooves thumped on the wet leaves and then all was silent.

Betty was too lethargic to do anything other than warm herself at the hearth for a while, the blanket wrapped tightly around her. She sipped at the milk, tucked into the dark farmhouse loaf and considered her situation. So much had happened in so short a time and nothing had turned out as she expected. Well, she would have to resign herself to fate and make the best of it. Even though Betty's plans had been thwarted, she was obviously not totally alone. Her friend Giles, the old carter, was too decrepit to have rescued her on his own, so he'd obviously found someone else who cared enough to help. As Betty warmed and fed herself she cheered up. She was usually a happy girl and her glooms never lasted long.

The fire had died down a little. Betty flung off the blanket and stoked it with the poker. Soon it was blazing and crackling merrily. She must take off the damp clothes, else she'd catch a cold. There was no one about to see, and Betty was beginning to feel uncomfortable and steamy. The small room was now very hot and somewhat smoky, as the chimney had not been swept for years.

Betty fiddled with the small buttons at her breast, trying to poke them through the damp, shrunken buttonholes. And whilst she took her time, the two young men peeping through knotholes in the door made short work of undoing the buttons that threatened to pop off their distended breeches.

Outside, balancing on a ledge halfway down a shallow well which was hidden under a tumbledown hut, poor old Giles was tied up, gagged and blindfolded. Through sheer misfortune on his part and no judgement on theirs, Parslow and Kit had accidentally come across the cottage and discovered their enemy chopping firewood. They'd threatened him with his own axe, and though Giles gave nothing away, they guessed he'd been plotting to help Betty, so they waited. It was not in vain. Meanwhile, they'd been arguing fiercely as to *who* would do *what* to Betty first. Kit was unaware of how Parslow had used Betty at the mansion, and the young sadist was not about to tell him. Neither would Kit admit to having tried to fondle Betty himself. Now the lovely virginal girl was there in the flesh again, soon to be completely naked. What a prize! But they'd still not come to any agreement.

Betty happened to be facing the peepholes, and as she managed to undo each button, a little more of her delicate white flesh came into view. Watching the innocent striptease, the young men frigged quietly but furiously. Parslow dreamt of how he'd torture her lovely breasts, and Kit of how he'd rub her cunt and put his fingers inside. Under the muddy dress, Betty wore a low-necked camisole beneath a corset that stopped just beneath the breast. Once she'd undone the restraining garment her taut breasts plopped out freely, and although they were now unsupported, the pert orbs hung high and firm.

Two faintly audible gasps came in unison from behind the door. Betty started and automatically covered her breasts. She looked around her, but could see nothing. 'Must be the wind.' Indeed, the wind had picked up; a twig was a-tapping at the shutters, dark clouds had blown over, and it was now raining quite hard. Betty shivered, moved nearer the fire, and threw off her top layer of clothing. Her petticoats were still snow-white at the waistline, though the hem had acquired some watery mud which had seeped halfway up, streaking the cloth grey. Her blue pocket containing her valuables – the choker and the red stone – was tied tightly at the waist. Betty poured water from the kettle into a bowl and rubbed her face and breasts with a washcloth. She began to sing happily. Kit and Parslow were transfixed.

Despite all she'd endured Betty was so fresh-looking, so innocent, that for a moment she touched Kit's heart. Reminded of the time he'd watched her wash in the attic back at the mansion, his usual coarseness softened. 'I don't know as we should take 'er now,' he whispered, still frigging rapidly. Kit was used to sharing his women, but suddenly he wanted Betty to himself.

'Don't be soft, Kit. I never 'eard such a stupid thing!' Parslow drew his foreskin right back and glanced down admiringly at the purple top. 'Any girl'd swoon to get a load o' me spunk down 'er! It's on'y nat'ral.'

'She's an angel, jus' the same as when I seed 'er up at the mansion, on'y more so. It wouldn'a be right.' As they stared, a bright sunbeam pierced the clouds, streaked through the skylight and illuminated Betty's golden hair and white breasts. 'See, she's a real angel an' she's got a halo an' all!'

'Don't be daft. She's got a cunt jus' like any other wench. Yer soft, Kit. I never seed you so soft! If you don't jump 'er, I will. Never 'eard nothin' like it! Spunky Kit soft on a girl! Ha! Wait till Grace hears. She won't 'alf thump you!'

'What if Giles escapes? If we ain't tied 'im proper.'

'He won't!'

'What about Adam? He'll frigging kill us both! I seed the pistols.'

'Let's hurry up. The quicker we do it, the sooner we can get 'er away from 'ere.'

'We ain't got much time to do things proper.' Kit thought quickly. He didn't believe he could stop Parslow once he'd made up his mind, so he went for a compromise. 'Why don't we get the chit to suck us off an' swallow our spunk? We can do the rest later.'

'Good idea, Kit. I'll pinch 'er little nippies! Jus' think o' those ruby lips a-sucking on yer cock. Come on.' He nudged Kit in the side.

Kit held back for a second. 'It won't be a good idea to make 'er cry, Pars, not today anyways. You never knows who might be in them woods.'

'Let's give the trollop a surprise!'

Simultaneously, the two men burst into the room, their erect cocks bobbing up and down in their excitement.

Betty screamed.

'It's on'y us, Bett!' Kit ran up to Betty, grabbed her and silenced her with a sloppy kiss on the lips. 'Yer old friends.'

Parslow groped Betty's breasts, found her nipples and pinched them hard.

'Get off!' Betty wiped her mouth and wriggled. 'You ain't me friends.' Parslow hung on and her breasts stretched out under the tension. 'Ow! Yer hurting!'

'It's meant to hurt yer silly rabbit!' Parslow laughed. 'Where's the fun if it don't hurt a bit?' He leaned nearer and whispered. 'How'd you like us to bite yer cunny-lips?'

'I s'pect you'll do what you want, anyways.' She knew firsthand Parslow's capacity for extreme cruelty. 'Where's Giles?' Betty looked half-scared, half-angry. 'You better not've hurt Giles.'

'We din't hurt 'im, but we know where 'e is.' Betty

squirmed as Parslow twiddled her nipples. Fortunately for her he restrained from squeezing as hard as he'd have liked, and the sensation was not unpleasant.

'Tell me, oh please do, kind sirs?' Betty pleaded.

'We'll tell you, arter you done what we want.'

Betty sighed deeply. She knew what Parslow wanted and she knew it would hurt her, and because she did not love him, she thought it might hurt her more than she could bear. But she could not let Giles down. She spoke almost in a whisper. 'All right.'

'You must suck us off! Swallow us both, deep down yer little throat! All the way.'

'Both of us. Good an' hard. Suck our balls an' suck our toolleywags an' swallow all the spunk!'

'All of it! Swallow it slowly an' taste it. Every bit. Else we won' tell.'

Betty shrugged her shoulders. 'I might.'

'You will! You will, if you wan' to see Giles alive!'

'And how do I know as you'll tell me where Giles is?'

'You don't. You gotta trust us.'

'I don't trust you. Tell me first. There's two o' you. I couldn'a get away, any case.'

'We'll show you. He ain't far. You can call him.'

'Let me get dressed.'

'There ain't no need for tha'. Come as you are.'

They dragged Betty outside and over to the tumbledown shed which, unbeknown to Betty, covered the well. 'He's in the hut. Call him.'

'Is that you, Giles?' She looked anxiously at the young men and shivered as her body sprung with goose pimples. 'He ain't answering.'

'He can't, he's gagged!'

'You horrid boys!' Betty screamed, jumped at them and gave them both a smack on the head. 'He's an old man! How could you?'

Kit laughed at her pathetic effort, but Parslow was angry.

He grabbed Betty's wrists, and looking her straight in the eyes spoke viciously. 'You do tha' agin, Bett, and yer for it!'

'Let me call agin. Oh please do!' Betty's naked breasts wobbled as she pulled her hands free. 'Giles, Giles, knock if yer there.' Betty listened intently, and sure enough she heard a faint knock. 'Are you all right? Give one knock if you ain't, and two if you is.' Betty was relieved to hear two knocks. 'You'll be out soon, Giles. I won't be long.' She faced Parslow. 'Will you let him out if I do as you want? Promise?'

'Course we will!'

'Swear it! Swear on the Bible!'

'We ain't got no Bible, but we swear it all the same.'

'Let Giles out first. Then I'll do whatever you likes.'

'Why not?' Parslow rubbed his hands gleefully. 'An' Giles can watch us, like, eh Kit!'

'Don't make him do that. It ain't fair.'

'Better than that. He can join the party. We'll soon see if he's man enough for Bett! You can suck 'is shrunken ole toolleywag an' all!'

Betty was horrified. 'But he's like a father to me. I can't do that!'

'Either 'e stays there an' waits, or you suck 'im off an' all. Makes no difference to us!'

Inside the cottage Parslow and Kit sat on a rough oak bench, legs apart, their proud members rearing up monstrously. Betty knelt on the floor with the intention of getting the whole business over and done with, in as short a time as possible. 'Well, what d'you boys want?'

'We want to see 'ow good you is at suckin' pintles. You got to get us both right down yer little throttle!'

'Who goes first?' Betty licked her plump lips. She'd done it so many times before. What did two more pintles matter?

'You can do us together.'

'How can I suck two pintles all at once? They won't both

go in me mouth!'

'Frig us fer a start.' Parslow had an idea that suited him. 'Then choose the cock you wan' to milk first. Take turns to suckle our cocks an' do yer best, like, to make us come down yer throat. The first man to spunk does it on the bench and the last man to spunk gets to do it in yer mouth an' you swallow it right down. That's fair.'

'No it ain't. She's gotta swallow both lots.'

'Tha's easy, she can lick it off the bench arterwards. Ready Betty? We both got stiff-standers!'

Betty cradled her palms under their distended ballocks, weighing them and wondering who she should start on first. The boys were quite similarly proportioned in the nether regions, though their colouring gave them a different appearance. Parslow was fairer than Kit, his flesh redder and his thatch thicker and more wiry. His ballocks hung slightly lower. But both virile members reared up stiff and straight from the root, of almost equal thickness and length. In their youthful urgency they looked equally good to Betty. Her expert fingers dug into the soft sacs gently. She pulled at their ballocks, bent over their laps in turn, and rubbed her soft white cheeks against their hard cocks. Once she started on them they'd soon forget their need to be away quickly, and perhaps the man in the mask would return to save her. As Betty nuzzled she began to breathe more heavily. Their youthful scents excited her, her cunt was beginning to run with juice, and her own strong sexual needs drove away her thoughts of Giles.

'She don't need no instruction.' Parslow laughed wickedly as Betty fixed her lips over his hard cock and sucked deeply. 'God's ballocks, she near enough swallowed me right in 'er little throttle an' down to 'er belly.' He held onto the back of a chair for support as Betty's vigorous sucking threatened to overbalance him. 'She ain't no angel, Kit, she's a trollop. Do you know wot I did to 'er up at the big house?'

Kit's eyes flashed jealously. 'You didn't do nothin'. I never seed you do nothin'.'

'Oh, ho! Didn't I?' The thought of his earlier encounter with Betty sent Parslow's blood boiling to his swollen member and it grew even bigger. 'Didn't I get them screws out? Didn't I put 'em on her nippies? Didn't I turn 'em tight?' Parslow grabbed Betty's hair and rammed his groin hard against her face, pushing himself deep inside her throat. 'Body o' me, she ain't half milking 'ard!'

'Ah! Bett! Bett! Come on, it's my turn!'

But Betty could not get away, being practically glued to Parslow's groin, forced so close that his wiry hair tickled her nose.

'Come on, Parsy. Gimme a turn.'

Betty grabbed Parslow's balls, tickled them to take his attention away from his toolleywag, and was just about to draw away slowly when nature pre-empted her. She sneezed! The boy's surprised cock slipped neatly out of her mouth, pulsing the contents of his balls into the air.

'Od's nobs! I'm a-spunking, dammit!' As Parslow's ejaculate fountained, he swung round to direct the spurtings onto the bench, but too late! The pumping stream landed off target but directly on the purple tip of Kit's cock.

'You didn't half tickle me nose!' Betty couldn't help laughing. She latched her plump lips over the engorged head of Kit's cock, which was still dripping with Parslow's creamy spunk. Eagerly the boy thrust forward, and holding her head in his hands, fucked her mouth, shoving in as deeply as he could.

Betty swirled her tongue around the solid shaft and swallowed, tasting the combined essences, but the expert motion was too much for Kit. 'Hold on, Bett, else I'll be spunking afore me time. Ah, save it, save it afore you swallows deep!'

It was not to be.

Concentrating on Betty, the boys had failed to hear the sound of an approaching horse, the footfalls of the highwayman as he strode up to the cottage door, and the clink of the latch. Not until the door thudded shut and the man brandished his pistols did both boys look up in surprise. Parslow hurriedly tucked his genitalia into his breeches and edged towards the window. Kit's cock slid from Betty's lips. He was rigid with fear rather than passion, and could not prevent the course of nature. His spunk oozed slowly onto the floor, followed by a torrent of acrid pee.

'Kit, I told you to listen out, you poxy whoreson! Now we'll all be killed!'

'No you never. Yer a damn liar an' a coistrel!'

'Get out! Yer a pair o' beggarly cowards! And don't you never come arter Betty agin!' The man shook the pistols wildly as if he'd only just got used to handling them. 'If'n you do I swear I'll kill the both o' yer!' He turned to Betty whilst the boys took the opportunity to jump out of the window and run away. 'Don't you know me Bett?' He took away the kerchief that half-covered his face.

'Why, if it ain't Adam! I'm so glad you come!'

Way down the path leading away from the cottage, Kit and Parslow paused for breath. 'Now wot'll we tell Liza?'

'We ain't come away with nothin',' Kit boasted, drawing a small purse out of his breeches. 'We got the diamon's.' He tipped the jewels onto his palm. They gleamed softly pink.

'Gissit here!' Parslow grabbed the choker and held it up to the light. 'Them's not diamon's! Them's pink! Diamon's is white! Them ain't worth nothin'!' He tucked the choker into his shirt. 'What else you got?'

Kit held out the ruby. 'On'y this ole stone.'

'That ain't worth a toss on a dog's tail.'

'I'll keep it to 'mind me o' Betty. Wot shall we tell Liza? She won' half be wild.'

'We'll tell 'er the truth!' Parslow folded his arms smugly.

'You mean, tell 'er Adam's taken Betty?'

'No dogbolt, don't be daft. Tell 'er it were tha' highwayman as the redcoats ain't catched yet. No one as we knows.'

'So you lost the girl, you damn fools. You can't be trusted with nothing.'

'She got away, the bugger!'

'It weren't our fault, Liza, honest it weren't! We didn't 'ave no pistols, an'...'

'Don't bother telling me that tale no more. I can smell a pack o' lies when I sees it. Jus' get back out there an' find Betty. An' don't bother to come back on yer own! I'll be buggered if I'll 'ave you!'

Chapter Eleven

Skulduggery in the Scullery

A cock skinned back – Dangling breasts – Dying fer a fuck – Fredericks turns the screws – A price in pain – Father Loughran's punishment – Evil plans afoot

Grace stood on tiptoes, opened the shutter a little, and peeped in the scullery window. All was silent, save for the drip, drip, drip of water somewhere in the vicinity.

She'd been travelling a while, and having stopped for a glass of ale or two her bladder was full. The sound of water triggered her subconscious. 'I couldn't half do with a piddle.' She lifted her skirts where she stood, splayed her legs and let go a stream of hot, steaming urine.'

'I see you ain't changed.'

Grace ignored the familiar voice and carried on peeing until only a few drops clung to the long hairs of her motte. 'That were good.' She sighed in relief and wiped the wetness from her pubic hair with her petticoats. The touch immediately sent her thinking: I ain't half dying for a bit of rantum-scantum. Grace turned to the young man and held up her skirts, showing her cleft to good advantage. 'Wot you a-doing on, Fredericks?'

'Nothing until now.' The groom came up to Grace, grabbed her full cunt in his hand and squeezed. 'Yer frigging juicy.' He smelt his fingers. 'You been finger-stinking?'

'No, but you 'ave! Let's 'ave a sniff!' Grace laughed coarsely. 'It don't stink much considering I been travellin' a coupla days.'

'Come inside the scullery. There ain't no one about.'

Fredericks pulled Grace's hand and led her inside. 'Wot you come back fer?'

'Promise you won't tell?' Grace wriggled her arse. 'I come back to find some papers. If'n I do I'll be a lady. I don't mind doing a favour if that's wot yer arter.'

'Huh! If anyone's about to do a favour, that's me! I know where them papers is hid!' He dug into his breeches as if to retrieve them, but pulled out his cock instead. It was fully erect, skinned back, and the tip gleamed in the semi-darkness. 'I know where them papers is hid.' He pulled Grace over to him and pushed her into a kneeling position. 'Now suck me cock an' I'll fetch 'em arterwards.'

'Will you fuck me an' all? I ain't half dying fer a fuck!'

'I might. Then again I might not. Get on with it, I ain't got all day! An' get yer dugs out an' all.'

'Do you want to spurt all over me bubbies?' Grace untied her front fastenings, lifted out her enormous breasts and allowed them to dangle freely.

Fredericks tipped his head to one side to observe them more fully. 'I'd like to hang you up by 'em! That'd make you scream.' Laughing, he grabbed her nipples and gave each one a sharp tweak.

'Get off! That hurts! You ain't a-doing any o' that nasty stuff with me, you ain't!'

'Ain't I just? You gotta do wot I say, else you won't get them papers.'

Grace gritted her teeth and smiled grimly. 'I'll suck yer balls, if you like. An' you can fuck me arse.' She cocked her head to one side. 'But don't hurt me, Freddie, dearie.'

'I were on'y joking, like,' Fredericks lied. 'I'll come in yer mouth first. Then jus' let me tie yer bubbies up a bit, you know I likes to tie up a girl, an' I'll give you a good fucking when me cocks hard agin!'

Grace grabbed Fredericks by the cock, shoved it in her mouth and sucked hard. She was fairly desperate by now, since she'd not coupled for two days. Her work in the brothel had increased her sexual appetite and she'd found no one on the road who was willing to satisfy it.

'Here, Gracie, watch you don't swallow me toolleywag.' Fredericks grabbed a tuft of the girl's hair, rotated his hips and then began to thrust in short, sharp jerks which he maintained for several minutes. Since he frigged regularly, he was able to control his emissions and could delay the final ejaculation for hours if desired. At last he shuddered to a slow, grinding halt, and holding Grace's head close to his groin he poured his hot salty sperm down her throat. 'Now for yer tits!'

Grace swallowed the sticky liquid and wiped her mouth on her dirty sleeve. 'You don't half have a lot o' spunk!'

'An' you fair sucked me dry, Grace.' Fredericks fondled his balls, then tucked his equipment into his breeches. 'Drained me ballocks dry as empty corn sacks.'

'Here, wot you doing? I thought you was gonna gimme some rumpy-pumpy.'

'Gimme a rest, Gracie. I ain't made o' spunk! Now stand still while...'

'Wot now? Get off!'

'I tol' you. Jus' tying you up like. Tying up yer bubbies.'

Fredericks had taken out a length of twine and was now winding it around Grace's upper body. He crossed it over her breasts and wound it around again so that they were lifted into an unnaturally high position. And then, before Grace could protest any more, he had her arms behind her, tied up and then fixed to a ring in the ceiling.

'Stand up, Gracie me dear.'

'You won't hurt me, Freddie?'

'Not much, I won't!' He pulled on the twine so that Grace was forced to stand. 'Now fer them screws!'

'Oh no!' Grace's expression was a picture of horror. 'You said as...'

'Never mind wot I said. I changed me mind. It won't hurt much, honest!' The young man took two lethal-looking iron screws from his pocket. 'Know'd where I got these?'

'I don't know as I do. Now untie me!'

'I got 'em from a sailor wot'd bin to foreign parts. He stole 'em from a priest wot used 'em on witches afore they were burnt to death!' He grinned maliciously.

'Well, I ain't no witch. Untie me, I say!'

'You be lucky. Do you want them papers?' Fredericks affixed one of the screws to Grace's left nipple and slowly tightened it.

'Yes, I do!' Grace drew in a sharp breath at the initial pressure.

'Well then.' He smiled. 'If'n you want 'em, I gotta do this first.'

'How do I know you ain't lying?'

'You don't. But I'll show you, anycase.' Fredericks disappeared into a dark corner of the room, and reappeared with some documents. 'Now, you agree to let me torture them bubbies an' you can 'ave them papers. Otherwise they goes on the fire!' He waved them in front of Grace's face, and her eyes lit up with greed. 'Well?'

'On'y if you give us a good fucking arterwards.'

'I might.' The young sadist attached the screws to both nipples and tightened them, all the while watching gleefully as Grace's face contorted with the pain. 'Do it hurt, Gracie?'

The girl pouted and her ugly expression softened. She was more used to inflicting pain and humiliation than receiving it. 'Course it don't.' She shook her head. 'You can't hurt me.'

'Ha! We'll see!' Fredericks turned the screws, causing Grace to wince and grit her teeth. 'How about that then? Don't it hurt you?'

'No! It don't!' Another turn, and Grace's mouth opened wide as a rush of air filled her lungs. The pain was excruciating at first and then, as Grace reached her plateau, the hurt seemed to subside. Her face took on a beatific air and her facial cast was quite transformed. Fredericks, a connoisseur of ugliness rather than beauty, watched, fascinated. Grace, fat, ugly, dirty Grace, was suddenly beautiful, radiant.

'You's lovely, Grace, like that.' Grace smiled weakly through the pain. 'You's lovely. You's an angel like Betty.'

Grace half smiled again as Fredericks attached each screw to a length of twine which he fixed alongside the others in the ring. 'But you pays a price fer beauty.' Gradually he pulled the twines tighter so that eventually Grace's full breasts were lifted high by the nipples. 'An' it don't half look good to me.' The young man stepped close up to Grace to observe her breasts. Her large nipples were fully stretched upwards and the creases under her full orbs had disappeared under the tension. 'You pays a price in pain!'

For a moment Grace was alarmed. It would certainly cause considerable pain if the twine was tightened more, but she was well supported by the ropes attached to her arms. Then he proceeded to untie her arms, thus leaving her attached by her breasts alone. 'There. I said as I'd do that!' He stepped back to admire his handiwork, then sat on a stool holding the twine in one hand. 'Right, Gracie, me dear. Kneel down an' then up, then down an' give yerself a frigging at the same time. Go on!'

'Ain't you gonna fuck me?'

'Arter you done it. Kneel down!'

'But I can't go no lower. Me tits is all pulled up.'

'I'll let go o' the rope a bit. When I says down, you kneel, an' when I says up, you stand. Easy. See?'

'Wot if I catch it wrong.'

'It'll hurt you.'

'I ain't never gonna trust no one agin!' Grace glared angrily at Fredericks.

Suddenly there was a movement at the door, which slowly creaked open to reveal the black silhouette of a man.

'But you would trust your spiritual master, would you not, Grace?'

Grace squinted and stared into the doorway.

'I don't know as who you are, sir.' The man stepped inside and Grace instantly recognised the corrupt priest. 'Why, Father, if it ain't you?'

'"Master", my dear, "Master". Not "Father". Have you already forgotten I am now the master here?'

'No, sir.' Grace hung her head. She had left the mansion quickly, much to the disapproval of the priest.

'And have you forgotten your disloyalty to me, your new master?'

'Oh sir. It were Liza. I didn't wanna leave. She made me. I wish I never left wi' Liza. She's a trollop, no mistake. An' she makes me rump an' pump wi' gennelmen all day. I gets right sore.'

'So, you have been perpetrating the devil's work in a bawdy house? Tempting men to sin? You are a harlot, a fornicator!'

'Yes, sir,' Grace knew she must not look him in the eye.

'And the fornicator has returned to beg forgiveness, no doubt?' Father Loughran took the rope from Fredericks and began to jiggle it. 'Do you wish to be cleansed of your sins?'

'Why, yes, sir. I come back fer confession,' Grace lied as convincingly as she could. 'An' to serve you master an' all, so I did. I can work in the kitchen like I did afore.'

'So, my dear, your soul needs cleansing. You have come to the right place for forgiveness and repentance.' The priest smiled, but his eyes were stones.

Grace nodded fearfully. 'Yes, master.' She had no intention of staying in service at the mansion, and would make her escape when the opportunity arose, but she dared not anger him. She'd watched through the peephole many a time and had heard the girls and women confess to the priest. She'd heard their screams as, in return for absolution, he'd satisfy his lust in the forbidden passage. For the meantime she'd play his game. 'I come back to you, master, humble, like.'

'Since your previous position has been filled, you will enter into the household as a servant of the lowest order. To make amends for the inconvenience you have caused, you will forfeit a year's remuneration. Those are my requirements. Will you confess and do penance?'

'Oh yes, sir, yes, gladly! If yer wants to poke me cunny, you can do it night an' day. It's allus nice n' juicy.' She tried to smile appealingly.

The master's face was grim. 'You are not to be "poked", Grace. It would hardly constitute a punishment in your case. No...' the priest stroked his chin with one hand as if in deep thought, 'if I am to purge you of your sins and drive the devil from your soul, I must use the only safe method, which is to enter the passage wherein he resides, the place where you have driven him with your endless fornication! In other words, I would enter you from behind. Your "cunny", as you put it, is of no use to me in this respect. It is the other passage I prefer.'

'Oh sir, not there, sir, not me bum. Not me bumhole!'

Grace was frightened. Having witnessed the depraved sadistic behaviour of the priest she knew he would stop at nothing to get what he wanted.

'Kneel, and I will hear your confession.'

'But I can't sir, er, master.' Grace tried to lower herself, but the ropes were taut and the movement stretched her nipples painfully. 'Sir, oh please, master, let me down, else I can't do it! The ropes is tight. I'll do anything you say. You can fuck me mouth, fuck me cunny, anythin' you likes, sir, on'y don't fuck me arse. Oh please let go them ropes.'

'But you must be punished for your misbehaviour, my child, your disloyalty.' He relaxed the tension slightly, but still Grace could not kneel. 'It would be a simple matter to leave you here, hanging by your bubbies. No one would hear your screams, Grace. The house is deserted.'

'Master, I promise as I'll serve you proper. I promise. You can fuck me arse, anything, but please don't hurt me dugs. Them's tender.'

The priest was enjoying the exhibition before him. True,

though she had lost some of her puppy fat since leaving the mansion, Grace was nowhere near as beautiful as Betty, nor as innately innocent, but she had a virgin arse. And she wriggled and squirmed before him in the most helpless manner, her large breasts bobbing like huge fruits as she tried to lift herself up on tiptoes to ease the tension on her nipples.

'Lift her and hold her still. I wish to inspect the hussy for signs of the devil's work.'

Fredericks had been watching fascinated, wishing it were he administering the torture. He positioned himself behind Grace and lifted her in the air, holding her in such a way that her legs were spread open. For a moment there was relief on Grace's face as her breasts resumed a more natural position, then she grimaced as the ropes went taut again, her initial relief disappearing as she realised her helpless position.

'Hm.' The priest tied the ropes to a hook and lifted Grace's petticoats. He then slid his hands up her calves and over her thighs. Pressing his thumbs to her cleft he pulled her cunny-lips apart, then pushed his thumbs inside the soft flesh. 'She is extremely wet. The Devil's milk, no doubt.' He bent over and sniffed between her legs. 'And the smell is strangely potent, the smell of countless emissions! Well Grace, how many innocent men have you tricked of their manly juices, robbed of what is due only to their loyal wives?'

Grace decided to string out the confession as long as possible whilst she thought of a way out. 'I don't know, master. Not many, I reckon.'

But the priest was determined to make her suffer one way or another. 'You lie! Lower her Fredericks!'

Fredericks began to lower her to the floor, but the priest still held the ropes as taut as ever and her nipples began to take the strain.

'Oh, Father, I on'y got two hands to count with, see.'

'My child, if the number exceeds the count of two hands,

then you are deeper in sin than I thought. Lower her Fredericks!'

'Please, Freddie, don't do it! I shan't bear it!'

'So,' the priest pressed his thumbs in more deeply, 'you admit to fornication with at least a dozen men?'

'Oh yes, master. Yes, I done it wi' dozens an' dozens.'

'Do you renounce the Devil and his Work?'

'Yes, Father, yes!'

'And you will serve your earthly master, your spiritual guide?'

'I will serve you. I will!' By now Grace was panting with fear and she could hold control over her bladder no longer. 'Father I'll serve you. I swear it! Oh, please let me go!' A golden trickle ran down one leg.

'Shall us carry on, master?'

'Continue to lower her until I give the usual signal.' He relaxed the rope ever so slightly, but all Grace could feel was the continued tension. She began to panic and the tears came.

'Please, Father, please.'

'Tell me, Grace, why are you wearing Betty's clothing?'

'Oh, let me down, oh please, an' I'll tell you everything.'

It did not take long for Grace to tell all, and for Father Loughran to concoct his evil plan.

Chapter Twelve

Too Much Excitement!

At the mercy of Adam – A proposal of marriage – Gentleman Jim and One Ballock Billy – A Poetry of Cunts – A prickly story – Silks and sapphires – Tasting spunk – Banqueting – A spoiled dress – A drunken orgy thwarted – The press-gang – Return to the mansion

'I loves you, Bett. I loves you so.' Gently, Adam stroked Betty's curls away from her face.

'If you loves me so much, you would o' told Giles the truth and let us go off together. And you wouldn'a tied me up stark naked.' Betty glared at Adam crossly and twitched her head away from his caressing hand. He'd bound her limbs to a sturdy oak chair, her wrists secured to the armrests, her ankles to the stout legs.

'Why won't you be mine? Why won't you love me?'

'I don't love no one no more.' Betty pouted. 'Least of all you.'

'But I rescued the old man, an' I saved you from them boys. Don't that count fer nothing?'

'No! You don't care 'bout me nor Giles, on'y yerself.'

'I loves you, Bett!' Adam's calloused hands stroked her marbled shoulders, then he bent over to kiss them, but Betty shrugged him off again.

'Anyways, I been a-thinking on what you said about saving me. That's just what Lord Clancy said. Yer all the same. You just want me body. And when you got it you just do as you please with me. That ain't love!'

'What is it then, if it ain't love?'

'Lust and fornication, a sin o' the flesh. That's what the priest would say. And you don't want nothing else, 'cept the money o' course. Everyone wants me fortune.' She pulled away from Adam, but he loomed closer. 'Yer all the same! 'Cept Giles.'

'Well, I ain't the same. I've allus loved you, Bett. Ever since I first saw you.'

'But you didn't save me from a-whipping, did you? When I first went up to the big house. I never know'd pain as bad as that. Yer a coward!'

Adam coloured at the taunt, for he knew the accusation was true. 'Neither did Giles! He didn't save you from the Squire's whip neither!'

'He's an old man. He ain't young and strong like you is!'

'I wouldn'a hurt you, Bett.'

'And you wouldn'a help me neither, not if it meant *you* got hurt.'

'But I changed. I love you, Bett.' Adam went down on one knee and clasped his large hand over Betty's. 'Marry me, Bett, oh please. I'm nothing without you. I'd do anythin' for you.'

'I won't marry you. I won't. Yer worse than Kit and Parslow. Leastways I know what they is. Liars and cheats and vagabonds. You pretend to be a friend, and then you let us down.' Betty curled her lip angrily. 'Yer a low-born peasant!'

'I'm as good as any gennelman!' Adam drew himself up to his full height. 'An' I got gold to prove it!' He pulled out a purse and threw the contents down. Gold, silver coins, ornate brooches and strings of precious jewels gleamed softly in the failing sunbeam. 'All fer you, Bett!'

'You ain't never a gennelman.' Betty spat at the pile of stolen jewellery. 'And no gold'll make you one! I on'y know one true gennelman, and that's Giles. He's me on'y true friend. And you sent him off on a wild goose chase!'

'Huh! Why don't yer marry Giles? If he's so fancy!'

'Giles is like a father to me. Me real one's dead an Felan's a no-good drunk.' Betty glared angrily. 'And you better fetch him back!'

'I give 'im the horse an' cart. He'll be far away by now.'

'I hate you, Adam!' Betty pouted, but she knew Adam was right. 'I just wish you'd let me see Giles afore you sent him off, that's all.'

'Betty, I jus' want you to marry me! Say yes!'

'I'm married to William.'

'He don't love you like I do, Bett.'

'He does.' Betty tried to stamp her foot but the bonds held her tightly. 'He does love me. I know he does.' Suddenly she burst into tears. 'And I love him. I don't want no other man. And I don't know why you rescued me if you weren't going to take me to him.'

'Don't cry, Bett. Don't cry. I loves you.' Adam was distressed, but his feelings were shallow. He looked on Betty much as a collector might view a butterfly. She was beautiful, and he would possess her one way or another.

'Well, if you loves me so much, take me to William. Take me to the mansion, now!'

'I will, I promise I will,' a crafty look crossed Adam's face, 'but it's getting dark, see.'

'That don't make no difference.' Betty looked up at the small window, high in the roof, and the thin beam of dwindling sun that pierced it. Suddenly she was cold and afraid. Although he'd helped her before, she could not trust Adam. 'Take me to William!'

'Not yet, Betty. Not yet.'

'You promised.'

'We's a-waiting fer a new friend o' mine. We rides the highway together. He'll be here jus' arter sundown.'

'Why didn't you tell me afore?'

'I forgot. I were thinking on you, Bett. Yer so pretty. Be nice. Give us a kiss.' Adam planted his lips on Betty's, but she twisted away.

'What's the man's name? You better let me go afore he comes.'

'No one as you know, personal like, but you may have heard on 'im.' Adam paused meaningfully. 'Jus' a close friend o' mine,' he boasted. 'Gennelman Jim. I'll untie you afore the sun sets.'

Betty's eyes flashed. 'Gennelman Jim? It can't be! Why, they say he tups the ladies arter he's stolen their silk clothing and their jewels! And they say he's hung like...'

'Like an ox,' Adam laughed. 'But he allus thanks the ladies. He's as polite as they come, a fine gennelman, a friend o' mine. An' he'll travel with us to the mansion.'

'Well, he ain't no friend o' mine! And he ain't a-tupping me neither!' But Betty was excited at the thought of meeting the infamous highwayman. The services she'd performed for Kit and Parslow, coupled with her present vulnerable position, had set her blood boiling. A stream of juice ran from her cunny and pooled onto the wooden seat. 'Don't let him tup me, Adam. I'll never forgive you.'

'What'll you do fer me?'

'You ain't a-tupping me instead, if that's what yer after.' Betty's black eyes flashed.

'Oh no, you don't 'ave to do that! Oh no!'

'And I ain't a-sucking yer nob.' She tossed her golden hair. 'I'm fed up with the taste o' spunk!'

'You don't 'ave to do that, neither.'

'Nor a-licking nothing else.' Betty bit her lip.

'You don't 'ave to suck nor lick nothin'. Honest.'

'What then?'

'I wan' to look at you close, Bett, look at yer cunny right close up.' Adam settled himself cross-legged on the floor and peered between Betty's legs. 'An' jus' touch it a little bit. I want to see as how the pretty lips curl open when you's juicy.'

Betty shook her head. 'You can look as much as you like, but I won't never love you.'

'It's beautiful. I ain't seen another cunny like it.' Adam leaned forward, breathed over the golden-haired mound and gently pulled on Betty's pubic curls, revealing the pink gash of her delicate slit. 'It's perfeck… perfeck!'

Betty shifted position. 'What's beautiful 'bout a cunny? They's all the same ain't they?'

'Oh, I don' know about that. I seed a few an' they's all different, an' pretty in their own ways.' Adam stroked along the outer lips. 'Why, some has dark hair an' some has light, an' some has none at all! Some has large lips here,' he gave her inner labia a little pinch, 'as hang down in a pretty, wavy frill. An' others…' Adam's enthusiastic description was interrupted by the early arrival of the aforementioned highwayman.

'A cunt, missy, is a cunt, just as a rose is a rose. However, as with roses, there are many varieties, in varying stages of bloom. Yours, I would say,' he paused and took an appraising look between Betty's legs, 'yours me dear,' he took a pinch of snuff and another searching look. 'Yours, your cunny that is to say – we shall forgo the more common appellation – your delicate cunny is at the budding stage, barely curling open but, by the look of the splashing dew on it, ready to burst into flower at the slightest provocation of Mother Nature or perhaps Father Time.'

'Why, who are you, sir? You startled me! Goodness, I never heard such poetry afore!'

'Gentleman Jim, at your service.' The highwayman winked his eye, cocked his head to one side, and with a flourish of his hand introduced his older, shorter companion. 'And this is my man, One Ballock Billy.'

The servant bowed low and slightly to one side, for he was as asymmetrical as his name suggested, the lack of symmetry applying not only to the aforementioned ballock, but to each and every limb. 'At your service, missy.' He smiled, his body tipping sideways in the other direction and at an odd angle.

Bemused, and thus forgetting her nakedness, Betty gazed in awe at the speaker whose appearance and demeanour contrasted so dramatically with his confederate. Gentleman Jim, dark-haired and white-skinned, with unusually fine-cut features, wore his opulent clothing with a swagger that befitted his title. Over the close-fitting velvet coat and moleskin breeches that hugged his muscular form, he'd flung a loose cloak, and his soft leather boots moulded his calves like a second skin. With costly lace at his throat and deadly weapons at his side, he was a formidable yet ravishing sight.

'We right wrongs, see, missy. We taxes the wealthy, and returns their ill-gotten gains to the rightful owners, the poor!' One Ballock Billy squinted another smile.

'Young lady,' Betty's eyes now turned to Jim. 'I am an expert in many matters, relating not only to the highways, which it behoves one in my profession to fully understand, but to the fairer sex, in particular to the pudendum. Which is why I could not help but remark earlier upon the delicious attributes of your sex, thus beautifully displayed.'

Reminded she was stark naked, her legs wide apart, her cunny splayed rudely for all to see, Betty tried to jerk her legs together. 'Oh, sir.' She blushed as the highwayman's eyes travelled unhindered over her nakedness to rest once more at her cleft.

Gallantly, Gentleman Jim removed his cloak and wrapped it around Betty. 'Spare your blushes, missy. You are safe with me.' He winked at Billy.

Now she was covered, Betty lifted her eyes to gaze upon his proud forehead, over his luscious, sensual lips, over the broad chest and downwards to the prominent bulge that threatened to burst from his fine breeches. Strong-looking handsome and virile, he paled Adam into insignificance. Betty's breast heaved with a deep and shameful desire for this dark stranger, and the juice from her cunny began to run freely. Automatically she tried to close her legs, then dropped her chin to her chest again.

'Missy,' the highwayman lifted her chin and gazed into the deep black pools of her eyes, and tried another poetical metaphor, 'such ripe fruit is far too luscious to rot by the wayside, or be bruised by rough hands. I shall eat the fig before, over-ripe, it bursts! You are a virgin, I take it? And in need of protection?'

'Indeed, kind sir, my virgin state is most precious to me. It is all in the world that I have of value.' It was the first time this thought had ever crossed Betty's mind, and a small tear ran down her cheek. 'And if it be taken, why, I have nothing to recommend me to a husband, and I'll end me days in the almshouse.'

'Betty, a maid as beautiful as you must not be allowed to shed even the tiniest tear of sadness.' Jim took out a fine silk handkerchief and wiped Betty's cheek. 'There will come a day, perhaps sooner than you thought,' he winked at One Ballock Billy, 'when you are only too willing to give up that innocent state.'

'That time is far away, sir, for me virginal state is precious to me for other reasons, not merely for the sake o' propriety, but because if it is retained, I stand to inherit a vast fortune. Do not, I beg you, attempt to force me.'

The man's eyes flashed with increased interest at the mention of a fortune to be had. 'So,' Jim turned to Adam and dramatically waved his arm at Betty, 'this beauteous creature is the angel you spoke of: excessively celestial, more charming than the cherubim on high, a rose without thorns, innocent as the snowdrop in spring, as perfect as the driven snow, as pale as a primrose, as—'

'I told you, sir, she were a flower,' Adam spoke doggedly. What chance did he have of Betty's favours now?

'Then why is she used so badly?' Gentleman Jim glared angrily at Adam. 'She is clearly innocent of crime or deception. Why, for the sake of all that's in heaven, is she bound with ropes to a chair? Surely the beauty is a lady, not a wench nor hussy? Untie her forthwith! If I am to eat of the fig, and I fully intend to do so, I would want such luscious fruit offered to me freely. Untie the lady, I say!'

Adam was immediately jealous, and he fleetingly thought to protect Betty from the possibility of Gentleman Jim's rampant advance. However, as usual, his cowardice got the better of him. Fearing the wrath of his new companion and mentor, Adam hastily untied the bonds, set Betty on her feet and drew the cloak tightly around her shoulders.

'Oh sir, you flatter me.' Betty was impressed by Jim's fine words, and though a little suspicious that there was a motive behind it, was relieved to be released.

'Billy, fetch the bags. The lady must be dressed as befits her station.' Jim threw himself onto a low settle and put his calf leather boots on the stool. 'Adam, if you look in the saddlebags there is port a-plenty and cold roast meats to boot. We shall celebrate in style!'

A few moments later the men returned, Adam with several bottles and the cold meats, and Billy with a large carpet bag containing stolen property. 'Wot would the missy like?' He tipped out a pile of expensive silks, satins and velvets in colours that astounded Betty's eye. 'Take yer pick.'

'A glass o' the finest port, I warrant! Open a bottle. No doubt the lady is thirsty. Good health to you all.'

Pewter goblet in hand, Betty knelt on the floor next to Billy as they sorted through the pile of clothing.

'Why'd they call you "One Ballock Billy"?' she whispered.

'I were a-waiting fer you to ask, missy. There ain't a girl on earth can resist the question.'

'And Billy cannot resist giving you the reply! Proceed, my man. Tell the tale. Entertain your audience. Amuse dear Betty.'

'Well, missy, it's like this. Long time ago, when I were a lad, no higher than a door knocker, I were a-playing in them fields nearby. An' I happened to fall, like a stuck pig, upon a sprig o' dried up holly. Now holly is prickly at the best o' times, as you know, but a dried-up sprig is pricklier than ever.

'Being only a small sprogget, I couldn'a pull the damn thing out, an' I ran home a-crying and a-wailing to find me ma. I remember her very words: "Oh," she says wi' a smile on 'er face, "The little sprog has sprung a sprig. He's sprung a sprig o' prickles. And the sprig o' prickles has missed his little prickle and pierced one on his baby balls!" An' she fell about laughing at the joke.

'Well, it weren't no joke to me. The little ball swelled and swelled until it weren't small no more. It swelled an' swelled till it were as big as me head. An' spite of all the cobwebs laid across it, it would not shrink. Would it shrink? No, it would not!

'Fer near on two week, I lay in a fever. An' then, do you know what happened?'

'I can't hardly guess!'

'It shrunk clean away! Why, it disappeared altogether. An' that's how I come to be called "One Ballock Billy".' Billy folded his arms and grinned, very pleased with himself. 'There, what d'you think o' that?'

'I don't hardly know what to think, Billy. It's a tale and a half, it is. Is it really true?'

'I ain't never averse to showin' a fair lady the proof o' the truth.'

And before Betty could protest, Billy had exposed his entire manly tackle to view.

'Why, Billy, so it is. I can't say as I've seen the like afore.' Betty smiled. 'But now I have seen it, why, it ain't so bad.' Betty turned over the garments. 'Here, these clothes, these jewels, they ain't a-stolen, is they?' Betty longingly fingered a silk dress and a matching sapphire necklace. 'I ain't a-taking them if'n they ain't yourn to give. But they's so pretty!'

'My dear, who do you think I am?' Goblet in hand, Gentleman Jim jumped up, drawing himself to his full height, and in the process almost spilling the port. 'A common thief!'

'Oh dear, missy, you gone an' done it now.' Billy shook his head. 'Don't upset the gennelman. He won't take it kindly. Find summat to wear afore 'is Lordship gets cross!'

'These clothes,' Jim paced the floor. 'These satins and silks, these trinkets and baubles, etcetera, etcetera, are the levy which must be exacted from the wealthy. They are given freely in exchange for an extension of their dissipated lives on this mortal coil! A bargain at half the price!'

The rich fabrics were tempting, and Betty was cold and naked. What else should a girl do in such dire circumstances as she found herself? Amongst the dresses Betty discovered one only that fitted to perfection. It could have been made especially for her since its original owner had much the same figure. Under the covering of the cloak, Betty stepped into the pale blue silk, drew it up and over her bosom and arms and laced the front. The décolletage was very low, and the bodice so tightly fitting in the cut that a corset was unnecessary.

'Oh, sir, it's lovely!' Betty's eyes shone with delight as she smoothed the exquisite material with her palms. 'I ain't never wore such a lovely dress. I don't know what to say. How can I thank you?'

'Do not speak, my dear, do not utter one letter, one sound, one word, do not let a syllable cross your pretty, ruby lips.' He patted the settle. 'Take your rightful and honourable place here beside me, and plant your delicate juicy flower petals upon mine own. Ah, to taste such innocent sweetness! That is thanks enough.' He winked at Billy again.

Gentleman Jim pulled Betty to him, kissing her full on the lips, and Betty responded warmly. What joy to have the arm of a strong young man around her waist, to have his searching lips and tongue upon hers. Oh to submit once more to the power of Nature, to feel the vibrations of the earth itself coursing through her veins.

Betty was aroused and her flowering bud, as no doubt Jim would have named her cunt, expanded as if to say "Take me". But Betty could not utter those words of betrayal, for in the background always, always, the presence of William loomed, and so she withdrew coyly. 'Oh sir, you ain't half warm. Oh my goodness, oh my, oh my! What shall us do? You have quite over taken me with yer charms.'

'Betty, ah, sweet Betty, if you were free to give what is yours alone to give, then I *would* take it.' Suddenly the man was hot, but nonetheless still hopelessly poetic: 'I would have your bud for mine own. Not that I shall, dear one. I would take that pure, virgin flower. Later, that is. I would open it. Gently, mind you. I would mount your lovely limbs, part the portal, fill the interim space with my stamen!' At this point and with practised expertise, he pushed his hand into the placket of his breeches and lifted out his throbbing member.

'I would plunge my puissant proboscis deep within,' he shook his cock and a bead of spunk flung onto the floor, 'and, dear heart, this strong and stalwart stamen has such staying power. It would fertilise you to the very core!' He grabbed Betty's hand and held it around the shaft. 'Full, lusty, vigorously rampant with Nature's fertile essences, ah, ah!' And Gentleman Jim, prior to his own expectations, spunked in Betty's little hand.

'Why, sir, what is this juice? It quite fills me hand to overflowing.'

'Drink deep of the effervescent cup of life, my sweet one. Lick and lap the very sap of life itself, its sticky fulsome essences.' Betty poked out her tongue and wriggled. 'Oh, such a delicate appendage, how pink, rosy, rubicund it is! The tongue that so delicately peeps from between those crimson portals.'

'What if the cream should spill and stain me dress?'

Running out of poetical expressions, Jim became more practical. 'There are plenty more where that came from. The previous owner will be only too willing to oblige. Forget the dress and let us drink!'

Gentleman Jim lifted his goblet to his lips, and Betty's hand to her mouth.

'Why, sir, I ain't seen nothing like it afore. Shall us taste it? Why it's nice. It tastes o' salt and musty bibles and old stone, all rolled in one. And yet it has a freshness about it too.'

Jim smiled at Betty, playing along with her pretence at innocence. 'The essence of manhood you taste so unexpectedly, but so willingly, is but an hors d'ouevre; a preliminary course to the evening's revelry! Set the table, Billy, and we shall dine as befits the beauteous flower by my side, this unparalleled example of pulchritude!'

'It don't look like Adam'll be a-joining us, sir,' said Billy, ignoring Jim's rhetoric. 'I reckon he's been drinking port as if it were ale.'

'And I don't know as I'd want him to eat alongside us!' Betty cried. 'Why, I thought he were me friend and he pretended to help me, then tied me up and goodness knows what he'd have done if Gentleman Jim, and your kind self, Billy, hadn't come to the rescue. Why, I may have lost summat precious to me!'

'My dear,' Gentleman Jim patted Betty's arm, 'in my company you have everything to gain and nothing to lose. Feel free to partake of my humble hospitality.'

The threesome settled around the homely cottage table. Billy had set it with a fine lace cloth and filigree napkins, booty stolen from an unfortunate bride's bottom drawer, exquisite candelabra, silver cutlery and rare bone china plates with a strange oriental design. The pewter goblets had been replaced by enormous golden chalices which had been appropriated from a number of churches, and Billy had filled them to the brim with the finest of the ports.

The cold meats were piled high: chicken's legs, thin slices of mutton, pheasant, and the tiniest of partridges and quails. They all ate heartily. At first, Betty supped in a delicate manner, her little finger awry as she's seen the ladies do.

But as time wore on and the effect of the port took place, her manners became somewhat less refined.

'When I's a real lady I shall dine like this, with rare things atop the table. And I shall wear the finest silks. And I shan't care if the grease off the chicken runs all down me chin. I shall eat little birds,' Betty bit into a quail, 'and big birds.' Now Betty bit into a leg of chicken, and as predicted the fat ran down her chin, over her uplifted breasts and onto the beautiful embroidered bodice of the silk dress. 'Oh, goodness me, I's drunk as Adam!' Betty simpered, putting a coy hand over her lips. And, indeed, for the first time in her life, Betty was truly drunk. 'Oh sir, the dress, the silk is ruined! Oh look, the juice is a-running on me bubbies and on me dress.'

'Billy, fetch a cloth.' He winked. 'The lady must be sponged. Meanwhile, I shall lick the offending juices with my tongue.' Jim wobbled his drunken way around the table. He was extremely inebriated, and although capable of imbibing much liquor before collapsing, he would shortly reach that unhappy state.

'Betty, my dear.' Now his arms were around her neck, his nose tickling her back, his tongue dribbling on her shoulders and his large hands holding a breast apiece. 'Such beautiful orbs were made for man's pleasure. Such roundness,' he squeezed, 'such firmness, ah, dear Betty, ah!' And Jim turned Betty around to lap the grease from her décolletage.

'Oh, sir, what shall us do? You are so kind to me and yet it is me husband William that I truly love. Will you take me to him, sir, else I shall die on a broken heart?' Suddenly Betty thought of Giles. 'And me old friend, Giles. Find him, sir, do find him, else I shall have no one to confide in.'

'Gennelman Jim, at yer service, milady,' and Jim began to wave his arms around madly. 'I shall save you, me dear, save you from…' he paused, forgetting exactly what Betty should be saved from. 'I shall save you from certain death. But first, give me a little taste o' yer sweet nuts, yer cherries, yer little booby-buddies.' He sat Betty on the table amongst the half-eaten meal and with little difficulty, prised her nipples from the dress.

'Oh, sir, what are you a-doing on? You must not, I declare, you must not! Take me to William, I say!'

'It shall be done!' But the lusty highwayman could not resist Betty's beautiful nipples. 'A little squeeze, a little suck me dear, will do no harm!' He milked each one in turn. 'See, your virginity is safe with me.' A hand crept to the edge of her petticoat. 'I know the ways of women, and make it my business to study each one.' The hand crept further up Betty's leg.

'But sir, what are you a-doing on?'

'Aha!' Suddenly Betty was lying on top of the table, her petticoats flung up and over her belly.

'Studying, for the purpose of my profession you understand, that which most interests me.' And Jim's large hands were immediately at Betty's cunt, roving over the mound, down the sticky thighs and between the cleft. 'Such exquisite beauty must be thoroughly examined.' He breathed heavily and his face gradually snuggled into Betty's pubic hair. 'It is in the interest of humanity that such discoveries be made.'

'Oh sir, you are strong and hot and I's so weak. Oh, sir!' Betty's heart had begun to melt. Oh, what a perfect opportunity for the lusty highwayman. But all of a sudden Adam was wide awake, and Adam was very, very jealous.

Billy had gone to sleep in a corner, so it would have been an easy task to overpower the highwayman, but as it turned out there was no need.

'Oh, sir, I must pee, else I shall do it on yer face!'

'Do it where you please, my head reels.' Jim helped Betty from the table and she ran outside and into the safety of the bushes, followed by Adam.

'Let me watch, Betty.'

'I don't know as you should!' But Betty was desperate all of a sudden and she lifted her skirts, without shame peeing hard onto the leaves.

'Shh! What's tha' noise?'

'It ain't me!'

'Listen.' Having spent much time in the forest, Adam was attuned to the familiar night-time sounds. 'I hear horses. Quick, we must hide!'

Adam and Betty crouched low and waited for what seemed a long while. All was quiet in the cottage since Jim had now collapsed unconscious.

'I can't hear nothing.'

'Soon, you will soon. Be patient.' Adam was right. In a while the soft sound of hooves on turf became evident. And then the shouts and calls of men.

'After this one, we'll have men enough to satisfy the Captain.'

'Good, the cottage is still lit and all is quiet.' A man laughed with glee. 'There is much gold in this one! He has a price on his head!'

Moments later two men appeared from the cottage with Gentleman Jim and One Ballock Billy slung over their shoulders. They hung so limply, it was obvious that it was not the port alone that had rendered them unconscious. The men from the press-gang slung their bodies over the horses' backs and led them off into the night.

'It's safe now, Bett.' Adam had his arm around Betty's shoulder. He would not bother to take advantage of her just yet, for his plan was going as intended.

'Who were they?'

'The press-gang, Betty. I doubt we'll see Gentleman Jim an' his cohort for a long while. They'll soon be bound for Botany Bay in our Majesty's Service.'

There was nothing to be done to save the highwayman and his companion, so early the next morning Betty and Adam had ridden to the mansion. Adam had promised to reunite Betty with William, and they were now in the maze of underground tunnels leading to the dungeons. They'd sneaked quietly onto the premises. Not that they need have taken this precaution, since the mansion was empty save for a few disloyal servants who could be bribed to do anything. Emma was at a watering spa and Father Loughran had resumed his parochial duties.

The underground tunnels were damp and had been strewn with straw to make the passage safer. Adam was reminded of the day he first saw Betty, the day he'd helped the Master prepare her for a whipping. He'd held her slim waist, removed her clothing and supported her against his body as the Master delivered his cruel punishment. He had a sudden urge to repeat the exercise, only this time he would be in charge. In a moment he'd open the trap door to the cell where William was imprisoned and force the man to watch as he whipped and then debauched his virgin wife.

'What you waiting fer, Adam?' Adam did not reply. 'You ain't a-tying me up an a-whipping me!'

'I wouldn'a do that!' But Adam was lying, for it was precisely what he intended.

'What then? What you arter?' Adam had both arms around her waist and was squeezing gently but firmly. 'You promised as you'd take me to William!'

'Jus' a little kiss first. Won't do no harm.' He pressed his lips to hers. 'There, that weren't too bad, were it? Now open yer mouth. I wants to feel yer tongue.'

'I ain't—!' But Adam held her tightly, pressed his mouth on hers firmly, and pushed his tongue between her lips.

Betty gasped and her mouth opened. Her natural inclination to submit was strong within her breast, urging her against her own wishes. Betty struggled free, panting. Adam's young firm body was hot against hers and it was difficult not to respond. 'Just a little kiss then, Adam.' Betty felt a trickle of juice flow down her inner thigh. 'No more.' She closed her eyes and relaxed into Adam's embrace.

Now was the moment of opportunity. Betty did not envisage

Adam's next move. It took only a second for him to hold her arms in a fierce lock and tie them behind her. 'Now you is mine, all mine, me lovely butterfly! I can do jus' as I like!' Another second and he'd twisted the rope around a ring in the wall.

'How dare you, Adam!' Betty glared angrily.

'Ha, ha! I dares! I dares! If you won't marry me I'll have you anyways.'

'You said as you'd bring me to William.'

'Better. Better than that. I shall bring 'im to you. I shall.' Adam laughed gleefully. He couldn't believe how well it had gone. William was imprisoned in the next dungeon. All he had to do was to strip Betty naked and open the panel behind her. The grille would prevent William from entering but he'd see everything at close quarters. He'd hear Betty's screams as the lash cut, hear her begging for mercy, hear her cries when he took her virgin passage! Adam looked at the scar on the back of his hand. The wound had healed but it was a constant reminder of his servitude to William. How sweet revenge would be!

'There, now you know exactly what's what!' Adam smiled gleefully.

'Adam, I beg you,' Betty pleaded as she swung gently on the rope, 'grant me one favour afore you do yer worst.'

'What's that then? I ain't a-cutting you down, if that's what yer thinkin' on.'

'Cover me eyes. I don't want to see nothing nor feel William's eyes on me.'

'Yer a rum one, no mistake.' Adam took out a large kerchief and tied it around Betty's eyes. 'There. Now don't say I don't do nothin' fer you.' Adam walked over to the grille separating husband and wife, and slid the panel across. He peered into the darkness. 'William, are you there?'

But there was no answer. Betty waited fearfully. She could hear nothing but what seemed like the rats scuffling. The kerchief had muffled what little sounds the press-gang made as they seized both Adam and William, knocked them unconscious, and carried them away to a waiting vessel bound for Botany Bay.

Betty and Giles sat side by side in front of the kitchen range in the mansion, each immersed in their own thoughts. Giles had managed to escape and had made his way back just in time. Betty had been hanging in the cold dungeon for some while, and she'd chilled thoroughly. He'd cut her free, carried her to the kitchen and set her in the blankets amongst the litter of puppies. They'd crawled all over her and gradually she'd grown warm. For a few hours she'd felt well, but then developed a fever. Giles bathed her brow with cool water and fed her a sop of bread and milk until, after the third day, she gained her strength.

It was by a sheer fluke that Betty had not been captured by the press gang alongside the men. The arrangements of the pillars supporting the dungeon ceiling had concealed her, and since they'd only come to collect William, Adam was a bonus. Had Mistress Emma known that Betty was to be there she would have been sure to order her capture too, but the evil woman had left for Bath where she intended to partake of the spring waters. Emma had taken her retinue of servants and the remainder, being overworked, had taken themselves off to the local hostelry with the other servants, so Giles and Betty had been left to their own devices.

'Giles, I can't help but dwell on me husband.'

'Ah, Bett, you don't wan' to think o' William. He be far away by now. He won't never come back, if the truth be told.'

'Don't say such things.' Betty began to cry.

'There, there, me dear. I wouldn'a hurt you, but life is harsh.' Giles patted Betty's golden hair. 'Ah, you are so like Wylmotte, me dear, so like. An' I loved yer Gran so.'

'Giles,' Betty reached out and took Giles's gnarled hand in hers, 'I don't know as I love William or no. What shall us do?'

'Forget William for the time being. If God wills it then you shall be reunited. Meanwhile you must keep yer promise to Emily. A promise is allus a promise. When yer better, I'll take you to Madame Farquar's and then send word to Rowena.'

The old man and the young woman snuggled up together beside the fireplace, and slept.

Chapter Thirteen

Madame Farquar's establishment

Making new friends – A surrogate mother's love – A large breast relieved – A light whipping – A reunion with Candace – The Cleric of Clerkenwell

'My dear,' Madame Farquar glided forward to embrace Betty, gently kissed her cold cheeks and grasped her gloved hands loosely, 'I have waited *so* eagerly for this moment. And you have been *so* long coming I feared t'would snow and you'd be delayed till spring!'

Betty smiled shyly. Though her cheeks were apple-red with winter cold, she looked the picture of health. She curtsied politely. 'I am yer obedient servant, ma'am.'

'Nonsense! In this house we ladies are equals!' Madame held Betty's shoulders at arm's length and studied her face carefully. 'Your beauty surpasses all description, my dear. And what's more, you are plumper than I imagined. Excellent.'

'Yer too kind, ma'am.'

'You must call me Clemmie, dear. All the girls do, unless we are in the company of our clients. Now sit with me for a moment. The fire is well stoked.'

The two women settled themselves by the hall fire. There was an immediate rapport between them, though their ages, experiences, and lives were very different. So they sat silently for a while, and it didn't seem to matter one jot that they were not talking.

Madame Farquar untied the ribbons of Betty's bonnet. 'My goodness, such magnificent tresses!' She ruffled Betty's golden curls. 'Why, you are gifted with the hair of an angel.'

'Well, it's an odd gift as allus brings me nearer to hell than heaven.' Betty sighed and wrung her hands.

'Oh, it was merely an expression. And in this house we talk only of paradise, not the other place. But don't take on so! You are safe in my protection.

'Hm. I heard that afore.' Betty looked around the reception room. 'Ma'am...'

'Yes dear. Let me take your gloves. No, show me how you remove them first.' Betty obliged, slipping the kid gloves slowly and neatly over each finger. 'Excellent. You are perfect Betty. Completely perfect for the task. A natural dominator.'

'Ma'am?' Betty looked surprised. 'I ... what is that?'

'More of that later. I won't bother you with long words before tea is served. Are you ready for refreshment?'

'Not yet awhile. I already eaten along the route.'

'And how was the journey?'

'Well, thank you.'

'And you, my dear? How are you?'

'I been in a fever for some weeks, and I had some sickness and such strange dreams.' Betty bit her lip and twisted it coyly to one side, then smiled engagingly.

'Do you know what we do here, Betty?' Madame squeezed her eyelids together, panther-like.

'I got a fair idea, ma'am. Ain't the ladies to please the gennelmen as come here?'

'In a manner of speaking, my dear. And would you like to join us in doing so? There is no compulsion.'

Betty sat thinking a while. She immediately trusted the Madame and her judgement, though spontaneous, was not wrong for Madame Farquar was, in spite of her profession, a good lady. 'I think as I would, though I may need some training. I don't know much about the ways of men.'

'Tell me, with your limited experience of course, how you would best please a gentleman.'

'Well, I done certain things afore, see.' Betty was too

embarrassed to be more specific.

'Yes...?' Madame Farquar gave her an encouraging smile. 'What things, dear?'

'I don't know as a high-born lady such as yerself will unnerstand.'

'I'm not so high, though I may look the part. Now, my dear,' she took Betty's hands in hers and smiled reassuringly. 'You have performed certain, shall we say, services, for gentlemen, I presume? What did you do to please?'

'Yes, ma'am. I done things with... with me mouth and me lips.' Betty hung her head. ' I never... I'm still a virgin, ma'am, but I sucked...' Betty could not think of a suitable word that would fit with the luxurious surroundings. She forced out the words awkwardly. 'I sucked pintles, ma'am. That's what I done mostly.'

Madame Farquar burst into peals of laughter which only embarrassed Betty further. Her face grew redder and redder. 'My dear, you are so quaint, so quaint!' she wiped the tears of laughter away. 'So you are an accomplished fellatrix! I can see we shall get on very well, very well indeed.'

'Oh, ma'am, you ain't cross! I ain't done many other... other things. I don't know much about yer trade, see. There must be a deal to learn.'

'You know enough my dear. But we don't call it a trade, here. It is a profession, and it is the oldest in the world, so they say. We have a job to do, true, but it elevates us far above other trades. Indeed, if we must call it a trade, then we trade in love, but not that alone.'

'But ain't this a bawdy house, ma'am? It don't look like what I imagined. It's too fine. Why, there's more gold here than a palace, and them paintings, why they must be worth a fortune, and the furniture it's, it's...' Betty was lost for words.

'It's fake, my dear. It's all fake!'

'But the wood. It's beautiful and...' Betty stroked the arm of the chair and suddenly realised she was stroking a shiny wooden penis. 'Oh, I ain't seen nothing like it. Why, these chairs has got rude things all on them.' Her eyes widened as she realised that all the furniture was carved with innumerable sexual motifs.

'And you won't see the like unless you travel to forin climes, me dear. For the Great Catherine has the very same articles in her palace, only many more. These are copies. As for the gold, the only real gold here is what you'll find in a gennelman's, I mean a *gentleman's*, purse!' She patted Betty's knee. 'There! And you will see there is no need for you to lose what is most precious to you.' She drew Betty close and whispered. 'You are chaste. And may stay that way.'

'You mean, there ain't no tupping?'

'Only if you wish it. You see we specialise in this house. We deal not only in the coarse pleasures; the runting and the grunting of men – you understand what I mean, dear, the animal side of the beasts, for some of them, poor things, must fuck to get their pleasure – but in the painful refinements of punishment!' Madame smiled warmly, an amused glint lighting up her eyes.

'But if they's gennelmen, don't they have servants to please them in the art?'

'It is a matter of expertise. The ladies here...'

Betty looked alarmed, but she was excited too, and her eyes grew wider and blacker. 'Does they use the whip?'

'All manner of instruments, my dear friend, according to preference.' Madame took Betty's small hands in hers and smiled into her eyes. 'Why, you are trembling. There is no need to be afraid. You will not be hurt.'

'Madame,' Betty hung her head, 'sometimes I feel ashamed o' me feelings, but I ain't afeard o' pain.' She lifted her chin and looked hard at the older woman. 'But I think, p'raps, I need to love a gennelman afore I can submit to the cruelties of the lash.' Betty went quiet. She was thinking of William and how far away he would be now.

'My dear, you do not take my meaning. There is no need for you to take the lash.'

'But how does the gennelmen chastise the ladies?'

'Mostly they do not wish it. In this establishment it is quite the contrary, my dear. It is exactly the reverse.'

'You mean...' Betty's expression was puzzled. Although she was intimately familiar with the pleasure-pain divide, it had not occurred to her that a man could share her desire for submission, the need for complete abdication of self.

Madame took Betty's hand in hers and squeezed it affectionately. 'Most of the gentlemen who visit the ladies here come for a beating themselves, not to administer it, but to receive it! What do you think of that?' Madame laughed at Betty's expression. 'My dear, your face tells all. It is quite a picture, quite a picture.'

Betty pouted and shrugged her shoulders. 'Is it true that Squire William come here?'

'My dear, surely you know...' Madame's eyebrows lifted to impart some significance of which Betty was obviously ignorant.

'I don't know nothing.'

Madame patted Betty's knee. 'And we'd better keep it that way, for now.'

Betty frowned. 'That ain't fair! No one tells me nothing.'

'My dear, do not delve too deeply into the why's and wherefore's.' The older woman smiled. It was a genuine smile for, in truth, she had very much warmed to Betty.

'Gita said as I should accept things as they are.'

'She was right. You must tell me of your friends later. We have much to share. For now listen to my advice. You are a handsome young woman and in need of guidance, for although your innocent appearance and manner can work to your advantage, it will undoubtedly bring danger from the stronger sex.'

'But I thought as you said they wouldn'a hurt me.'

'Indeed, but were you to be unleashed into society, which

is my eventual plan for you, who knows whom you would meet. Will you trust me and place yourself in my care?'

Betty responded warmly. 'Why yes, madame.' She took madame's hands in hers and kissed each one gently. 'I do sorely need a friend, and I see in you, oh I don't know how to say it.' Betty trembled and suddenly burst into tears. 'I ain't seen me ma in a long while and I do miss her.'

Madame Farquar arched her beautiful, dark brows. 'And you are in need of a mother's love?'

Betty gripped madame's hands tightly as she let the tears flow. 'I see you are a lady but I trust you, madame, like a mother.' Her voice was husky with emotion.

'Ah, sweet thing.' Madame fondled Betty's curls. 'Betty, you have unwittingly touched upon, well, shall I say a 'motherly' streak in me.' The woman smiled strangely and her breasts seemed to tighten and swell under the cloth of her dress.

Betty was suddenly aware of a milky smell reminding her of her mother's full, comforting breasts, with their huge brown nipples dripping with excess milk. She nuzzled her face into madame's breast and sighed at its soft ampleness. 'Ma were allus full o' milk, with bubbies so huge they allus hurt. She let us biguns suck her dry just to give relief, and then the milk would come again and she'd feed the babes.'

'My dear, I had not thought to come to this so soon, but the time seems right for both of us.' Madame Farquar slowly unbuttoned her dress, and lifting her left breast, placed it at Betty's mouth. 'Would you relieve me, Betty dear? Come, lean into me and drink to your heart's content.'

Betty snuggled up, sucked the large teat into her mouth and drank deeply while madame sighed and writhed with pleasure. Madame leant back into the cushions of her chair and spread her legs as she pressed Betty more firmly to her breast.

'Now, my little love, did you enjoy that?' Madame's hand had found its way up her own petticoats and she fondled her cunny as she spoke.

The teat stretched then plopped out of Betty's mouth. A dribble of milk ran from the corner of her smile. 'It were lovely. And me cunny's wet an' all.'

'Mine too, my dear.' She guided Betty's hands between her legs. 'Feel.'

'Did I please you, madame? I allus like to please.'

'Then, if you please, call me aunt.'

Betty laughed excitedly. 'Shall us really call you aunt?'

'Indeed, my dear. Now I have an idea, which I believe will please both of us. Do you love me Betty?'

Betty smiled shyly. 'Madame, I mean aunt, I do love you.'

'And would you like to please me more?'

'Why, yes!'

'And take a punishment too? Are you ready for that?'

Betty gasped, blushed red, then looked away. 'Yes, aunt,' she whispered. 'But I thought as you said...'

'You will not be asked to do anything you do not deeply desire. Are you ready?'

'Yes aunt, and I's sorry I showed a lack o' trust.'

'Oh, you are a bad girl, Betty!' Madame laughed, and Betty smiled too. 'We must call for assistance.' She stroked Betty's cheek tenderly. 'Now don't be alarmed. Your suckling has delighted me and you shall delight me more. But we must share our pleasures. It would be selfish not to do so. Go and ring the bell. I have a surprise for you.'

Within a few moments there was a discreet knock on the door and a tall dark figure in a footman's uniform – red jacket with brass buttons, tight black breeches and buckled shoes – appeared in the doorway. The woman, for such it was, wore a mask covering her eyes, and as her breasts were bound she gave all the appearance of being masculine.

'Betty, you will kneel at my feet. I have heard you are well practised with your tongue. You must show me how good you really are.'

Madame's voice took on a steely tone and Betty

automatically responded to its authority. She knelt humbly, and lifting the petticoats away, nuzzled her face into the woman's groin. Slowly she parted the lips with her fingers, and ran her tongue along the slippery edges. Pressing one finger inside she licked up and over the clitoris. As she did so Betty felt a hand adjust and smooth her skirts over her behind.

Then, suddenly and without warning, the crack of a whip and the lash descending over her rump. Betty jerked, more surprised than hurt. But the stimulation caused her to lick, suck and finger madame's cunny more vigorously.

Madame grabbed a handful of Betty's curls. 'Ah, my dear. You will be much in demand with the ladies. I can tell... ah! Your tongue! Ah! It is exquisite! Exquisite! Ah! I can bear it no longer!' Suddenly the woman's hips shuddered. 'Ah, I am spending... spending.' Betty licked harder as the lash struck her again, but ever so lightly. She could feel the cunny beneath her lips tremble, and at last a huge spray of liquid engulfed her tongue and she swallowed greedily. Madame slumped, exhausted, as Betty withdrew.

'Why, aunt, you don't half spend! Why, its a-dripping from me chin.' Betty wiped her hand across her mouth. 'It don't seem possible to have so much juice! I never drunk so much afore!'

'My dear, there are some ladies who spend in this way. It does not always apply, of course. And they can spend time after time. It is a matter of the opportunity and the right stimulation. Your tongue, my dear, is very long and firm and tickles in just the spot!'

Betty rubbed her bottom. It was not sore, for she had been struck over the cloth, but it throbbed a little and her cunt was very wet.

'Don't look so surprised, Betty. I know you can take more than that little punishment. That was nothing, as you well know. Did you spend, too?'

Betty pouted, then smiled. 'A little, aunt, but not so much

as you.'

'Now for your surprise.' Madame glanced at the uniformed servant. 'Reveal yourself,' she ordered.

The young woman in question tore off her mask and walked forward out of the gloomy area where she'd waited, and into the light of a lamp. As she approached Betty gasped in surprise, then laughed in delight. 'Candace. Aunt, if it ain't Candace!'

The two friends hugged each other delightedly. 'I never thought as I'd see you again, Candy.'

'Our friendship is far too precious to let it go.'

'What happened? How did you come here?'

'We will share our stories and our secrets later.'

Betty was impatient. 'Do tell me now.' But Candace shook her head.

'Did you know as I were a-coming?'

'My dear, when I heard from Emily that Adam had taken you to the mansion, I was sorely troubled. We heard news of what had happened and madame sent money for your care.'

'So Emily is here too?' Betty smiled happily.

'Indeed. We'll talk later.'

Madame Farquar had adjusted her skirts to cover her cunny, but her right breast was now very swollen and in desperate need of relief. She drew out the large blue-veined orb and the milk spurted under the pressure.

'Candace, you will call my client. Is he dressed suitably?'

Candace laughed. 'Why, yes, madame, he surely is.'

Madame turned to Betty. 'You will see strange sights and learn of ideas which may surprise you, as they did me at first. However, show no sign that you think anything unusual, for you will soon learn that there are many different tastes and appetites to be satisfied in as many ways.'

'But what shall us do, aunt? Shall us see Emily?'

'All in good time, my dear. For now, remain seated on the stool until the opportunity presents itself for you to join in the fun. Candace, off you go and fetch the Cleric of

Clerkenwell. And do not forget to attend to the Bishop of London.'

'The Bishop of London, aunt! Is he to hear me confession?'

'Not today, Bett. Later. As for the present, the Cleric of Clerkenwell is to be my baby. And a very naughty baby he is, too!'

Betty raised her eyebrows and wriggled excitedly on the stool.

'Now, remember what I said, Bett. Listen carefully. When my naughty baby arrives he must be treated exactly as a real baby. Do not on any account think of him as a man of the church, nor call him by his title. To us, today, and only for today remember, he is little Freddie. Naughty little Freddie, and a very bad boy indeed!'

Chapter Fourteen

Changed Allegiance

Fucking a red-faced magistrate – Impersonation – Anilingus – Grace's torture – Plotting and planning – An ancient secret – Grace escapes – Liza and Parslow

'Well, young hussy, what is your name? And hurry about your business. I do not have all day to deal with the likes of you!' The red-faced magistrate sitting at the centre of the three men glared fiercely at Grace. Standing before the bench Grace felt smaller than she'd ever felt before. She was thoroughly scared. The three distinguished men represented authority, and in their presence she felt intimidated. Suddenly she felt vulnerable. What if they should discover she was only posing as Betty? The papers in her possession would be seized and she'd be thrown in prison. Grace stood quite still, staring dumbly ahead of her. She might be under Father Loughran's instructions to claim the fortune and seduce the magistrate for good measure, but she could not move. She was paralysed with fright.

At last she managed to stammer a few words: 'Sir, sir... I... Yer Honour, sir...'

'Yes, out with it girl. Speak or leave now!'

But Grace could speak no more. She let out a frightened scream, dropped the papers, clapped her hand over her mouth to suppress the noise, and immediately swooned to the floor. Grace had genuinely fainted in terror.

The next thing she knew was that she was lying stark naked on a soft mattress with her hands and feet held by four servants who strained to keep her legs wide apart. Atop her was the red-faced magistrate wildly thrusting his virile member against her motte until at last, after several vain attempts, it pushed inside.

'Hussy! Whore!' The magistrate plunged his enormous cock deep in her cunny and Grace nearly swooned again, but this time with pleasure.

'Oh, sir, you ain't half big. You cock is right up me womb.'

'Not yet whore, but it will be!' Pulling back and summoning his energy, he plunged deeper. Grace flinched slightly, but she was a big girl with plenty of room to take the large member inside her. 'Stuff it up, sir, stuff it up, yer honour.' Grace bucked her hips. She'd not had such a good fuck for months.

'Well, Betty,' the man growled. Of course he knew very well who Grace was, but he was in league with the priest and so kept up the pretence on purpose. 'So you no longer wear the chains and ring of shame.'

'No, master,' Grace simpered in an attempt to sound like Betty.

'But you are a self-confessed sinner.' He continued to thrust in and out with tremendous vigour.

'Yes, master.'

'And to seduce a magistrate is indeed a punishable crime!'

'Yes, master.'

'But you are rich, are you not? The papers say so!'

Grace's eyes lit up. 'Why, yes, sir. I am near on a lady now an' I could give yer money.'

'Ha! But a lady would not fuck and buck as you do my dear. A lady would not enjoy this bestial pleasure as you do.'

The magistrate thrust increasingly quickly and Grace screamed with delight as her orgasm came in huge pulsing throbs. 'Oh sir, oh, sir! Would you marry us, sir, an become a true gennelman?'

'What a fool you are! Bribery and corruption of a magistrate. Impersonation...' He slumped heavily on top of her. Meanwhile the servants had tied Grace's limbs to each corner of the bed. 'The list of crimes is endless. Do you wish to go to prison, Grace?' But she could not answer since he was now heavily astride her with his wilting cock stuffed into her mouth. 'Lick me clean, Grace, and when you have cleaned me thoroughly we shall consider your position.'

Grace swallowed and set to work upon the huge member, working as hard as she could. 'Now for my greatest delight.' The man moved and settled his massive behind over Grace's face, positioning his arsehole over her mouth. 'If you do not wish to go to gaol, then you must work to please me, Grace, in whatever way I choose. Put your tongue right up, my dear.' The magistrate wriggled his hips over Grace to increase the pleasurable sensation. 'Ah, Father, so pleased to see you.'

Father Loughran closed the oak door behind him. 'I see the girl has been exposed in more ways than one. How are the services she performs?'

'So-so.' He grinned. 'Though she does not work as well as one might expect.' He pressed down harder. 'After all, one in her position...'

'Her tongue is obviously in need of some practise, some encouragement. Perhaps she will respond to the demands of the whip!'

'She is already trembling beneath me, Father. The very words are enough to frighten her!'

'Good. We'll omit the confession for today. She will have much sin to confess before the night is out!'

'So, the penance, Father?'

'Indeed, and here is Zillah to help "restore" the ring and chain. Meanwhile, I'll take a turn of her ministrations.' The evil priest lifted his cassock, and as the magistrate stood up, so the priest mounted Grace's face. 'Grace, as you are so willingly to play the part of Betty, we shall allow you to do so. At least while it is convenient to us.' He laughed nastily. 'You are to be pierced, exactly as Betty was. If you are willing, then wriggle your tongue faster, if not, you may go to the dogs!'

Suddenly the priest felt Grace's tongue pushing the tight anal muscle open. She did not relish the thought of wearing the ring and chain of shame, but the thought of the fortune made her desperate to please. Frantically she moved her tongue, wriggling this way and that until she thought it would drop off.

'Do not stop, my child. Do not stop for heaven's sake. You must lick and suck until I spunk! At which point you must open your mouth to receive the vital juices in your throat. Zillah, you may prepare yourself.'

The old gypsy woman took out her instruments, laying them in a neat line along the nearby sideboard. She rubbed her dirty hands together. 'Master, all is ready.'

'One moment, Zillah.' With a final twist of his hips the priest lifted himself up and then aimed the tip of his member at Grace's open mouth, spurting the spunk over her face. 'Lick, girl, lick.' Suddenly the cock was in her mouth and then, almost as suddenly, it was out again. He untied her legs and lifted her buttocks. Then, with her feet over his shoulders the priest pushed his organ into her arsehole. Grace's eyes popped wide open in surprise as her muscles dilated to receive him. 'For your penance, you will say twenty Hail Mary's and you will receive this self-same punishment on a daily basis until I have driven out the Devil. Do I hurt you, my child?'

'No, Father.'

'I thought as much. You are enjoying the Devil's cock! You are, indeed, deep in sin, and cannot receive absolution until you are cleansed to the very core!' And the priest continued to rump away at Grace's bottom until he orgasmed for a second time. After the last tremblings had died down he spoke. 'Zillah will fit the ring and chain and then you are to be married.'

'Married, Father?'

'Yes, married. That is the plan. Of course, if you have any objection...'

But Grace was hardly in a position to object.

'Then all is settled. I shall leave you in the care of Zillah.'

'Well, Richard, what think you?'

'An excellent if somewhat devious plot. We will leave the dates blank on the marriage documents. I doubt your bigamy will ever be discovered. As for the death certificates, they are all prepared and you can decide which ones are needed as the plan unfolds.'

'Have you all the legal documents to hand, the entitlement to the lands and fortune?'

'Do not think, Father, that I am a fool. I must keep these in my possession until it is all over.'

'I thought as much.'

'Tell me, Father, how did you discover the method of insemination? I am sorely puzzled.'

'Ha! And if I tell...?'

'I will be eternally grateful.'

The priest looked thoughtful as he stroked his chin. *You will be eternally grateful sooner than you think!* As he planned to dispose of the magistrate very soon, it would do no harm to give away his secret. He had a boastful streak within him which was rarely exercised. 'Much study and work was involved. In the old Squire's library I discovered an old tome, in an ancient and foreign script. By dint of perseverance I learned its secret contents.'

'Which were?'

'Quite simple. Be patient whilst I explain. Apparently the idea originated in the Himalayas and travelled to Carthage, from whence the theory came to England via the spice trade. The tribesman of the wild mountains have long known that the juices of man contain fertile seeds which grow within the woman's womb to produce a child. But these bandits were constantly warring, and in these circumstances how does one protect one's womenfolk? One of the young bandits, knowing he would eventually be called to ride in battle and leave his betrothed, was particularly concerned. The girl was unusually small and had not begun her natural courses. She was also still a virgin. Worried that she might be accosted by another male in his absence, he summoned his magician who found the solution.'

'Which was? You are tantalising me, Father.'

'Firstly, he devised a kind of chastity belt to prevent even the smallest of male members from entering the beloved's virginal passage. Thus she could be kept chaste. Secondly, he collected the husband's fertile juices and stored them in order to inseminate the girl once she reached the menarche, but without destroying her virginity.'

'How is this done? Surely it would become stagnant and rot!'

'The male must firstly spend into a thick glass container. Immediately this has been done, the contents must be covered in a special paper and then waxed. Thereafter the glass must be placed in ice. Of course in the mountainous climes there is ice to be found at any time of year. The jars can be stored for some while in this condition without affecting the vital fluids. This process can be repeated many times and with as many or few men as is liked. When the female is at her peak of fertility, the middle of the moon phase, she must be filled to capacity with as much of the liquid as is possible for her to take. Day after day the spunk must be fed into her vagina. If she is secured upside-down, so much the better.'

'And that is how Sarah became pregnant?'

'Exactly, for I could not bear to enter a woman in that usual passage the common man appears to find so delightful. That is a revulsion I cannot overcome, so must work around it.' The priest frowned as memories of his childhood spent in a brothel surfaced. Quickly he dismissed the painful images.

'And what of Betty? The real Betty, that is.'

'She too may have my child. If my spunk is stronger than William's and if there was enough, who knows? When the child is born we shall see.'

'Are you certain she is with child?'

'Without a doubt. I discovered the virgin under the tender care of The Sisters of Nommerci.'

'Ah, from your dear friend, the good and trustworthy Sister Ignatius.'

'Exactly, the innocent fool provided the information by accident rather than design. Meanwhile I must keep every possibility open. I cannot fail the church.'

'Do you truly intend to give up all to Rome?'

Father Loughran began to chuckle until the sound developed into a loud laugh and finally an enormous guffaw. His whole frame shook until the tears ran. 'What do you think, Richard? Am I a loyal servant of God and his representative on earth, the Pope?'

'Of course, Father.'

'But the Pope is not here. Indeed, his followers are presently outcasts in England, and as such are not entitled to the ownership of lands. To alert the proper legal authorities would endanger everything. As far as the laws of inheritance are concerned this is a simple case. As far as Rome is concerned, there is the matter of the girl's virginity. If we satisfy Rome in secret, there is no problem. Do you understand?'

'I follow in as far as I can. It is so confusing.'

Father Loughran looked hard at his simple companion. There was a note of derision in his voice. 'I have friends in high places, friends who are prepared to bend and stretch the law providing there is something in it for them. I provide that something. These village girls who confess to me are as clay in my hands. They provide services that even the most experienced whore would blanch at.'

'I see.' But the magistrate was very puzzled and did not "see" at all. However, he'd been promised a fair share of the fortune and thus would go along with the wily priest.

'For goodness sake man. It is simple enough. Ever since the wretched will was written in the first place, those who had an interest have lied, bribed and cheated in order to get their hands on the money and the lands. They have lied to Rome about the girl's virginity and they have pretended that all was within the law of this land. Those who could have exposed the plotters were paid handsomely for their silence.'

'But if the Church of Rome was illegal...'

'It matters not. The Squire's family were convinced that their land would, at some date, be seized. And as a result they have kept possession and accumulated a vast fortune through the spice trade, ready for such time as the Church comes into its own again and makes its presence felt in this land.'

'Ah!'

'And there are other families who have been kept in similar bondage with other, equally ridiculous stories. Avarice is a powerful force.'

'Ah! I think I see it now.'

'Again, it matters not. Suffice it to say that we have a means of keeping the lands and of accessing a vast fortune. Of course I can rely on your discretion, Richard.'

'Naturally.' But the magistrate had begun to have ideas above his station. If he were to get rid of the priest and marry Grace posing as Betty, then the fortune would be his. Or perhaps he could get rid of both Grace and Betty, then wed Betty's sister Sarah instead.

The two men sat thinking for a while, each dwelling on his own greed. But their thoughts were soon interrupted by the sound of screaming. It was Grace. Although in her greed she'd willingly agreed to the piercing of her delicate flesh, she was making as much commotion as possible. Zillah had never liked Grace and had made the whole thing as unpleasant and as painful as she could get away with. Now the two women entered the room. Zillah walked in front, leading Grace who was naked, save for a red corset and the chain around her waist, which joined the ring in her clitoral hood. She was crying and rubbing the tears away with her fist.

'So, the penitent is ready.' But the penitent was *not* ready. The pain and humiliation was more than she could bear. Suddenly Grace gave Zillah an almighty shove and ran out of the room, down a corridor and out into the night air. Shivering, she ran off into the bushes and hid.

'Shall us call the dogs, master?' Zillah rubbed her hands gleefully at the thought of Grace wobbling across the fields chased by a pack of barking hounds.

'Do as you like, Zillah. I have God's work to perform, confessions to hear, penances to give and punishments to deliver. It will occupy me throughout the night, I am certain. The womenfolk of the village are confirmed sinners! Goodnight, Richard.'

Liza and Parslow were settled at the hearth as usual. The kitchen was warm and stuffy, and since they'd consumed a vast quantity of port they'd both nodded off and were snoring loudly. Neither heard the gentle tap tap on the shutters. Outside, wrapped in a miserable sackcloth, stood Grace. Her feet were cut and bleeding and her white body was smeared with mud and covered in scratches. She knocked again, this time more loudly.

'Oi! Parslow! What's that noise you lazy punk? Get up an' find out!'

'Go yerself, you ole hag!'

'Don't you speak to us like that or you'll feel the back o' me hand!'

'Promises. Promises.' Reluctantly Parslow got up, staggered to the door and after a few failed attempts, managed to lift the latch. 'Why, lookee 'ere. If it ain't Grace. I'll be damned and blasted to hell and back again if it ain't Gracie.'

Grace walked in and collapsed into a chair, but the oddly-matched lovers continued arguing and took so little notice of her that even the ring and chains went unobserved.

Liza turned to Parslow, her voice bitter. 'You'll be damned if it is, an' damned if it ain't! Either way you be going to a very warm place. Warmer'n that fire. I promise you!'

'Shut yer mouth, Liza. I ain't ready to leave yet.'

'I know'd I shouldn'a let you back agin! Don't you give me no more on yer cheek. I ain't a-havin' it!'

'No, you ain't a-havin' it no more! You 'ave too much on it. I'm fed up o' you a-havin' it. I'm wore out. See this little man 'ere.' He delved into his breeches and pulled out his cock. 'He were right big an' you shrunk him all up wi' working him too much. Lookee 'ere.'

Suddenly Grace was alert. 'Yer big enough fer me Pars.' Her eyes widened. 'Fancy a bit o' rantum-scantum?'

'No fear. Me cock'll drop off. I'm a-going to bed to sleep. I'm right wore out.'

'Hm. He don't know what work means. I'll catch up on 'im, so I will!' Liza glared at Grace. 'What you a-doin' of?'

'Not much.'

'I can see that. What you done wi' them clothes?'

'I lost 'em.'

'I can see that. Well you'll 'ave to pay. There's no two ways about it. Goodnight!'

'Where's Kit?'

'Run off wi' a whore. Now I said Goodnight.' The door banged after her.

Grace jumped up and was about to follow Liza when she thought better of it. She stood forlornly in the middle of the kitchen. No one here cared whether she lived or died. She had no friends to speak of, no one to help. She sat down again and cried heartily, her breast heaving in distress. Apart from Kit, whose interest was entirely sexual, Betty was the only person who'd ever been kind to her and she'd not done one kindness in return, in fact she'd done quite the opposite. She would find Betty, make it up to her and be her friend.

That's what she would do. Grace lay on the floor next to the dying embers of the fire and wrapped the sacking around her. Exhausted, she soon fell asleep.

Early the next morning, Grace awoke to the sounds of birdsong. She was an early riser and was used to little sleep. The household had not stirred. Grace sat up and decided she would leave as soon as she could, but she would need to find some suitable clothing without disturbing Liza. In the corner there were some dirty clothes, set aside for washing. Grace picked out a blue silk dress last worn by one of the larger whores. Red wine stains were splashed across the bodice and around the full skirt. It smelled slightly musty, but it would do. Hanging behind the door was a large, homespun wool jacket belonging to Kit. That would do as well. Grace took the jacket off the hook. Underneath hung Kit's pocket, bulging with oddments. She tied the pocket around her waist, took a lump of stale bread from a crock on the table, and filled a wooden flask with water from the jug. Once outside, she stopped for her usual pee and then set off in the direction of the City.

Chapter Fifteen

The Cleric of Clerkenwell

Eating sprouts – A stiff-stander – A spanking for Betty – Confession

'Come in, Freddie. Come in.'

The oak door swung halfway open with a creak, and Candace entered holding the plump hand of a large, fat man, who shuffled awkwardly into the room behind her. He was dressed entirely in oversized baby garments; a long robe with smocked yoke, a knitted woollen jacket and stockings, a pair of leather booties, and lastly a bonnet tied under his chin. In his mouth was a large dummy, tied to a ribbon which was pinned to his chest.

'Come to mama. She wants to see you. You've been a naughty, naughty boy.'

The Cleric of Clerkenwell, for it was he, hung his head in shame and blushed to the stubbly roots on his masculine chin. 'Mama,' he cried, attempting a high voice, but with some difficulty since his voice was unusually deep and the dummy stuffed in his mouth was particularly large.

Betty watched, half in fascination, half in dread. She'd thought she might laugh but the scene was deadly serious and she entered into the drama of it quite naturally.

'Mama,' the man cried again.

'Are you ready for your punishment, Freddie?' The man nodded. 'Then come here. And since mama is very full today, you may drink first.'

The cleric got down on his knees and very slowly made his way across the carpet to arrive at madame's feet, whereupon, as a token of respect, he removed her slippers and kissed each dainty foot in turn.

'Oh, Freddie, you naughty boy. Mama did not say you could do that. You will earn a double punishment. Come here and take your drink before I smack you!'

The cleric nuzzled at madame's large breast. She was eager for him to suckle her since her other breast had become very distended and was beginning to pain her. But the cleric in the guise of Freddie was determined to be naughty. He banged his head against her breast and pretended to seek her nipple with his tongue, but all the time avoiding it.

'Nurse!' Madame turned to Candace. 'You must smack him very hard. Agnes, help me with the brat. Can't you see he's playing up?'

Betty sprung up from the stool and took her part. 'Yes aunt. I'm sorry aunt, I were dreaming.' She stuck a finger in the Cleric's mouth and jerked it open. Then, grabbing madame's teat, she pushed it inside and squeezed the nipple so that the milk ran. 'Oh, he is a naughty baby, aunt. I don't know as how you bear it, but once he gets a taste, he'll be good.'

Meanwhile Candace had lifted the nightdress to expose the cleric's naked bottom. She began to beat the fat cheeks mercilessly with a little stick. 'Naughty, Freddie! Naughty boy!'

'Mm. Mm. Ah,' the man murmured and sucked vigorously.

Madame was breathing heavily by now and was obviously enjoying herself immensely. 'Oh, you naughty boy, you naughty boy! What shall I do with you? You will die if you do not eat properly. Nurse, bring me the sprouts.'

Candace left off the beating and fetched the cold vegetables from the sideboard.

'Freddie, you will eat these every day until they are all gone. Look what a mess you are in!' Madame pulled her teat from his mouth and deliberately sprayed the cleric's face with the warm milk. 'You have wasted my lovely milk.

You will go in the corner and eat your sprouts.' She pushed the man away. He crawled abjectly into the corner and bent over the dish of sprouts Candace placed in front of him.

'Set the sand-timer, Nurse. An hour will be good enough to teach Freddie the lesson he deserves. Come niece, we will repair to the other drawing room.'

'Oh, madame, don't go yet a-while. The naughty boy has a stiff-stander.'

'Goodness gracious! Whatever next? I must inspect it. Niece, have you ever seen such a thing!'

'Why no, aunt. I never did. Upon me word.'

The three women were now gathered around the cleric as he knelt humbly in the corner, a dribble of mashed sprouts at the corner of his mouth. Candace lifted the nightgown to reveal his virile member. It was of sizeable proportions and the foreskin had slipped back to reveal its purple tip.

'Why, aunt, whatever is it? I never seed such a thing in all me life. Is it a snake of sorts?'

'In a manner of speaking, my dear, but it won't bite.'

'It don't half *look* poisonous. Can I touch it?'

'By all means play about with the little snake as you wish.'

'I shan't hurt the little snake.'

'Oh, but you should! It is a very naughty thing and deserves a good smacking with the cane!' Madame drew out a small, silver-tipped cane. 'Here, niece, try this.'

Betty took the cane in one hand and held the cleric's member in the other. She felt the veins throbbing under her touch.

'Thprouth,' Freddie demanded.

Candace stuffed a large sprout into the man's open mouth and nodded to Betty, who tapped the penis with the stick. 'Harder than that, my dear. Freddie has been very naughty. Do it like this.' Candace grabbed the cane, and with a glint in her eye, administered several vicious strokes to the stiffened member. Immediately Freddie began to howl. His mouth opened and the mashed sprouts fell out onto the floor.

Candace continued to beat the organ until it seemed as if the very veins would burst. 'Take your punishment you wicked boy, and eat the sprouts off the floor. Lick it clean or else!' Candace allowed the man to bend over and follow the instructions as she began to smack his bottom soundly.

'Why, his behind is quite red!' Betty watched as the cleric's skin flushed redder and redder.

Whilst the girls were thus occupied with the Cleric, madame wheeled out a large commode which she set in the centre of the room. 'Time for business, Freddie.'

Freddie let out a howl, stood up, waddled over to it and sat upon the seat, his prick standing up proudly in front of him. 'Nurthey,' he lisped.

Candace knelt in front of the cleric. 'Oh, Freddie, what a big stiff-stander you have. You cannot use your po with such a big thing there. Nursey will milk you.' Candace took the cock into her mouth and the Cleric sighed as madame then sat beside him and allowed him to suckle her huge teat once more.

'There, there baby. Drinky milky… drinky milky…'

Betty sat on the low stool, her eyes fairly glued to the scene. Madame's breast was softening as the milk drained away, and Candace's head bobbed up and down as she worked skilfully upon the cleric's organ. His eyes had begun to glaze over and his cheeks were flushed as if he were about to reach his peak. But no, for all of a sudden Betty saw his cheeks go rigid and felt his hard gaze upon her. Despite the softening effect of the baby's clothing, his eyes were steely, probing. She lowered her eyelashes and looked away in discomfort. A moment later she could not help but meet his look again. Betty shivered and shook with a strange fear. There was power and cruelty in his eyes. With a slight smirk on his lips the Cleric pulled away from madame's nipple and lisped his orders. 'Thmack lazy Aggie.' Betty sneered in return, meeting his challenge whilst Candace continued to minister vigorously to his virile member.

'Come Agnes. What a naughty girl you are! Sitting there, doing nothing whilst all the household try to please our darling Freddie! Over my knee!' Within seconds, madame was on the stool with Betty over her ample lap, her bottom in the air. With a flourish and a great pretence she began to belabour the girl's rump, and Betty pretended to wail in pain.

But the cleric was not to be fooled so easily. 'Thmack botty! Bare botty!'

Betty lifted her skirts to bare her rump. What a strange picture the scene would have made to any observer; the Cleric still wearing his baby bonnet, Candace sucking his cock and tickling his balls, and madame smacking Betty's bare behind.

The cleric, however, was not yet satisfied. 'Fweddie thmack Aggie!'

Betty started. She was oddly afraid and yet excited too. Madame had not spanked her hard, but her cheeks were glowing and the blood had rushed to her cunny.

Madame bent over Betty, a look of fear in her eyes. She dare not disobey her powerful client, but she'd assured Betty that she'd not be hurt against her wishes. 'Do you wish it, my dear?' she whispered. 'He has only asked for this once before and...' She raised her eyebrows, but refrained from telling Betty that the girl in question had fainted.

Betty hesitated before answering. She was both drawn to and repelled by the man. But she sensed madame's predicament and did not want to disappoint her new friend. 'I wish it, aunt,' she said softly.

Madame stroked Betty's curls gently. 'Do not do it for my sake, dearest girl. You may regret it.'

'Fweddie thmack Aggie. Now!'

'He may hurt you Betty. He is a strong man,' she hissed in Betty's ear. 'The last girl swooned in pain.'

Betty jumped up and smiled at madame. 'I ain't afeard o' pain. Why, a little smacking never hurt no one.' She stepped proudly over to the commode, meeting the cleric's challenge once more. He'd pushed Candace away and his cock stood up, as rigid as a rod of iron. Betty glanced at it scornfully. 'Oh, Freddie, you do have a little, stiffy-stander! What have you been a-doing on? I's a good mind to bite it all off!'

'Freddie thmack naughty Aggie!' There was an odd glint in the man's eye that Betty could not quite make out.

'If you must, but I ain't as naughty as you.' Betty lifted her skirts to expose her pinky rump and settled herself over his large lap, pressing against his distended member. The cleric nodded in dismissal to madame and Candace. Reluctantly they left, leaving Betty at his mercy.

As Betty lay across the cleric's legs, her breast heaving, she became aware of the slow ticking of the clock and of hot breath at her neck. She shivered and her skin prickled into goose pimples as she waited, the hot member pulsing beneath her. Suddenly the cleric's strong left hand gripped Betty's wrists in a vice and his right hand struck her rump.

'Fweddie make Aggie cwy!' There was a vicious element to his voice.

Betty was expecting a sharp slap, at the least, but though the cleric was strong, his touch was nevertheless light and playful.

Behind the panelling, peeping through a hole in the wall, madame and Candace watched the scene.

'Fweddie make Aggie cwy,' he repeated, and a series of light smacks descended upon Betty's vulnerable arse.

'The poor girl seems unperturbed, Candace. Look how she takes it. It is remarkable.'

'She is used to it, madame, and it gives her great pleasure. She receives pain as one tastes the finest champagne and finds it good.'

'I have seen so many strange and wonderful things, Candace, and yet, in truth, I find this "taste" for submission so hard to understand.'

'Perhaps, madame, you have not tried it for yourself.' Candace smiled. 'They say the proof of the pudding is...'

'In the eating... true.'

'And you have not eaten of this fruit. You might find it would excite you, too.'

'I admit that sometimes I am a little bored with the administration of punishment. Perhaps I should... my goodness, Candace, see what is happening now.'

The cleric had torn off his baby's clothing and was completely naked. Betty was crouching over the stool, gripping its legs to prevent herself from slipping. Her arse was covered with the faintest of red blushes and her cunt was split apart so that the gash showed pink. In one hand the cleric held the dummy, which he was alternately pushing into Betty's cunny from behind and then putting in his mouth. In the other hand he held his excited member.

'Naughty, juicy, Aggie.'

'See what the rogue is about to do, Candace! We must stop him! His intention is obvious. A spanking is one thing, a tupping is quite another! Quickly, before he slips it in!' Both women ran into the room, madame keeping up the pretence to avoid upsetting the cleric. But at the selfsame moment, the cleric, who had no intention whatsoever of rumping with Betty, jumped up, threw himself on the couch and gave "Aggie" her orders:

'Aggie suck Fweddie!' he demanded, and spread his legs.

'You naughty boy, Freddie! Nursey, take Aggie to her room. Bread and water for a week! The hussy is far too bold!'

The cleric was livid. 'What is the meaning of this outrageous interruption?' He stood up, and despite herself, madame could not suppress a small giggle. Indeed he did look rather ridiculous, for he was stark naked, sporting a giant erection, and he still wore a pair of pale blue woollen baby stockings. Petulantly, he stamped his foot.

Madame looked at Betty who smiled in affirmation. Even though the spanking was light she was very excited and her cunny was sopping wet. She knelt before the cleric, and pressing her lips to his groin, sucked him in deeply, moaning softly as she breathed his manly scent. She'd enjoyed the fun and games of the last hour and the spanking had greatly titillated her. Now she would indulge in the greatest of pleasures. She would submit to this strange man, perform any service for him, lick and suck him until the fertile juices burned her throat. Betty set to work with a vigour which was astounding, even to herself. She knew she did not love this quirky but powerful man, at least not as she'd loved William. But in some odd way he reminded her of Father Loughran and her desire for submission was strong. The cleric sensed her acquiescence, and placing his hands heavily on her shoulders, began to thrust back and forth deep in her throat.

'Why, Freddie, you are grown into quite a man!' madame exclaimed. 'And Betty, why…'

'Betty? Did you say Betty?' The man paused in mid-stroke. 'Leave me with the girl. When she has finished I would hear her confession.'

'Is it necessary to do so immediately? Surely you can wait until she has committed some more sins? It seems hardly worth the trouble.'

'Leave me, Clemmie. She will not be harmed, I assure you.'

Betty started in surprise. The cleric's natural voice was deep and very gruff. How strange that he should suddenly change so from a baby to a man. But she continued to pleasure him in the best way she knew, running her tongue up and down his member, nibbling his balls from time to time, her small finger creeping slowly around to his arsehole.

'Enough! Betty, you may now grasp that devil's organ, whilst I hear of your sins. And Clemmie, you may leave!'

'Bless me Father, for I have sinned.'

'How long is it since your last confession?' The cleric put his hand on Betty's head. She felt an almost imperceptible pressure.

'Oh, Father. I used to confess every day, but I only just come to the City today. Why, I ain't done it fer a long while.'

Kneeling before the man she clasped his soft hand and kissed the large ring which he'd placed on his finger.

'And yet you are with child, girl.' The cleric stroked Betty's rounded belly. 'Recount your sins, and remember you cannot hide from God.'

'With child, Father? I did not know it. Surely, it cannot be. I am still a virgin.' Betty pressed her hands together and then twiddled with her hair. 'Can it be true?' She thought back to her wedding day. She'd rubbed William's spunk in her cunny in the hope that the old wives' tale would come true. But why was there so much spunk?

'My child, Sister Ignatius informed me of the details of your condition. She did not guess it herself, even though the signs were obvious. She was eager for you to confess your usual sins and in the conversation much was revealed.'

'What shall us do, Father? If what you say is true, I cannot stay here in me present state.'

'I shall consult with Clemmie. Though sinful, she is a good-hearted woman and will do her best for you. I think, perhaps, I should advise a trip to Italy.'

'To Italy? To forin parts?'

'You will be safe there. Remember, there are many parties interested in your inheritance. You must give birth in secret and when the time is ripe, claim the fortune for yourself.'

'Good, good!' Zillah rubbed her hands wickedly. *'She bears a child, but whose child? William's, the Black Prince's, or the priest's? Show me! Show me!'*

Chapter Sixteen

Past is Past, Present Calls, Hereafter Beckons

Liza learns a secret charm – A pact with the Prince of Darkness – Harold's grief – A virgin's birth – Liza and the fucking post

It was chilly in the cottage so Zillah drew a thick woollen cloak around her shoulders and then arranged the shards of crystal in a neat row on the oak table.

'Why ain't you replaced the big glass?'

'The pieces will suffice, Liza, have no fear.'

'Well, you don't have to make do no more.' Liza shivered as she fiddled with the stolen splinter glass in her pocket. She'd tried to conjure the forces by herself, but to no avail. *'There's plenty o' gold to be 'ad, you knows that!'* She looked around the miserable hovel. *'Why you won't spend any o' yer money, I don't know!'*

'Quiet, woman, and watch closely. You might learn summat. Remember, the power to shape hearts and minds is greater and more valuable than all the gold on earth!'

Liza was quite happy to watch since she was hoping to learn more than the old witch had bargained for. She'd watched Zillah closely, listened to her chanting and remembered the spells word for word, but there must be more to it than that. If only she could discover the secret.

Observed by Liza, Zillah began to rock back and forth, chanting her customary spell to conjure the scene. At first all seemed as usual, and then an extraordinary thing happened. As she conjured the dark forces, the separate shards responded differently, each one showing its own picture and telling its own tale. Zillah had accidentally discovered a remarkable quality in the glass, for the stories and scenes they were about to witness would be diverse, though never contradictory.

'There, Liza.' Zillah's bony fingers shook with glee as she held up one of the shards. 'See the trollop at the mercy of Father Loughran. She is confessing, the fool, and he has his hands all over her innocent bubbies! Ha! Look how she trembles in shame!'

Liza leaned over the table to see the picture, jealousy and hatred rearing as she recognised her hated foe. 'She deserves to be shamed, the hussy! Whipped to within a hair's breadth of her life! What would I not give to see her suffer the filthiest poverty on earth, and after a long life of misery, damned to the fires of hell?!'

Zillah smiled craftily. 'Your soul, perhaps?' She spoke soothingly. 'Your soul, Liza, would you give your soul?'

'Soul! Soul! There ain't no such thing, an' if there were I'd give it willingly to see the chit debauched in the foulest way imaginable, suffering from all manner of poxes, reduced to penury, rags an' the poorhouse!' Liza pursed her lips grimly and her voice lowered. 'Oh, what I would not give!'

One of Zillah's eyes had begun to fail her and she'd been finding it very tiring of late to read the scenes, so it would be useful to have an able companion in her old age. 'If it be within my power you shall have your desire,' Zillah dissimulated. 'A pact with the Prince of Darkness is easily made.'

'Then do it, and do it soon afore I change me mind!'

Zillah grasped Liza's hands in her own and began to whisper all sorts of profanities, spells, and strange unintelligible mutterings. 'Try for yourself, Liza, try for yourself.'

And Liza followed the wicked hag's example, only this time it seemed to work.

'See, see the shards are clearing! The Prince of Darkness

has accepted you as one of us! Ha! Ha!'

Zillah and Liza watched each splinter in turn as they gradually began to changed from opaque, to a light cloudiness, finally to clarity.

'Find a clear one an' tell me what you see.'

Liza picked up one of the shards and threw it down. 'There ain't nothin' there.' She picked up another, then another. 'Why, Zillah, they's all different!'

'Gimme, here!' Zillah stared at the fragments in her hand. 'So it is possible, after all.' She looked at Liza admiringly and spoke under her breath. 'You are more tainted than I thought. Ha! The Devils progeny to be sure.' And then aloud: 'Choose one and tell me what you see.'

'I see Harold. He's staring out of a window high in a Tower. And the fool is crying at Betty's loss. I can hear him muttering to himself.'

'Why, oh why, dear Christ, did You take her to Your eternal bosom, to be Your bride and not mine? Why, oh why, my darling Betty did you have to go! I would have married you! Oh, oh my love, my love! Without your sweetness and your light, life is meaningless. My heart is as empty as the barren hills before me. What does it mean that I own these towering stones and these desolate lands if I have not you to hold in my arms? See, see this knife, my sweet. I shall plunge it deep in the flesh till it reaches the heart and makes the fatal wound. Thus I'll be reunited with you forever!'

'He has a knife! Ah, the picture fades.'

'So he goes to Clancy Towers after all. Good! Just as I planned. Good! And he mourns Betty's...'

'Death, Zillah... death?'

'Be careful of your interpretation, Liza, the girl may merely be incarcerated in a convent. It does not do to surmise too much. There is often trickery in the glass. Try another.'

'I see Betty's Aunt Rowena, an' she's surrounded by

children o' many hues.'
  'Many hues, eh? It fits, it fits!'
  'Hush, they's speaking.'

'Aunt Rowena. When will mother come? I miss her so.'
  'Soon, Felix, soon.'
  'But you always say that and she never comes.' Felix, the youngest of Betty's boys and the progeny of the priest, was very tender-hearted. He began to cry.
  'Don't cry, Feli. Aunt is right.' Little Gita, the middle child, who was named after Betty's dear friend, stroked his head. 'I know mother will be here soon. I dreamed it.' She smiled vaguely. Gita was the very image of Betty except for her dark skin which, by contrast, rendered the blondeness of her curls a pure white. 'An' I have the letter!'
  'Goodness, you haven't been a-reading again?' Rowena pretended shock. 'It did your mother not a jot of good. It will land you in all sorts of trouble.'
  'Well, how am I to understand ma's letter if I can't read?'
  'That is exactly the sort of thing Bett would have said herself.' She turned to her female companion. 'Isn't it marvellous, she has spent so little time with her mother and yet she is so like, so like.'
  Gita stamped her foot and nudged William. 'She *will* come, won't she Will? Ma *will* come to see us? An' she loves us too! Why, she sent us gifts.'
  William, the firstborn of Betty's triplets, pulled an ugly face and spoke up rudely. '*I* do not remember when I last saw mother. Indeed I wonder sometimes if we *do* have a mother at all!'
  'William, how dare you say such things!'
  'I do dare! And what of these gifts? I can't wear pink stones around my neck like Gita, and the silly red marble mother sent is no use at all! Why, it won't roll!'
  'William, be silent!'
  'Furthermore,' William continued, his father's aggressive

demeanour and gift of speech evident, 'it does not appear we have a father either, for none of us has seen him!'

'I have.' Felix thought of his recurrent nightmare. 'I saw father in a dream. He had three heads and they were all different. One was...'

Rowena sighed. 'Quiet, Felix. Enough of your nonsense.' She knew the ugly subject would arise again. The children were growing up rapidly and constantly asking questions. Naturally they did not ask Rowena directly, but enquiries had been made through the servants. Of course the triplets need not be told the bizarre story of their parentage at all, but the information would be better coming from her rather than the kitchen. But how on earth could she bring herself to tell the triplets the whole truth? It was barely believable to an adult, let alone a child. Suddenly she decided that something must be done.

'Children, gather round. It is time you heard Betty's story.' And so Aunt Rowena told some, though by no means all, of the truth. She was a sensible woman and thought to make concession to their tender age, but being unused to children, she knew not how. However, she told the tale as well as she was able. What the small things made of it is anybody's guess.

'Some while ago Squire William, your mother's husband, had been conscripted to serve in Our Majesty's Navy. Your dear mother, being on hard times, was forced to make a living as best she could.

'She was pure in heart, and like the Virgin Mary, kept herself intact, though for a different reason. If she gave birth and remained a virgin, she would inherit the family fortune. Well, without sacrificing her hymen, Betty became with child, but there was witchery and plotting afoot and it was necessary for her to escape from her enemies. With the help of Madame Farquar I travelled with Betty to hide in the mountains of Italy, where I remain as your guardian under the garrisoned protection of madame's esteemed brother.

'Here, within these very walls, she gave birth to triplets,' she smiled at the children as she came to the difficult part, 'each one very different, my dears, as you well know. Different my dears, because each one has a different father.'

Rowena had expected one of the children to ask how that had come about, but since they knew nothing of the processes of reproduction, their innocent minds did not beg the question.

'So you see, my children, each of you has but one shared mother and yet each of you has your own father.'

'Well,' said the quarrelsome William, 'I expect *my* father is *far* more handsome, stronger and *far* more gentlemanly than yours, Felix!' He pushed at his brother, who began to cry.

'I don't see how your father could be more handsome than *mine*,' Gita argued. 'I am more handsome than you, so *my* father must be more handsome than yours.'

'Well, I am taller than you, so mine is taller, and taller is bigger, and bigger is better, and better is wiser!' William gave Gita a small push on the shoulder, to which she responded by a hard kick on the shins.

Poor little Felix, good-hearted but the runt of the litter, sat sucking his thumb and fingering the ruby in his pocket. He dared not enter the quarrel. Gita would be sure to get the better of him in words and William would punch him if he did not agree. 'Aunt Rowena,' he plucked at her dress, 'why did mother go away?'

'My dear, against all sensible advice, she walked outside the walls and was spirited clean away.' Rowena pulled the little boy onto her lap. 'She is in a faraway clime, high in the Himalayan mountains, but she is safe, for her letters tell us so. She awaits the Master. Soon we will be reunited with her and...' she paused, for this part was difficult, '...one of you will meet your father, who must needs be a father to you all.'

'Curses, the picture fades!'

'It is the way of the glass, Liza. Try another.'

'Hm. I see Edmund. We knows him of old.'

'William's older brother, the scoundrel, and his beautiful Indian princess, no doubt?'

'It must be her, for she's a little darker complexioned than he, an' she wears them forin robes, same as wot Gita wore when she arrived at the mansion, only they's richer an' she wears much gold.'

'What are they doing?'

'Quarrelling. An' she's big with child an' all!'

'I care not for this cold country of yours, and as for the ridiculous Will, why, it is a madness! I shall not endure your so-called "virgin" birth! I shall not! Not for all the riches in the world. And that is the end of it!'

'It is only a little stitch, just for show. Once the priest has seen the closed aperture, along with your large belly, he will be satisfied. It can then be cut.'

'Stitched, stitched! Stitched and then cut! How dare you suggest it!' The princess was near screaming point. 'I shall not be stitched! And I shall not be cut!'

Edmund was beside himself. 'Where is the humble, obedient wife your father promised?'

'Ha, you fool, I was sold to you because I would not submit to his authority! I refused to lower my eyes before my father, my brothers and even my husband-to-be! No matter how they beat me, I would not submit! I would not lower my eyes! My father was all for turning me out with the clothes I stood up in but my mother begged him to sell me instead, claiming it would be more profitable, which, of course, it was. Sir, you have been entirely fooled! If I would not surrender to those who had the power of life and death over me, do you think I would defer to you? A paltry lover who thinks more of a man's rear parts than women's charms!' The princess stormed out of the room.

Liza turned to Zillah. 'Poor Edmund,' she laughed. 'It don't look like he's a-getting his way!'

'Pah, he is more of a fool than I thought. Here is the perfect opportunity to claim the fortune. With Betty presumed dead, with William away, his wife about to give birth, what better advantage can he have?'

'He's weak. Allus was.'

'Not as weak as you think. The belladonna Mistress Emma gave him was enough to kill a horse. I should know. I sold it to her.'

'Well there's that forin fever, Yellow Fever. I hear 'e still 'as the bouts.'

'They say the Yellow Fever addles the brain, not that Edmund ever had much brain to addle!'

'They says right. I know how to master a wife more'n he does. Mind you, Zillah, they allus said he prefers the company o' lads to that o' women. An' where 'e wants to put his cock is nobody's business!' At the thought of the man's cock Liza's hand went straight up her skirts to her cunt and she began to finger herself furiously. 'Mind you, he had big enough ballocks when he was a lad hisself.' She paused to take a breath. 'What wi' him an' William, an the grooms, old Nursey had as good a time as can be got by an old maid wi' the care o' lads. Why, I remember...'

'Never mind that, choose another glass.'

'I think as I'll 'ave this one. It's smaller'n the rest so may be it won't 'ave so much in it.' Liza carried on rubbing her cunt with the other hand. 'To tell yer the truth, Zillah, I could do wi' some rantum-scantum. This crystal lark 'as fair wore me brain out, I can tell yer!'

'Finish with the glass, then try the broomstick, dearie, now you're one of us.'

'Who'd ha' thought it, eh? I see Grace. She's standing in the street a-crying. I reckon she's gone an' got 'erself lost in the City o' Lonnen. Serve 'er right, the bitch. She *shouldn'a left, that's what I say!'*

Liza put down the glass. 'Well, I ain't done too bad, 'sidering I ain't never done the like afore. What say you, Zillah?'

'I say, it's time to fuck and buck and suck! Go fetch the fucking post, me dearie, and we'll conjure what we will!'

Chapter Seventeen

Into the Fire

The conjuring of dreams – Prepared for the Master – Sucked by a slave girl – Dance of the Sacred Snakes – The yoni and the lingam – A pee before a prince – Sucking an arsehole – Strict punishment – Betty finally fucks

Zillah petted the black familiar settled half-sleeping, half-awake in her lap. She stroked his smooth fur, running her craggy fingers from his head to the tip of his tail, which he extended especially for the purpose.

'Well, my own dear prince, we must reach Betty in her dreams.' The cat winked his yellow eye, as if in agreement, stirred slightly and began to purr. Meanwhile Zillah peered into her glass and started to rock back and forth as usual. 'Past is past, present calls, hereafter beckons... Yes, there she is. Ha ha! We shall see, we shall see, shan't we black one? Such clever dreams must be carefully conjured! Ah! The mountain air again and the Black Prince riding, riding... and Betty falling, falling into the fires of hell!' The witch uttered a scream, thus startling her feline companion who jumped up and ran out into the black of night.

'Wake up. The time has come!' Vashna pulled Betty to her feet. 'You are to be washed and dressed.'

'I can wash and dress meself.' Betty spoke petulantly and shrugged the intrusive hands away. 'I don't need servants. I ain't used to them.'

'You'll become accustomed in time.'

'But I ain't staying here that long.'

Vashna took no notice of the last remark. 'Surely, in your own country, the favourite of the prince has many slaves to do her bidding.'

'But you ain't doing me bidding. I tell you I can wash meself.' Betty frowned at the ring of dark women surrounding her bed. Then she jumped up and stamped her foot crossly. 'Go away!'

Vashna put an arm around Betty's shoulders. 'My dear, we are here to pleasure the prince but also to help you achieve your pleasure too, for here in this mountain hideaway, the two are one. The art of erotic awakening is ancient. You must know that the prince is a Tantrik, and as such he must be nurtured.'

'A Tantrik? Why, Gita told me o' such men and it seems they have powers o' giving and receiving pleasure beyond a woman's maddest dreams.'

'Indeed, our prince is such a one. But since he has been delayed on his arduous journey he has sent word that we should begin the preliminary stimulation. Your pleasure will be increased if you are thoroughly prepared for the Black Prince. Our ritual will cleanse both body and soul, rendering you the perfect receptacle, the lotus flower to his bee.'

'So I must accept his...'

'My dear, you are playing too naïve. You know why you are here, and in reality you do not object.'

'How can the prince need me, with all these beauties about the place? I ain't never seen a man here. Where is they?' Surreptitiously Betty slipped her hand under the voluminous silk robes. She'd been dreaming of the absent prince, of how he might couple with her, and her cunny was quite wet already. She slipped a finger between the lips, which parted in readiness.

Vashna smiled; although the bedchamber was dark she knew exactly what Betty was doing.

'Your delicate maiden yoni must be prepared for the entrance of the Master's lingam tomorrow. Together we will find the saspanda and play with it until the kama salila flows, and your lotus flower expands in readiness to receive your masterful prince.'

Betty carefully studied each of the women in turn. Their faces were not unkind and they appeared eager to carry out their assigned task. Although she'd not come willingly, there was no escape from this mountain palace, and little point in resisting when exquisite pleasure was to be had.

'What shall us do?'

'Good, good. Her thoughts are as malleable as wetted clay!' Zillah suddenly realised the black cat had gone. *'So you have flown, dear Prince, flown to the darkest corners of the earth, whence you will poison innocent dreams.'*

'We are experts in the art of self-loving. Remember, we spend much time alone. It is so much more rewarding to contemplate one's yoni rather than one's navel.' Vashna held Betty's hand in hers and squeezed it. 'Come.'

Together with the other slaves, Betty was led from her dark and cosy bedchamber, across the internal courtyard, and into the bathing area. Here they stripped Betty of her clothing, bathed her in a deep pool of perfumed water and rubbed her skin in scented oils, paying particular attention to the most intimate parts of her body.

'What a funny little flower she has,' Chandra, one of the younger slaves, laughed as she rubbed at Betty's cunny. 'Even smaller than mine. I doubt if the tip of the Master's member would fit there.' The woman bent over Betty who by now lay supine on a padded bench, her legs relaxed and splayed apart, thus giving the women complete access to every part of her naked body. What they were most interested in was her cunny.

'Haven't you tried stretching it a little?' She wriggled a finger inside, then another. 'Not quite as tight as I thought. Mitra, will you help tickle this lotus bud?'

Using her two fingers, Chandra stimulated Betty's unstretched vagina, whilst Mitra gently centred on Betty's clitoris. At first Betty kept still, delaying her orgasm as the fingers worked, but it was almost impossible. 'Oh, Chandra, I can't bear it! I shall go mad!' Betty arched her back to avoid Mitra's infuriating finger, which was rubbing and rubbing deliciously over her swollen clitty.

'Mad, mad with what?' Chandra asked in innocent pretence. 'Do you like this, Betty? Your beautiful saspanda swells so under my fingers.' The young woman's expert fingers had begun to thrust against the upper side of Betty's vaginal passage with firm, rhythmic strokes. 'The plum swells! I feel the plum swell so!'

'Oh, Chandra... ah! Ah! I shall spend!'

Mitra's fingers were now circling firmly around Betty's clitoris and then between the cleft, sometimes meeting Chandra's hand, which continued to pump evenly, and then a finger titillating Betty's anus.

'But you must not spend, not yet. Wait for further pleasures if you can.'

'I cannot help it. I cannot help it! Ahhh...' With a shudder, Betty's hips bucked and reared so fiercely that the women had to hold her limbs for fear she should roll off the bench.

'Quick, Vashna, quick, she is one of the chosen, see, see, gather round.' Chandra withdrew her dripping fingers and showed them to the women. 'See how much juice she has.'

'We must try to make it flow again.'

'And drink of its life-giving properties, before we release the flower, fully opened, for her Master.'

'Come, Betty, you must kneel up.'

'What you going to do?' Betty's face was flushed with her release. 'Is summat wrong?'

'No, my dear Betty. Listen, it is well known amongst our people that the flowing juices of the third stage emanating from a virgin have life-preserving properties, which to many are extremely valuable. And we aim to collect as much of your juice as we can. Some we shall drink and some we shall sell.'

'Sell? Sell me juices? Why, them as buys and sells it must be mad!'

'Not so, for it will fetch a good price. Now, there are three distinct juices of the yoni. The first is small, a little trickle, similar to the pearl found dripping from the man's glossy head. Then there is the abundant and sticky juice of lubrication, enabling the thickest of member to penetrate and plunge deeply without hurt to it. Lastly, there are the spraying juices. Few women possess these. Even fewer find them, but once discovered, a girl can learn to spray almost of her own volition. Put your legs apart Betty, and I will show you from whence they come.'

Mitra fetched a silver mirror and placed it in a convenient position. The metal had been highly polished, and beautifully reflected every contour of Betty's flesh.

'Have you studied your flesh, my dear? Studied your sacred parts, your beautiful flower?'

'Why no.' Betty was suddenly both surprised and ashamed. 'I never thought to look close up since I were a child.' Betty stared at her reflection. 'It do look so nice.'

'See, here is your delicate clitoris.' Vashna pulled the ring piercing in Betty's clitoral hood to expose the tip of the delicate organ. 'See how pretty it is? What woman could resist tickling it with her tongue?' Her eyes gleamed as she licked up the slit in Betty's mound.

'Well, I sort o' seen me clitty. I bent over to look once when I were small, but Felan caught me and give me a whipping.'

'And here, Betty, is the tiny hole which gives off your usual water. And here, each side of it, the magic sluice, invisible to the eye, from whence your third juices emanated so rapidly just now.'

'It don't look much to me. I can't see nothing.'

'Perhaps not, but with more study you shall. Now we must

hurry and see if we cannot milk you of your essence and prepare you for the Master, too.'

'Yes, for our play will increase your passion for the Master and thus your most intense enjoyment.' Mitra laughed. 'When we have finished pleasuring you, your thoughts will dwell entirely upon the prince and his desires, and you will be unable to refuse him whatever his size.'

'Is he very large?'

'Beautifully so.' Mitra smiled dreamily.

'Well,' an older woman nudged Mitra and laughed coarsely, 'how should *you* know of the size of the Master's love stick, eh?'

'Oh, it's enormous!' The girl's eyes widened. 'So large, he plunges to the very depth of one's soul!' She giggled. 'Well, of course I haven't seen it for myself, but they do say so.'

The old woman laughed scornfully. 'Not seen it for yourself. What is this world coming to if the Master has not fulfilled his duty with every slave? In my day...'

'Never mind about *your* day,' Vashna interposed sharply. 'It is Betty's day and she must be prepared for the prince.'

At last the women were finished and Betty was now tired. She had not quite recovered from her long journey over land and sea, and she'd not yet acclimatised to the thin air in the high mountain peaks. She lay on the cushions in her bedchamber trying hard to get to sleep. Vashna had planned to wake Betty before sunrise, so it was essential that Betty rest. The Master could arrive at any time, perhaps at the crack of dawn, and all must be ready for him!

'You are sure to need a little stimulation beforehand, my dear. If you are not wet enough, it could damage the prince's sacred lingam. I would never forgive myself it that were allowed to happen.'

'Oh, I's allus wet, Vashna. Me cunny ain't never been dry in me life. I can't help a-rubbing it, you see. It's such a nice thing to do.'

'Would you like a little girl company to help you sleep?'

'I's so tired, I don't know as I need any help.'

Vashna persisted. 'I have a sweet little slave who would help you. She is a young woman, though she looks more of a girl since she is so tiny. The poor creature was born deaf and is therefore also dumb. She has seen you and has asked in her sign language if she may be *your* slave tonight? Your yoni slave. She is so willing, it would be a shame not to let her pleasure you. Besides, she is extremely beautiful and has a wonderful tongue.'

For once Betty felt too tired and the offer did not seem exciting, but she did not like to reject the girl, and so agreed. A few moments later the pair were settled on the cushions together, all covered with a light silk counterpane, the girl at Betty's cunny softly licking, and Betty laid back, her legs splayed wide.

'Don't forget, I shall fetch you early in person.'

Still tired, Betty dozed off with the girl still gently lapping at her cunt. It was not to be a restful sleep at first, for the dreams *would* come. Every so often Betty would moan in her sleep and her thumb would go to her mouth, but when her hand unconsciously sought to comfort her cunny, she found the slave girl had pre-empted her.

'Betty!' It was Vashna. 'Are you ready now?' Betty was still curled up on the cushions, the girl slave sleeping at her cunny, her nose buried in the cleft. The room was warm and the richly embroidered silk cloth had been sufficient to keep them comfortable but Betty, usually the early riser, was still tired.

'Not yet, not yet. I's still weary.'

'Then I shall awaken you, my dear.' Vashna crept under the coverlet, and by the time she'd finished her ministrations Betty was flowing with juices but was still sound asleep.

'Come, come! Dance for me!' The prince woke Betty from

her sleep and gently lifted her. She looked up in surprise, then quickly lowered her eyes.

'I would have you display your physical charms in all their detail. Let there be music!' Although the room appeared empty apart from Betty and the Black Prince, his order was immediately obeyed and a small group of plainly dressed blind musicians with various oriental instruments, filed into the palatial room. They set up discreetly in a corner behind an ornate carved screen, principally so that they could not be seen by the occupants.

Within moments, Betty was dancing to the unfamiliar but enchanting notes. Her lithe figure responded naturally, and the delicate silk robes, at one moment illuminated, at another silhouetted, flowed gently with the beat. At first her movements were slow, though never clumsy, but as the tempo increased, so she became faster and more frantic.

The Black Prince watched entranced, his head moving rhythmically with hers, his eyes following each limb as it traced flickering shadows on the walls. Apart from the head, his body was motionless, his face passive, but there was fire in his yellow eyes.

'You must dance with the sacred snake.'

Tossing her curls away from her eyes, Betty took a sideways view of the Master. Yes, there was the pink, swelling tip emerging from the dark furriness between his legs. She was about to move nearer to accommodate him when a young girl slave appeared with a large snake cradled in her arms. Betty's eyes started and she stepped back, in her haste treading onto the corner of her silk robe.

The Master laughed. 'Take it. It is not poisonous.'

'If it were, Master, I should take it all the same if it were your command.' Betty took the mighty snake over her shoulders. It was not as heavy as she'd imagined. The creature coiled its dry tail around Betty's waist whilst the head slithered over her hips and down one leg, its tongue flicking.

'The Dance of the Sacred Snake.' The Master clapped his hands.

Suddenly the music changed to a slow, pulsating, eerie rhythm, and the room was crowded with naked women, each one carrying a large snake. Moments later, Betty was naked too, the women having gathered around and removed every last stitch. Without speaking, one of them signalled to Betty to copy her movements, and before long she'd mastered the primitive swaying motions. Carefully the women held the snakes in their arms, for it would not do to harm the sacred beasts, slid them about their naked bodies, finally holding them high for adoration.

Suddenly the Master clapped his hands and the women were gone, taking the snake with them.

'Betty.' The prince's tone was at once strict and gentle. 'Show me your beautiful yoni.'

'Why, sir, you ain't kissed me yet.'

'I shall kiss your yoni. Come here and stand near me.'

Betty walked over to face the prince. 'Sir, Master, Prince,' she knelt before him, 'I shall do your will.'

'Then show me your most intimate and beautiful part.'

The prince, in customary fashion, was seated on the cushions. Betty placed a low stool before him so she could sit astride it and show him the object of his desire. With eyes downcast and with trembling heart she grasped the two lines of golden hairs that ran along the outer lips.

'There, sir,' she pulled her cunny-lips apart a little, 'you see it, do you not?'

'I see it but do not see enough. Can you not open wider?'

'Why, sir, I's small, but see, I shall try.' This time Betty tugged at the hair with greater force.

'There, sir, I can't show no more'n that.' Betty's face coloured pink as she opened her cunny as wide as she could.

'Hm, now for some discipline.' The prince leaned back and closed his eyes. 'Stay in that position, Betty, until I give you leave to move.'

Betty remained as still as she could, for as long as she could, all the while being examined by the prince's watchful eyes. But the urge to urinate had got the better of her.

'Master, may I move? I think as I'm going to pee!'

'You may pee, but do not, on any account move.'

'Pee here, sir? Pee here, afore yer very eyes?'

'Yes, Betty, yes, before my very eyes, and I shall draw closer to observe your humiliation and shame more fully.'

'Vashna had not spoken of humiliation, or of shame, only of pleasure. Did Vashna and the other slaves truly know their master? Or had they lied?'

'Oh, sir, I don't know as I *can* pee afore you. It will not come.'

'Oh, but it will.' The Master stood up and came behind Betty. He squeezed her breasts first, nipping the teats sharply. Then his hands went to her belly. 'Relax, Betty, relax. See how easy it is when you try your best.' The prince pressed her belly with one hand and her clitoris with the other. 'Good, good. Pee, Betty, pee...' He rubbed her clitoris, pressed her belly, then sought the inner petals of her lotus flower at which stimulation, Betty orgasmed and peed simultaneously.

'Oh sir, I am spending, I am spending... Ah... ah!'

'Have I given you pleasure, Betty?'

'Yes, Master.'

'Then give me mine. Worship and adore my divine body.'

Betty prostrated herself before the prince, who by now was seated on the low couch. 'Master, beautiful Master.'

'Attend to my feet.'

Betty crawled nearer to her Master and found his feet. With thumb and forefinger, she twiddled each of his toes in turn, then nibbled and licked around his ankles, her soft white cheeks rubbing against the bones.

The Black Prince purred quietly and leaned contentedly into the plump couch whilst Betty worshipped his feet.

'Such soft pads.' She quivered her eyelashes over the soft soles of his feet. 'A butterfly kiss for the Master.' Gently, her lashes fluttered over the tender underskin. 'Master,' she murmured. She latched her lips over his little toe and sucked it into her mouth, first curling her tongue over the dark hairs and then plunging it down the gap between that and the adjacent toe. The prince stretched his legs dreamily and spread his toes wide.

'Just as I hoped, she dreams only of her humiliation. Ah, my dear familiar, my Black Prince of the darkest nights, do your foulest work. Poison her dreams. Love falsely and be loved truly, eat her very heart with deceitful kindness. Stoke the fires of passion, pausing only to laugh afore the kill! Ah! Hereafter beckons.' Zillah rubbed her dry palms together, then cracked her bony knuckles one by one. *'Forces of evil, aid me!'*

Betty lay prostrate, her golden hair a wild frothy tangle tumbling over her naked shoulders and over the prince's black legs. 'I would serve you, Master.' She ran her face up his leg, licking and sucking until she reached the tender inner part, then nuzzled her face into his groin.

'Then, soft slave,' he gathered her hair, 'you must satisfy my every desire, obey my every command. No task is above or beneath you. When you have finished ministering to my extremities, then I shall allow you to tend to that excellent princely part which, in the grooming, will most abase you. At present, all I require is your abject humiliation, nothing more or less. Proceed.'

'Master,' Betty swallowed, her saliva catching in her throat. 'My sole desire is to obey you, whatever your whim. But I don't know as what you mean, sir. What part, sir?'

'Is this a wilful lacking in your character? A slave must, at all times, guess the Master's whim, and guess correctly too, for the punishments for recalcitrance are most severe. Do not think the whiteness of your skin will spare you.'

'Master, I understand. I have attended to your beautiful

feet and now must worship the lingam.'

'No, Betty, no, not yet. That princely part is last on the list. So you think it humiliating to worship the lingam? You must be punished for that blasphemy! You have one chance for a reprieve. Speak.'

'Sir, oh sir,' Betty sighed deeply. She was full of shame and yet excited too. 'Sir, must I pleasure the forbidden place?'

'Indeed you must, but I sense a degree of reluctance on your part. You will be punished all the same.'

'Sir, that ain't fair!'

'Fair, Betty, fair?! I am your Master and you must bend to my will. Kneel behind me and wet your tongue.'

The prince knelt with Betty behind him. She nuzzled into the soft flesh and parted his arse-cheeks.

'Lick, Betty, lick, and pray thereafter that your punishment be light!'

Betty gripped the prince's arse in her small hands and swept her tongue up the deep cleft to finally rest on the tight closure. She wriggled her tongue around and around the circular muscle, gradually insinuating it into the tight ring.

'Push, Betty, push. I must have your tongue deep inside me.'

Betty pushed with all her might and her tongue slipped inside the puckered hole and as deep within as it would go.

'Suck, Betty, suck!'

Betty withdrew her tongue and with her lips sucked hard at the flesh, simultaneously wetting it with her tongue.

'Now for your arse.'

Suddenly the prince was behind Betty, in one hand the enormous cock, in the other a short but lethal-looking cane.

Betty still knelt on the floor, but now her head hung low and her arse upraised.

'Open your legs to me! Open your cunt to me!'

'Master, Master, I shall do your will.'

The Black Prince lifted the cane and struck Betty's rump. Once, twice, thrice.

'There, have you punishment enough?'

'No, Master, no! Whatever your will, it is mine to endure. Lash me, lash me if you will. I am yours. My white flesh is yours for the taking, yours to discipline as you must. And I humbly accept me just chastisement.'

'Huh, a pretty speech, designed and rehearsed, no doubt, so that I might feel sorry for you and thus minimise the penalty.' Then the prince struck the cruellest of blows, right between the cleft, and despite her tolerance of pain, Betty howled louder than she'd ever done before.

'Take me, sir. Take me. Fuck me to the core! I am yours forever! Ah!'

The prince mounted Betty from behind. He felt for her tight cunny and pushed his fingers, then his hand, then his fist, against the closed door. 'Open, Betty, open!'

With the other hand he drew back the foreskin of his cock and then settled the tip at the door.

'My sweet, my sweet white slave, open to me, open to me.'

Betty stretched her legs as wide apart as they would go, and with one hand guided the prince to his rightful destination. 'Fuck me, Master, fuck me!'

'Betty, sweet Betty, I shall fuck you and whip you till the breath is drawn from your body!'

In her sleep, Betty's little hand went to her cunny and she rubbed madly, 'Oh sir, oh sir...' she murmured in her dream. 'Fuck me! Fuck me!'

And in the dream he plugged her to the very depths.

'Bless me Father, for I have sinned.'

'Tell me, Betty, and spare no intimate detail of your sin, for God sees all.'

If he sees all, thought Betty, why did she need to tell the priest what she done?

'Well, my child? I know by your voice you have been a-sucking. What did you suck, Betty?'

'I sucked eggs, Father.'

'Is that all? Did you perform anilingus?'

'Why, no, Father, I only sucked the prince's arse. I didn't do nothing like that.'

'And did you perform fellatio?'

'Why yes, Father, I sucked the prince's feet good and proper. That's what I done.'

'But, I repeat, did you place your mouth upon his member?'

'Oh no, Father, I never sucked the prince's nob. I's not guilty. But I would o' done it, only I never did.'

'Oh, but you lie! Did you copulate with him Betty, did you copulate?'

'No, Father!' Betty was indignant. 'I fucked him, that's all. I didn't do nothing else.'

'You are wicked, Betty, and deserve the fires of hell. But God is good. For your penance you will say a thousand Hail Mary's.'

'A thousand, Father? How many's that? I don't know as I can count that much.'

'Then you will burn in the fires of hell!'

'And you will burn with me!'

Betty tossed and turned, her body drenched in sweat.

Suddenly she was falling, falling. She jerked her foot to stop the pace and all of a sudden Betty was awake.

The Final Chapter

Betty Serves the Master

1783 – Hideaway in the Himalayas – The Master returns – Florence's poison – Mother of sons – Lesbian lust – A nasty tale – A surprise for Betty – The spilling of virgin blood – Just desserts for a witch

Shading her eyes from the glaring winter sun, Betty tried to make out the features of the distant rider ascending the ridge. The man was too far away to be recognised, but in any case his face was bandaged with a black protective cloth. In the clear Himalayan light Betty watched the stallion step delicately on the narrow ledges under the rider's expert guidance.

'Are you sure it be the prince, Florence?' Betty jumped down from the narrow stone sill where she'd been perching, her bracelets and anklets jangling musically. 'He's all alone. Don't he have no servants?'

'He likes to ride that path alone. Since no one but His Eminence has the skill to navigate a horse in these treacherous hills, he is perfectly safe.'

'Well I know an English gennelman as could ride up them hills. Why, William, he could ride them blindfold. He were the best...'

'I am sure you mean what you say, my dear, but I'm afraid there is no point in you hoping that William, or any other English gentleman, will rescue you.' Florence smiled strangely, thinking *more's the pity!* 'I wonder why he has come so early.' She glanced jealously at Betty, guessing the reason for the Master's hasty return.

'I don't know as I want to meet the prince no more. I had such dreams last night.'

'Why, my dear, there is no need to be afraid.' Florence lied with confidence. 'If you obey his every whim he'll be gentle with you. Remember, he knows the ways of women well. He has deflowered many a virgin in his travels overseas and in the confines of the temple has made short work of at least ten score girls, including myself.'

'More'n ten score virgins? So many lovers? That can't be true.'

'My dear, you look surprised.' The young woman laughed. 'Think of it this way. The Master, being in his prime, is bursting with seed which must be sown. It would be a sin against his God to spill the precious grain, so he must plant it. What better for a virile man in his position than to fertilise the wombs of many maidens?' Florence stroked her rounded belly. 'He is a just and good Master.' She smiled craftily to herself. 'I would not be with another for all the world.'

'Even in these climes.' Betty shivered, not with cold, for this part of the palace was heated, but with a growing fear. I see you bear his child. Is your time soon?'

'Indeed, I bear his son!'

'A son is important in this land, too? How can you know you carry a boy?'

'It is written in all the oracles.' Florence set her teeth. 'And I shall essay to have many more besides!'

'What of the girls?'

Florence waved nonchalantly. 'The mountain is very high, my dear.' Betty's eyebrows rose. 'The paths are slippery, the tigers prowl day and night. It is easy. But enough of that. The Master is extremely wealthy, and to father numerous male offspring is a sign not only of his virility but his immense riches. His chosen slaves are well looked after.'

'But they's still slaves and that means he can do as he likes...'

'Exactly! He can do whatever he wishes with his property,

including offering a recalcitrant slave for sale to the highest bidder, if he so desires. You too, dear Betty, or me, though I pray nightly that he will not.'

'What if the prince don't want me?'

'It is hardly likely. Your skin is very white, your golden hair...'

'What if I don't want the prince?' Betty trembled, excited but appalled by the prospect of serving this exacting Master.

'You have no option, dear, so you may as well get used to it.'

'I could run away!'

'You would be caught and whipped! I have seen it done, and although it does not kill the girl...'

'I been whipped many times afore.'

'Not by a eunuch in a harem!' Florence stroked Betty's white arms. 'Your ivory skin would mark too easily, and if you became ugly to him, well...' Her eyebrows rose and she shrugged. 'It is the way of the world here. I hardly dare tell you the possible consequences of disobedience in this wild country. You must not incur the Master's wrath.'

'He can do his worst, for all I care! I ain't being a slave.' Betty threw herself onto a great mountain of cushions. 'Not a real slave!'

'Betty, the Master owns you body and soul. A slave is worth less than a yak.' Florence sat beside Betty and held her intimately, her eyes flashing cruelly. 'Listen to me. This man has not yet been crossed and thus his mettle remains untested, but I will tell you of the old master's strict example.' Florence's eyes glared enviously at Betty's slender but voluptuous figure. 'A young virgin girl, barely sixteen, refused his favours. She was much like you, dear,' Florence played with Betty's golden curls, 'beautiful but proud. She did not wish to couple with an elderly and wrinkled man, preferring a young stripling of her tribe. Well of course, the master had his way with her.'

'Did he force the girl?'

'She had no option, Betty. She entreated the master, begged that at least afterwards she should be allowed to return to her beloved. But he wanted to keep the virgin entirely to himself. He decreed death to any man who tried to take her afterwards, lest his inferior seed sully the portal wherein the master had placed his own sacredness.' Florence closely watched the expression on Betty's face to gauge if her exaggerated tale was having the desired effect. 'Such is the custom here! The girl's very refusal fired his ardour to such a pitch that nothing would satisfy him until he entered her virginal passage. Since she would not comply and resisted every gentle approach, the eunuchs held her down, stretching her legs apart.'

'Oh my, oh my, the poor child!'

'Thus he lay atop her, groping at her girlish breasts, tore her hymen and thrust his member deep within.'

'So, along with her hymen, the poor girl's heart was broken.'

'Indeed. But that was not the end of it. Afterwards she became sulky and disobedient, refusing to submit to his authority. Her head was shaved and a hundred lashes ordered, to be administered weekly, ten at a time. After the final weals had barely healed, the young man, fired with the ardour of jealousy and unrequited love, was discovered whispering vainly at the window of his beloved's cell.' Florence paused dramatically.

'Thus, the slave was staked out on the mountain top in the dead of night, her legs bound apart. Huge flaming torches were placed about her to keep her from her death, and to ward off the tigers that threatened to attack her tormentors who were given leave to do as they would. All night he gloated over her torture and then at dawn he mounted her half-frozen body, plugging her to the very depths of her womb and ravishing the other orifice and finally her mouth. Afterwards she was offered thus to his men, each and every one. As for the boy she loved, the tale of his ghastly tortures cannot be repeated. They were both sentenced to death. For him, beheading was a blessed release.'

Betty's jaw dropped and the pink in her cheeks drained away. 'Such cruelty!'

'Cruelty, my dear? Why no! Here it is not considered cruel, for the female sex is accorded no importance, unless she be a vessel for the man's use. In these wild mountains, and far in the distance where the cold desert begins, it is just and right for the stronger sex to rule.'

'I don't know as I like it.'

'Like it or not, it is the way of barbarians.'

'Did this happen a long time back?'

'Not at all. Only a short while ago just before the old master died. The girl was spared, for the eldest wife, requiring a personal slave, interceded on her behalf. Thus she must now perform any number of menial and humiliating tasks at the whim of the widow. And, indeed, that woman abuses her position sorely.'

'Oh my! I don't know as I could bear it. I s'pose I must obey and think on how I can escape.'

'There is no escape. See the mountains stretch mile after mile, seeming to reach eternity before the lower slopes give way to the barren desert.'

'There must be a way. The trading routes, the caravans...'

'Perhaps, but it is more than my life is worth to assist another slave to escape. I have my unborn son to consider.' Florence shook her dark hair and spoke to her rival with barely disguised bitterness. 'The Master will wish to penetrate you.'

Betty tossed her head rudely. 'And mount me like a yak, I s'pose! I'm worth less than a stinking pack-animal!'

'Be silent! How dare you speak that way. Think yourself lucky to be alive. And do not resist his approach, for he will force you anyway.' Florence smirked wickedly as she slapped Betty's face as hard as she could. 'Will you cry, Betty? Will you cry, baby Betty?'

Betty's cheek reddened and she trembled as she tried hard to control her anger. It was obvious she'd have to feign submission and pray that rescue would come soon. 'I s'pose I must obey.'

'Indeed, you must,' Florence taunted. 'It will hurt, you know, when he takes your virgin passage. It will hurt you very much.'

'Why should it? He's a man, like any other.'

'But your passage is very tight.'

'And it'll stretch like any other woman's to accommodate the male member. It's nature's way.'

'Both passages, my dear? The natural passage, yes, but the other more mysterious entrance is his preference. I tell you, he is very large.'

'There ain't no one bigger'n William. No one!'

'Who cares about your precious William? You will never see him again! Never!'

'I shall! I shall!' Betty tried to suppress a wail, but unable to check her pent-up emotions any longer, she burst into a waterfall of sobs.

Florence flounced out of the room with a final parting shot. 'William! Ha! When the prince finds him he will kill him, just as he did the slave! And after the Master has had his way, you will be imprisoned here forever, a slave to *my* whims until you die in this cursed hell-hole!'

'Betty, don't take on so! You will spoil your precious beauty with your tears.'

'Is that you, Florence?' Betty lifted her red and puffy face. Her eyes were dry and salty with too much crying, but the cushions were soaked with tears.

'Why, yes, my dear.' Florence, worried that she'd gone too far, had returned to make a pretence at friendship. 'I have come to make amends. I was too sharp with you, my dear, but I suppose I can't help but be a little jealous.' She stroked Betty's curls and wiped away her tears. 'You are so pretty, and so innocent, I know the prince will fall in love immediately. He has so longed to fertilise a woman of your delicate complexion.'

Betty responded cleverly to the false flattery. 'Oh, Florence, I's so afeard o' the Master.' She wound her arms around Florence's neck, mingling their perfumes. 'And I's a little afeard o' you, too,' Betty breathed softly, 'an if you would be my teacher, I could love you so, and give you pleasures.' She kissed Florence's cheek warmly and lowered her lashes in false deference.

'But it is the Master you must learn to love and pleasure, since he is the reason for your very existence. Still...' Florence smiled treacherously, for what she was about to suggest would earn Betty a whipping, her own delicate condition rendering temporary immunity from the usual punishment, '...if the Master were to discover you, this very afternoon, in the act of tickling my intimate parts with your tongue, he will undoubtedly look on you more favourably. It often pleases him to watch such abandoned and sensual play amongst his female slaves.'

'I would please the Master, Florence!'

'Then do as I say.' Florence took Betty in her arms, and arranging herself on the cushions, pressed Betty to her groin. 'Pleasure me, Betty. Show me how your little tongue works on a woman and I shall teach you how you may do the same for the prince. We must be friends together.' Florence moaned happily as Betty followed her order, slipping her strong tongue between Florence's plump labia, searching for the clitoris and then delicately titillating it.

'The Master will surely be here soon, and there is nothing His Eminence would like better than to see you, a carnal slave to my wishes.'

But there was something in Florence's tone that alarmed Betty and with a pretence at interest in the Master, Betty withdrew from the soft and perfumed mound and with eyes as wide as saucers asked innocently: 'Is it true that he is *very* large and *very* dark?'

'He is over six foot tall, extremely handsome with refined features, a beautiful turn to his lips and an enticing curl of the nostrils... dear Betty, do attend to my parts!' Florence pushed Betty onto her nether lips and bucked her hips against her as she spoke: 'His skin is smooth and shiny as ebony, his form as muscular as an athlete. His...'

Betty took a deep breath. 'But what of his manhood?'

'Why, he's as brave and courageous as a tiger... ah Betty, do place your sweet lips upon mine again!'

But Betty would not be silenced. 'What of his member, Florence, his virile member? You have mentioned its enormous size, but what of the colour and shape of it?'

'Pray continue.' This time Florence held firmly onto Betty's curls, constricting her movements. 'I shall describe it whilst you minister to my tender parts, but do not make me spend. I should not be pleased. Well, the thick stem is darkish with the prettiest of black hairs curling around the soft and juicy plums. The delicate skin that magically draws back to reveal the glossy prize is firm and yet flexible, the velvet head a beautiful bright crimson, as a sweet and honeyed flower bud, luscious in the barren desert.'

Fired by Florence's description, Betty wriggled her tongue eagerly at the wetting cleft, but soon rose for another question. 'And the smell o' the Master? I likes the smell on a man's virile parts.'

'Betty, you must learn to concentrate on the task set. We will light the candle for one hour. That is the time you must spend on pleasuring me.'

'An hour. So long to wait.'

'The time will soon pass if you busy yourself.'

Florence settled on the cushions once more and Betty nuzzled her nose into Florence's cleft. 'Mm. You smell nice, dear. What o' the Master's smell? Do tell me.'

'Well, if you must know of the Master's sacred scent, it is exquisite, a natural Master's delicious perfume, fragrant with figs, smoke and the finest incense.'

'But I heard the slaves a-whispering and laughing in their own tongue. They was signing and pointing...'

'With admiration, no doubt, at its great dimensions. Naturally, I have little experience of men.' Florence laughed to herself since, apart from being an inveterate liar, she could hardly admit to her former life of prostitution. 'I have no idea of the usual proportions of a man's appendage, but the Master's member is reputed to be extremely large. When he entered the sacred grotto, I found it painful, but what is a little pain when one loves to distraction? My husband...'

'But I thought you was his slave?'

'I am the prince's slave, but I was married once to an English gentleman.'

'And still a virgin?'

'My ugly husband married me for my fortune,' Florence confided. 'Since he preferred the male sex, his withered member found no way of rising on the wedding night. I was captured by the prince on our honeymoon, dragged away in the middle of the night. So I discovered that my husband had sold me into slavery and taken my inheritance. After a long journey I arrived here in this mountain retreat, my virginity intact. It was more than my captors would dare to harm me.

'Now, compose yourself. No more questions. The flame is lit and the Master may be here very soon. If you are found pleasing me, he will be most pleased with you. 'Florence kissed her new companion. 'Work patiently until he comes.'

'But you ain't jealous no more?'

A strange expression briefly shadowed Florence's face. 'No, why should I be? My position is ensured since I carry the young Master's first son.' Florence patted her stomach again then lay back on the pile of cushions, her muslin robes raised, her legs spreadeagled. 'Lick, Betty, lick!'

It was some hours later before the Master deigned to visit

his women. Florence had grown weary of receiving the intimate pleasures and fearing the orgasmic contractions she experienced would hasten the birth of her son, she'd left Betty alone. But she would not be far away. Betty had slept for a while, grown restless, slipped into a dreaming state and was now lying fully awake. Through slitted eyes and with a heavy heart, she watched the arched doorway. High in this ancient palace, far from civilisation, she would have no option but to submit to the demands of the Master. At last, as the day wore on and the winter sun's rays failed, the gloomy room darkened, its sole illumination the soft light of the flickering candles.

The Master stood in contemplation for a while, his tall dark figure filling the doorway, a note of triumph in his muffled voice. 'Betty!'

Betty squeezed her eyes and immediately prostrated herself as Florence had told her she must. She heard the soft pads of bare feet as he walked near, and with her eyes closed she groped in the dark and showered his perfumed ankles in kisses. 'Master,' she whispered. 'Master.'

The man lifted her easily in his muscular arms and placed her on the cushions. 'Lay back, I must inspect you for myself.' He removed her thin silk gown and parted her legs wide. His hands roved at her cunt, exploring the delicate folds, feeling for the evidence of the unbroken hymen. 'So, by a miracle, you are still a virgin, Betty.'

'Master,' she whispered huskily. Her eyelids fluttered open, the delicate trembling of a butterfly clinging to a leaf, but frightened to meet the Master's dazzling eyes she lowered her head in submission.

'Just as the oracle predicted!' The Master grasped Betty's tiny hands, drawing her to her feet. She stood awkwardly, ashamed of her nakedness before this powerful stranger whose law was absolute in his own domain. 'You are mine at last, Betty. My property, my slave. Many suns have passed...'

'I changed these last few years. There's girls more lovely'n me in the harem.'

'You are a treasured possession of great pulchritude, a matchless beauty, a peerless prize.'

'But I ain't as comely as I were, Master.' Betty tossed her golden hair. It had grown a little darker and her face a little leaner, but her black eyes shone as bright and clear as ever.

'You are infinitely more beautiful than I could have dreamed.' Gently, he ran a calloused hand over the faint silver streaks on her white rump. 'Such loveliness,' he murmured, 'can only be enhanced by motherhood.'

The Master held her closely to his broad chest. 'Will you serve me as a woman should?'

Betty sank to her knees. 'What is your will, Master?'

'I demand that which is priceless, your virgin blood!'

As she knelt, her face tight against the rigid manhood, Betty was reminded of her husband, the feel of him, the smell of him, the taste of him. 'Master, it is William I have allus loved. You may own me but me heart's elsewhere.'

'If you wish to see William alive and your children too, then...'

Betty breathed heavily and sighed in resignation. 'I shall submit, sir, submit to your authority because I must.'

'Submission is not enough! You must swear your love for me, Betty, your true Master! That is my command!'

'Sir, how can you command love?' Betty's eyes filled with tears. 'I have but one love.'

'Then you must take the consequences of your refusal.' The Master unwound the black head-dress, his dark eyes probing the depths of her soul.

'Oh sir! What magic has been worked?' Betty rubbed her eyes. 'Am I deceived? It ain't possible! Is it really you, William?'

'So, Betty, after all your protestations, you *will* love me and me alone!'

'Yes, my love, yes.' Betty pressed her face to the Master's

hardened member, breathing his delicious scent. 'Sir, let me take you first in me mouth.' She rooted into his groin and he thrust his rampant organ against her.

'I wish to take you, sir, take you in me mouth. But there's summat else.'

The Master stroked the tangle of curls. He knew what Betty needed, but she must say it.

'Order me, Betty, and I shall obey.'

'I order you to whip me, sir!' Betty clung tightly to him.

'Ask me, Betty, and I shall oblige.'

'Kind sir, I would be honoured if you would whip me.' She held tighter.

'Beg me, Betty.' The Master grasped her curls and forced her head backwards, but she did not protest. 'Beg me, and I shall carry out your wishes with the utmost severity.'

'Master, I beg you, I beg you with all me heart to whip me! I am yours, sir, yours forever!'

'It shall be done. But we have so little time before we must leave. The Black Prince is not far behind! He will expect to find the virgin mother of his firstborn son!'

The Master reached out for his riding crop. His lip curled with intense pleasure. Shivering with desire and anticipation, Betty parted his robes, released his pulsating member and sucked deeply as the whip struck her marble shoulders.

'I would claim all that is mine!' The whip struck again. 'You shall love only me. The Black Prince shall never have you, Betty. I should die first! Ah, I have waited long to possess the mother of my son!' The Master cast away the whip and threw off his robes to reveal his form. As he pulled away from Betty's mouth, his ruby manhood gleamed in the light. 'And after I have finally possessed you, you will give me my first-born! Open your legs to me, Betty. This time I shall fuck you!'

William fell heavily on top of Betty, wedging his knees between hers to part them. His hot, thick member pulsed at the portal as he tried to gain entry to her virginal passage.

'You are mine, Betty, mine alone. No one else shall spill the virgin's blood!' The tip of his shaft slipped between Betty's outer lips, and with a mighty shove he battered at the door, but to no avail. The entrance was as yet too tight for his mighty weapon.

In his passion the Master neither saw nor heard the silent figure of jealous, eavesdropping Florence. Creeping slowly, a maniacal expression on her face, a deadly dagger in her hand, she approached the cushions.

'Kiss me, my dear Betty!'

Betty raised lips and hips in acquiescence. 'Master, Master,' she whispered. 'I love you. I honour you. I serve you.' And as Betty gave herself to her only love, the weapon drove home deep in the flesh and finally the virgin's blood was spilt!

Far away, in another land, in a time now past, Zillah held a single shard of the glass to her face. 'Ha! It is he! It is he! May a thousand yak's fleas infest his armpits!' She let out a curdled scream as her gnarled and bony hand felt uselessly for the comfort of the black cat. 'At last, the virgin's blood is spilt, but I am tricked by the blackest of all princes, the Prince of Darkness himself!' The evil witch lifted the glass to the light as if to see more clearly, and as she did so a single ray of sunlight, its power multiplied as it passed through the prismoid, blinded her remaining eye.

Exciting titles available now from Chimera:

1-901388-20-4	The Instruction of Olivia	*Allen*
1-901388-05-0	Flame of Revenge	*Scott*
1-901388-10-7	The Switch	*Keir*
1-901388-15-8	Captivation	*Fisher*
1-901388-00-X	Sweet Punishment	*Jameson*
1-901388-25-5	Afghan Bound	*Morgan*
1-901388-01-8	Olivia and the Dulcinites	*Allen*
1-901388-02-6	Belinda: Cruel Passage West	*Caine*
1-901388-04-2	Thunder's Slaves	*Leather*
1-901388-06-9	Schooling Sylvia	*Beaufort*
1-901388-07-7	Under Orders	*Asquith*
1-901388-03-4	Twilight in Berlin	*Deutsch*
1-901388-09-3	Net Asset	*Pope*
1-901388-08-5	Willow Slave	*Velvet*
1-901388-12-3	Sold into Service	*Tanner*
1-901388-13-1	All for Her Master	*O'Connor*
1-901388-14-X	Stranger in Venice	*Beaufort*
1-901388-16-6	Innocent Corinna	*Eden*
1-901388-17-4	Out of Control	*Miller*
1-901388-18-2	Hall of Infamy	*Virosa*
1-901388-23-9	Latin Submission	*Barton*
1-901388-19-0	Destroying Angel	*Hastings*
1-901388-21-2	Dr Casswell's Student	*Fisher*
1-901388-22-0	Annabelle	*Aire*
1-901388-24-7	Total Abandon	*Anderssen*
1-901388-26-3	Selina's Submission	*Lewis*
1-901388-27-1	A Strict Seduction	*Del Rey*
1-901388-28-X	Assignment for Alison	*Pope*

Coming soon from Chimera:

1-901388-30-1	Perfect Slave	*Bell (March '99)*
1-901388-31-X	A Kept Woman	*Grayson (April '99)*

All the above are/will be available at your local bookshop or newsagent, or by post or telephone from: B.B.C.S., P.O. Box 941, Hull, HU1 3VQ. **(24 hour Telephone Credit Card Line: 01482 224626)**.

To order, send: Title, author, ISBN number and price for each book ordered, your full name and address, cheque or postal order payable to B.B.C.S. for the total amount, and allow the following for postage and packing:
UK and BFPO: £1.00 for the first book, and 50p for each additional book to a maximum of £3.50.
Overseas and Eire: £2.00 for the first book, £1.00 for the second and 50p for each additional book.

All titles £4.99 (US$7.95)